BATTLESHIP: LEVIATHAN

©2021 CRAIG MARTELLE

This book is protected under the copyright laws of the United States of America. No part of this publication may be reproduced, stored in a retrieval system, or transmitted, in any form or by any means, without the prior permission in writing of the publisher, nor be otherwise circulated in any form of binding or cover other than that in which it is published and without a similar condition including this condition being imposed on the subsequent purchaser. Any reproduction or unauthorized use of the material or artwork contained herein is prohibited without the express written permission of the authors.

Print and eBook formatting by Steve Beaulieu. Artwork provided by Vivid Covers.

Published by Aethon Books LLC. 2021

All characters in this book are fictitious. Any resemblance to actual persons, living or dead, is purely coincidental.

All rights reserved.

To those who support any author by buying and reading their books, I salute you. I couldn't keep telling these stories if it weren't for you and for the support team surrounding me. No one works alone in this business.

THANKS

**Beta Readers and Proofreaders -
with my deepest gratitude!**

Micky Cocker
James Caplan
Kelly O'Donnell
John Ashmore

SOCIAL MEDIA

Craig Martelle Social
Website & Newsletter:
https://craigmartelle.com

**Facebook:
https://www.
facebook.com/AuthorCraigMartelle/**

ALSO IN SERIES

Also in series:

Battleship: Leviathan
Leviathan's War
Leviathan's Last Battle

[1]

"*War is the natural state of things. Peace is a time to rearm and regroup.*" –From the memoirs of Space Operations Fleet Admiral Thaylon Loore

"Another Prog derelict? You remember the last one." With his arms crossed, Major Declan Payne rolled his eyes into a slow shake of his head.

"Your video is on, Major," Fleet Admiral Harry Wesson noted.

"What makes it different from the last thirteen derelicts? Whoever operated that fleet were experts at leaving nothing useful behind. But the Blaze Collective is advancing. Wouldn't we be better served with another behind-the-lines search-and-destroy mission? Sorry, Admiral, for being skeptical." He clenched his jaw and tried to calm himself, then uncrossed his arms and clasped his hands behind his back to appear more like the senior officer he answered to.

"Nothing to be sorry for, son," the admiral replied. "This Progenitor ship is bigger than anything we have or have ever seen before. I think its invisibility system failed. Otherwise, it would have still been invisible to us. The eggheads think it's been there for a thousand years." The admiral looked at someone off-screen before turning back to Major Payne and rolling his finger for the Space Ops team commander to hurry up.

"So it had some power until recently, which means it *is* probably intact." Payne followed the logic to why his team was being deployed.

"Cross-deck your team to *Cleophas*. Take your skimmer and be ready to deploy on arrival at Ganymede."

"Earth? We're going home?"

"No. You're going to Ganymede, the moon orbiting Jupiter." The admiral smiled. "I thought that might get your attention. I would have been disappointed if your first words had not been about liberty. Work hard, play hard. Isn't that your motto?"

It was, but Declan wanted to focus on why he was moving the team to a Kaiju-class ship. He waited.

The admiral continued, "We think the Blaze Collective has been made aware of this find. We're positive we'll get there before them, but you may not have completed your work by the time they show up."

Payne's mind raced with the planning. He tapped the secondary channel on the screen where a series of files showed up and scrolled through the pictures.

"I have the information," Payne confirmed. "I'll speak with Captain Malone and get this thing done. We'll be on our way within the hour."

"Do us proud, son. We need what this ship has if we're to stop the Blaze." He tapped a finger on his brow as an informal salute. "Wesson out."

The video channel went dark. Declan resisted the urge to read through the file. He could do that later while they were en route. Right now, he needed to brief the frigate's captain and then his team.

He jogged from his quarters toward the central corridor, where he nearly ran into Tech Specialist Seven Katello Mateus Andfen. Everyone called him Blinky because he worked with computers. Did the lights blink when they were supposed to? He said that had little do with computer engineering, but no one on the team believed him.

"Blinky, get the team ready to cross-deck in thirty. We'll take the skimmer."

Combat Specialist Seven Cointreau Koch leaned out from behind his fellow Spec-7. "We getting into the fight, sir?" He rubbed his hands together while beaming through a face-splitting grin.

"You gotta do something about that, Heckler. There's more to life than war. I'll brief you on board the skimmer. Thirty mikes. Get on it." Major Payne bolted down the wide corridor while his two senior enlisted launched into action.

Blinky headed for the lab and Heckler ran toward the workout facilities, which was where the rest of the team would be found. Blinky's first thought was about the equipment they'd need. Heckler was all about the people.

And weapons, because in Heckler Koch's world, the ones employing superior tactics with sufficient firepower were the only ones who walked away. Everyone else was carried off the battlefield in a body bag.

Payne made it to the bridge in record time, slowed to a walk, and stepped onto the command deck. It was located strategically at the exact center of the ship to increase its survivability.

Humanity had been at war for as long as they had danced among the stars. Every feature on board a warship had been implemented because of lessons learned through the blood of those who had gone before. Death was a great teacher for others to survive.

"Captain Malone, may I have a word?" Payne stepped close and spoke in a neutral voice. When he spoke loudly, Fleet personnel got nervous.

The captain leaned back in his chair, gnawing on a polyfiber toothpick, and pointed at the main screen. The frigate, Fleet Warship FW *Voeller,* was already within the close-in-weapons defensive perimeter of *Cleophas*, the newest of humanity's three Kaiju-class dreadnoughts. "I already heard. Orders from on high. You can go whenever you're ready, Major."

"Thanks, sir. See you on the other side."

"Gonna miss you and your team," one of the helmsmen muttered. "Gonna miss all that running and yelling. Gonna miss it real bad."

The corner of the captain's mouth twitched upward as he struggled to maintain a straight face.

"I feel a tear coming," Payne replied. "Nope. Must be dust in the air." The frigate's air was constantly purified. There was no dust.

He held out his hand. The captain took it and gave it a hearty shake.

"We'll be coming, too, but they want you on the big boy. Whatever you're doing, they're giving you a lot of top cover. BEP Central is sending half of their assets to join us. Or maybe that's just to protect their nubile youngsters from your team when the clubs open."

A joke, but he was serious about the Fleet. BEP. The Blue Earth Protectorate. That was what Earth called the military units that operated within the Solar System. *Cleophas* and the ships that operated in deep space and beyond were called Earth Fleet. They existed solely for offensive actions. Humanity had found that space was a violent place, and the only way to establish parity with aliens was by having an unrivaled potential for violence.

Humanity rose to the occasion.

Then they ran into the Blaze Collective.

"We're taking the skimmer. No need to airlock with that thing." Declan replied as the frigate violated the dreadnought's proximity safety margin. Payne hurried off the command deck and down the corridor to pack his personal effects. His go-bag was already aboard *Glamorous Glennis*, just like the rest of the team's.

"Stand off one thousand meters," the captain ordered.

The major didn't care about Fleet operations. They flew the ships. He was on board to ride from place to place. His team conducted their ops off the ship. Each Fleet warship had a Space Ops Force Team aboard. Fleet personnel called them SOFTies.

First stop was the weapons locker, where he found Combat Specialist Three Alphonse Periq checking the spare weapons and reserve charges. Periq was new to the Force and new to the team. He was also the youngest of the team's ten members.

"We ready to go, Fetus?" Payne asked.

The specialist handed over the major's personalized combat axe and pulse rifle. Payne checked the edge on the blade before tucking it into its sheath and putting it with his personal items. He double-checked his personal weapon loading system, a harness integrated with a body suit that could double as an environmental unit in an emergency.

He scanned the pulse rifle even though Fetus had checked that it was on safe before handing it over. It was standard procedure; both parties verified. It reduced the number of accidents, but unfortunately not to zero. There were still accidents, but not on Payne's team.

He slung the rifle over his shoulder and held out his hand, gesturing for more.

"Sir?"

"Plasma grenades! Don't leave me hanging, Fetus. It's all fun and games until you need grenades and don't have any."

The junior combat specialist counted out four and delivered them into Payne's waiting hand. The major tucked them into the four slots on his harness. "Carry on." He stepped past Fetus on his way to his quarters.

"Sir? Can I get a hand carrying this trash to the skimmer?"

Payne gave the youngster a thumbs-up and started walking, but the kid was new, and they didn't have time for him to fumble around with the weapons like two virgins in the dark. "No. If you were going to get company, Heckler would have already sent them here."

"But how am I supposed to move this stuff?" The specialist's face fell as if he'd been given an impossible task. A heavy laser with battery backup. A crew-served pulse weapon. Crates of grenades. Spare charges for the shoulder-fired pulse rifles. A solid two hundred kilos' worth.

The major sighed before opening the emergency bulkhead panel. He removed the hoverstretcher, activated it, and with a gentle push, sent it gliding across the corridor.

The specialist stood with his mouth open and pointed at a sign next to the panel door.

For emergencies only. Other uses will be prosecuted.

"If we don't have those weapons, we'll need that stretcher, but if we have our gear, then it's a lot less likely we'll need the stretcher. We'll bring it back when we're done." He winked at the specialist.

Fetus held the stretcher, glancing at it, the panel, and down the corridor. Payne walked away. He had his personal kit to grab before heading to the skimmer, their team combat landing craft.

He had a feeling this wouldn't be a quick operation, and he liked keeping his face clean-shaven. The others generally didn't shave during an op in a long-running challenge of who could grow facial hair the quickest.

Beards stood as a testimonial to how long the team had been deployed.

Payne filled a backpack with his personal gear, kissed his small quarters goodbye, and left to meet his team.

On the ship's lowest deck, a vertical ladder descended into the top of the skimmer. It was a flat and wide spacecraft with a lifting body, optimized to skid through a planet's upper atmosphere and glide along an extended flight profile before firing up its engines to land.

Glamorous Glennis was the standard SOF insertion vehicle. Payne had named his after the first human craft to break the speed of sound. The next team leader would call it something else. It was one of many traditions within the SOF.

Like calling the youngest crew member Fetus until he was no longer the youngest. Then he'd be assigned a new nickname.

Payne descended into the ship and headed up front to conduct the pre-flight. His executive officer, Major Virgil Dank, was already on it and four ticks down the checklist.

"Virge. We got us another space junk mission."

The XO groaned. "I was just getting excited for this one, too."

"Don't lose that thought. This one might be intact."

"Instant woody! I'm ready to see what these things are supposed to look like inside as opposed to empty, where all we do is spray paint a big fluorescent orange X on the outside of the hull."

"We'll review the intel once we're settled on *Cleophas*."

They verified each system was operational one by one while the rest of the team loaded the ship. Declan glanced behind him to see Combat Specialist Five Marsha Skellig securing the stolen hoverstretcher to the rear bulkhead.

"You know that's stolen, don't you, Turbo?" Payne called over his shoulder.

"I figured," Skellig replied. She pushed Fetus toward his seat. "Watch what you're doing, noob."

Twenty-nine minutes after the Fleet admiral had called, Payne was ready to cross-deck from *Voeller* to *Cleophas*.

"*Voeller* Ops, this is *Glennis*, requesting permission to depart."

"Roger. Hands off, we have the con."

"Then why did we just run down the flight checklist?" Payne blurted before he could stop himself.

"Because it's SOP, and far be it for the SOFTies to violate a regulation."

Virgil snickered. "It's like they know us." He glanced at the hoverstretcher. "Or that they don't."

Payne nodded and smiled. The restraining clamps unlocked with a heavy *thunk*. The skimmer remained where it was, held firmly in place by a forcefield. The ship started to move as the field shifted it away from the frigate.

"Thanks for the warm send-off, Ops. We're happy to be leaving. If I want abuse like that, I'll go home to my wife."

"Handing off to *Cleophas*. Enjoy the ride, people. Ops out."

"I didn't know you were married," Virgil said.

"I'm not. It seemed like the right thing to say. We need another games night when we get back so we can put those guys in their place."

Someone cleared their throat. Payne scanned the faces of his team, looking for who wanted to speak. Tech Specialist Four Salem Shao. "What do you have to say, Shaolin?"

"They kick our ass in the antigrav race every time."

"But we destroy them in everything else. Are you saying we need to practice?"

"I didn't say that," Shaolin countered. "If we can't wing it and win, we got no business playing."

"You've summed up the entirety of Team Payne in one sentence, Specialist. Well done," Declan remarked before rotating his seat to face the team. Major Dank did the same. "Gentlefolk who have offered their lives to the greater good of the galaxy…"

Heckler rolled his finger to urge the major to get on with it.

"We have traditions in this unit." The major stared at the combat specialist, who continued to roll his finger. "I accept your lives as tribute! Now to the matter at hand. We've got us another derelict, but this one appears to be intact. It's also bigger than anything else we've boarded. Much bigger."

"What does that mean, Major?" Blinky asked.

"It means if we can make it fly, we'll make it fly, and we'll take it to the BEP shipyard."

"If they abandoned it, I suspect it can't fly." Blinky was convinced his logic was valid.

"Maybe. That's what we'll find out, but we could have some company. Seems the Blaze may be interested in this thing, too."

The XO played with his fingers while pursing his lips. "They are five hundred light-years beyond the closest they've ever reached toward Earth. I can't believe they'd travel to the Solar System."

Payne pursed his lips and slowly shook his head. "It's as far as we *know* they've penetrated. The fact that the pointy heads think they're coming says this thing is special. It appears that it was invisible until recently when the Prog ship's screening system failed and it showed up on friendly sensors. What would an invisibility screen be worth? This could make all of your mediocre careers worthwhile."

"Now you're talking, boss," Blinky replied. "If I figure out how to fly the thing, do I get to stay with it? I thought these alien systems were a bit more advanced than ours. I'd love to tangle with them, see who has the superior intellect. My money is on me."

"You make me wanna puke," Tech Specialist Seven Laura Walker, nickname Sparky told him. Her specialties were engineering, engines, and environmental controls. If they had to board a hostile ship, she was the one to help the team understand its weaknesses.

Blinky put on his contemplative face and replied, "Words. They are all we have, even as inefficient as they are. Do you feel like puking, or do you want to puke? Or do you only want to blame me that you can make yourself want to puke but not actually puke? At the end of all these scenarios, the only thing that's missing is spew. Regina Spews-A-Lot. You need a new nickname."

"Team law! No nicknames over two syllables. That's the way it has to be." Payne stabbed a knife-hand at Blinky.

"Can anyone be serious?" Sparky shot back.

No one nodded. Payne continued, "I'll read the full brief while we're en route, and after that, you will know what I know. We'll prepare our ingress plan together first thing tomorrow. Once onboard *Cleophas*, find the workout room and hit the weights. I'm not sure what kind of time we'll have for fitness when onboard the derelict."

"We'll make the time," Turbo declared, cracking her knuckles through her gloves. "We'll see if Blinky is any good."

"No shit. I haven't been tested yet. What's the count, Major? A dozen NBH?"

"Nothing but hulks? We're at lucky number thirteen. All foreplay and no bringing it home. The head shed thinks this one will be different. Maybe they'll be right this time."

The team snorted as one while *Cleophas* brought *Glamorous Glennis* into her landing bay and magnetically locked the skimmer to the deck.

"All ashore who's going ashore." Major Payne pumped his fist in the air.

[2]

"Just because there's peace doesn't mean you stop preparing for war." –From the memoirs of Fleet Admiral Thaylon Loore

By the time the two majors of Team Payne made it off the hangar deck, *Cleophas* had already transitioned to faster-than-light speed.

A ship's steward met them. "If you'll follow me, I'll show you to your quarters."

"Not until my people are taken care of," Major Payne countered.

"They will be escorted to a single space sufficient for all of them. You will be in a two-man stateroom."

"We've shared before, but this is a Kaiju-class ship," Declan replied.

"Space is at a premium, gentlemen. The majority of *Cleophas* is dedicated to power generation and raw materials. Those two things make everything else possible."

"And lots and lots of armor."

"There is a great deal of physical shielding, too. This ship is over a million tons in gross mass. The throw weight of the weapons systems puts *Cleophas* ahead of the Blaze's Linion-class dreadnoughts, and their battlewagons don't stand a chance against us."

"That's the attitude, but we're headed in the opposite direction of the front lines."

"We're not going to Kepler-186f?"

"No. We're heading back to our Solar System," Payne replied.

A wave of nausea passed over them. They stopped and leaned heavily against the bulkheads. When the wave passed, they continued on their way as if nothing had happened. Because nothing had. It was a drawback of FTL travel in that eddies caused flesh-and-blood travelers brief discomfort. It was addressed by dealing with it like a hangover. Steady oneself and move on when the urge to puke went away.

The wide corridor down the centerline of the ship had a constant breeze from air movement as the primary ducting for environmental control. During combat operations, the bulkheads closed, and a high-speed filtered and shunted secondary system took over. A tertiary system supported each self-contained space and activated if the first two failed. Combat operations were conducted in fire- and corrosion-resistant environmental suits, also self-contained.

In space, air could only be found inside the ship. Air was life. Pockets of air gave rescuers time. Pockets within pockets increased the survivability of a trained crew. Ships could be replaced.

Ice represented the greatest quantity of raw material on board. It provided both water and oxygen. Together, they were the guarantors of life.

"How long is this central corridor?" Payne asked.

"Twenty-five hundred meters." He pointed to a side passage labeled with a frame number that represented meters from the front of the ship, followed by deck number and meters from the central corridor port or starboard to the outer hull. "Your quarters are twelve hundred zero six tac twenty-four tac eighteen starboard."

He turned down a lateral passageway.

"I better write that down," Virgil replied. "I'm assuming everything is painted the standard ship's gray, and once lost, we would never find our way back here."

"Pretty much," the shorter man quipped. "Or you could check the interactive wall screen for your quarters." He led them back to the central corridor of deck twenty-four. At the corner, there was a dark screen. He tapped it and it came to life. He enunciated clearly when he spoke. "Temporary quarters for Major Declan Payne, please."

"Congratulations, you are almost there," the unit replied, displaying an arrow in the corner that turned down the lateral corridor and went a short distance to the room on their right toward the aft end of the ship. "It is keyed to your face. Look at the screen to the side of the door, and it will open for you. Welcome aboard *Cleophas*, humanity's latest and greatest technological achievement."

"Sounds like a vid ad. I thought the Fleet would be a little more bland," Payne suggested.

"Give it time. After six months in space, the AI will descend gracelessly to our level of perpetual despair." Their escort raised his eyebrows and nodded with his revelation.

"Now you sound like a true Fleetie. How much time you got in?"

"Five years. Three of it in space," their escort replied.

"Eleven. All of it out here," Payne said, clapping the shorter man's shoulder. "Where's the chow hall?"

Their escort tapped the screen. "Where is the officers' mess?"

"There are three officer dining facilities onboard *Cleophas*. The nearest is on deck twenty-two at location one thousand two hundred tac twenty-two tac one port."

Declan leaned close. "When is it open for chow?"

"Meals are served constantly, day and night. Whenever you are hungry or have time, please stop by. State your name, and a meal will be prepared based on your activity level."

"What the..." Virgil started to ask, but Payne stopped him.

"That is the big hairy coconut balls. Chow whenever we want it. One question. How does that thing know my activity level?"

"That *thing* knows all," the escort replied.

A group of Fleeties hurried past, looking like they were on a mission.

"Is there a club on board, a place to have a drink and relax after a hard day's work?" Declan joked.

"Of course," the screen replied and showed a map to the officers' club.

"Where can we find hookers and blow?" Virgil followed up. Declan rubbed his temples.

The AI shut him down. "There are no such vile distractions onboard *Cleophas*."

"Not that you know of," Virgil countered. "I've been known to do some shady shit for a few credits."

"Make the ugly noise stop," Declan mumbled.

"Just trying to figure out the left and right lateral limits on this here firing range."

"How long does the ship think we're going to be here?"

Payne asked. Their escort pointed to the screen. "How long are the august Majors Payne and Dank scheduled to be on board?"

"Major Payne and Major Dank are scheduled for thirteen days, with a potential extension of three hundred days," the AI replied.

"Three hundred? I like the *Voeller*. I'm not ready to leave her behind." Dank tossed his hands in the air. "I feel like I've surrendered what little control I had over my own life."

"The mirage is that you never had control." Payne threw his arm over his XO's shoulders while he looked at their escort. "Lead on, wild man. We'll dump our trash in our quarters, and then we'll find our people so we can work out and earn the egregious amounts of chow we're going to consume. And then we'll hit the club and see what's happening."

"I don't think so," the shorter man said. "You'll be dining at the captain's table tonight. Please dress appropriately."

Payne took a step back, almost running into a member of the ship's company who was strolling down the corridor. "This is what we wear." He held his arms out, showing off his uniform before turning a full circle.

"We have a uniform shop on board."

Payne vigorously shook the man's hand. "Thanks for all your help. We'll see you around. Is there a special number we call to get you?"

"No," he replied. He held Declan's gaze for a moment and walked away.

"I guess we're turned loose. Captain's mess, huh? Big first night, Virge."

"Do we need to get dress uniforms made? Seems like a waste." Virgil didn't follow Declan, who had already turned the corner on the way to ditch his small bag in their room but never made it. He returned to Virgil, who was waiting before the screen.

"Fine." Declan crossed his arms and waited.

Virgil tapped the screen. "O wondrous screen of all knowledge, I shall call you SOAK from now on..."

"I won't answer to that," the screen interrupted.

"This AI is much better than the one on *Voeller*." He moved close to the screen and studied it. "Is there someone behind there messing with us?"

"Welcome aboard *Cleophas*, humanity's latest and greatest technological achievement. No one is in here besides me. The ship. I am the ship, and it is me. We are one, the embodiment of a perfect symbiotic relationship. *Cleophas* gives me energy that I use to bring joy to those within."

Virgil and Declan looked at each other. "I could stand here all day talking to you, but then I wouldn't burn enough calories to earn a meal worth eating. Where is the uniform shop?"

"There is no uniform shop onboard *Cleophas*. Should your duty uniform get damaged, you can turn it in for a replacement at the supply center on Deck Twelve."

"I didn't even get that guy's name, and he tried to pull a fast one on us. Damn Fleetie can fuck himself." Virgil raised his hand to give their escort the finger, but he was too far down the corridor. Declan stopped him.

"We should have asked his name. We're guests onboard this bad boy. A tour would have been nice, but I didn't plan on being here long. We'll have to count on SOAK to show us around. Let's find Team Payne." He turned back to the screen.

"I told you not to call me that."

"When you are the SOAK, you embrace your exalted position. Please tell us where we can find Tech Specialist Seven Katello Andfen and Combat Specialist Seven Cointreau Koch, please?" Payne tried to be cordial, even though he was talking to a machine. It was trying to help him, even though he was giving it a hard time.

"They are in their quarters on this deck. Two thousand one hundred and forty tac one hundred and eight port."

Virgil started counting on his fingers. "That's almost exactly one kilometer from here."

"Almost exactly." The screen stayed on.

"Thank you, SOAK." Declan headed around the corner and toward their quarters. He presented his face to the room screen at eighteen starboard and the door slid open. "Sweet digs."

The room was plain, two beds in a bunk pattern to maximize the use of vertical space. It had a separate restroom stall. On the frigate, the majors had their own staterooms but had a communal restroom.

"I've seen worse," Virgil said when he arrived.

Declan tossed his bag in the lower bunk. "Think about it, Virge. This whole ship to support us."

"No shit. Bring up the info. Let's see what we're up against. It would be a shame to go all that way to have to beg the Fleeties for help."

"Which means we better have our shit together. Sounds like we have twelve days to figure it out. But we also have to ask the question, 'Why didn't the BEP handle this without pulling a dreadnought out of the combat zone?' Is it better to leave a weaker force on the front lines, or is the threat back home that great?"

"All three Kaiju-class were out here. Maybe Earth is feeling a little exposed." Virgil changed gears instantly. "You know I sleep naked, right? And I'm going to climb to my rack right past your face."

"You are all kinds of wrong, Virgil Dank. Don't make me call your mom." Declan pulled the portable computer out of his bag and brought it online. It automatically linked with *Cleophas'* systems. Declan accessed his file storage to bring up the Prog ship imagery. "It's bigger than this thing."

Virgil whistled as the vid traveled the length of the Behemoth's hull from stem to stern.

"We need to crack that nut, Virge. With all the assets at BEP's command, they called us back off the front lines. That's not sitting right with me. It's giving me indigestion."

"That's probably those chimichangas you had last night, but I get what you're saying. It's right there. The BEP could ride the gravity waves at sub-light and still be there before us. Hell, they've already been there because we got pictures."

Declan leaned back and crossed his arms as the panning video moved in close for its return trip to the bow of the massive vessel.

Virgil reached past Declan and toggled the speed to slow it down, then backed up and froze the high-resolution image. "You seeing what I see?"

"Access hatch or missile ports?"

"I think the latter since they are arrayed in a nice bank. Missiles from a ship that could make itself invisible? That could change the war."

"From a race that abandoned its ships across the galaxy. I'm not convinced that anything on that ship is a game-changer, but it brings me back to—"

A sudden pounding on the door interrupted him. "Come!" Declan shouted. The pounding continued.

"The door doesn't like you," Virgil said. "Open." The door responded to his command from inside the room.

"Bring the Payne!" eight voices called.

"Come on in. This is where the party is." Virgil stepped aside.

"Officer country, land of the spoiled little bitches," Heckler said when he entered, looking around the quarters. "Our room is something similar. Same size space, but two quad bunks and no toilet. Can you do something about that?"

"Major Dank, see if there is something else. Maybe a couple can sleep in the skimmer, take the edge off. It's less than two weeks. You could stand on your heads for that long if you had to. When we come out of FTL, the prize waiting for us will be worth it. Ladies and gentlemen, I present to you the Behemoth."

Payne stepped aside so the team could see the screen. Blinky leaned in. "Why don't you project it to the room's screen?"

The major shrugged and gestured for his computer specialist to take over. Blinky tapped a few buttons, and the image appeared on the big screen opposite the bed. The team spread out to better see it without any heads in the way.

"That's one big ugly summa-beyotch," Specialist Skellig remarked. "But no scoring or scarring. I'm not sure it was in a fight. Why's it parked?"

"That'll be for us to figure out. Turbo has designated what it looks like on the outside, but on the inside, that will be one beautiful piece of gear. It was invisible. Geeks think the system failed, so no matter what, it had power that lasted a thousand years and invisibility. Those two things alone make this a worthwhile project." Payne had already seen the video. He opted to watch his people instead and gauge their reactions as they saw it for the first time.

Heckler stopped blinking and stared at the screen. He started mumbling in a stream of consciousness. "Missile ports, close-in weapons, broadcast aerials, beams, lasers, particle beams...is that a railgun? Maybe. Hangar doors, fighter ports, I'm counting sixteen, eighteen, twenty on this side, probably same the other side. Damn!"

"What are you thinking, Heckler?" Declan asked.

"It's a heavy battlewagon, ship-of-the-line size, bigger than a superdreadnought and definitely a ship built for battle. A battleship."

Tech Specialist Six Augry Byle, a weapons specialist, bobbed her head as the vid continued to play. "I could spend a lifetime digging into that kit."

"Me, too, Byle," Shaolin, a ship weapons specialist, agreed. "That is ridiculous. It's nothing but guns, missiles, and fighters. Do we know if anything is intact?"

"We don't, Shaolin. And that's the rub." She paused the video. "Why are they sending us in there and not some team that's already in-system?"

"'Cause we've got more combat experience than anyone back home. All except Fetus because that rat bastard Slayer up and retired thanks to his cold black heart."

"Slayer was good but slowing down. Better to retire while he can still enjoy it, but that leaves us hanging."

Dank raised one finger instead of his arm. "Because Team Payne is the only SOFT unit with a mix of tech and combat specialties. Weapon systems-heavy with Byle and Shaolin and three combat specialists. Other team leads go all combat or all tech, with one token rating to say they have a diversified team. They don't."

"They suck," Blinky offered.

Payne held up his hands for calm before the team pounced on the easy target of making fun of the other teams. "No matter what the reason, we're it." He pointed at the frozen image on the big screen. "We have to penetrate that thing and secure it. I don't have any orders beyond that, but I expect it will be obvious. It's going to take all of us to crack this nut. We can't fuck this up. Do you understand me?"

"Yes, sir," they replied in muted voices.

"We are going to dissect every element of information BEP gave us. We are going to crawl up that video's ass until we know exactly where the most vulnerable points are and where we're going in. Then when we get inside, we're going to use our vast store of knowledge about Prog ships to guide us through the interior to find the heart and mind of that ship."

"I'm sorry, what? We don't know jack about those ships. The other dozen we went into were nothing more than a skin over interior framing."

"Thirteen, Sparky," Payne corrected.

"A baker's dozen. See how easy it is to lose track when you see the same thing over and over?"

"Aren't you forgetting that Team Payne is the hero of Hell's Canyon?" Fetus blurted. The team stared at him.

"Meant we were luckier than everyone else. Nothing heroic about that," Payne replied.

Fetus remained adamant. "I've seen the vids. You guys danced with death and made him bow. That's why I killed myself to get on your team. I hope one day I'm worthy of the Blue Planets that you won."

Payne sighed and shrugged while looking at the deck. "It's in a display case at my parents' house. Maybe their friends ooh and ahh when they see it. I'd rather have a plasma rifle that can reach to a thousand meters. That is something worth getting."

"But you're a Blue Planet winner!"

"Stow it, Fetus. There is only what we do today to prepare for tomorrow. I intended to have this meeting later, but we lost track of time as soon as we brought up the files for a quick look-see. Now that we've had it, tomorrow we'll start a more in-depth analysis, including the other scans to figure what we need to burn our way into that thing."

"Hold on," Blinky urged. "If the ship is still intact, what if there's aliens on board? And if not, they had to be able to get back in. I suggest we can hack our way to the inside without breaking anything."

"I like breaking stuff," Heckler remarked.

"Meathead," Blinky countered.

"Unapologetically so." Cointreau Koch remained stalwart in his convictions. He had cross-trained in computer analytics, but only so he understood what Katello Andfen was saying. Heckler had no pretensions of being able to do what Blinky could.

"Is it just me, or is it getting hot in here?" Major Dank wondered. The team members looked at each other. Turbo opened the door and stood in the doorway to keep it from shutting. Somebody whistled from down the corridor. She gave him the finger.

"On it, Fleetie!"

"Back at you, SOFTie," came the reply.

"An ex-boyfriend?" Byle asked.

"Aren't they all?" Sparky suggested, earning her the finger too. She gave it back, and within the span of a single breath, the entire team was giving each other the rude salute.

"People!" Payne's single word brought order to chaos. "This op will put Hell's Canyon to shame. Mark my words. Time check."

"Thirteen-oh-five," Dank answered. The others checked their timepieces. They were auto-synced with the ship and reported a constant health status to it. *Cleophas* used that data to keep track.

"If we want to enjoy the fine dining offered by this ship, then we need to burn some calories. Next stop, the workout facilities. Oorah, hardcore. Bring the pain."

"Team Payne!" they shouted and hurried into the corridor. Fetus stopped, and Turbo ran into him.

"What the hell, Fetus?"

"Where are we going?"

"The gym, dumbnuts."

"I know the gym, but where is it?"

"Get out of the way, Fetus." He moved to the side of the corridor. She bumped him as she passed.

The majors were the last two out of the room as the rest of the team marched single-file down the corridor.

"What are you waiting for?" Payne asked.

"I didn't know where the gym was, and Turbo bumped me out of the way."

"No one knows where it is. She's going to ask that touch screen around the corner. Get up there and ask first, then lead this parade. C'mon, Fetus, show some initiative."

"Yes, sir!" The CS3 bolted down the corridor and almost missed the turn before disappearing around the corner.

Dank shielded his mouth with his hand as he spoke to the team's commander. "Do you think he's going to make it?"

"Kid is a techno wiz. Probably picked combat arms because he got beat up for being the smart one. He's going to make us proud. Just not right now. I'll pull Turbo aside to lay off. She's mad that Slayer retired. She looked up to him."

"As Fetus will look up to her if she earns his respect." Dank spoke loud enough for all to hear. "Turbo!"

She hurried down the line to answer her summons. Major Payne spoke. "Why are you so mean?"

"Sir?" She recoiled from the question.

"There's a big difference between being hard and being mean. I challenge you to learn it. Carry on."

"Yes, sir." She fell in at the back of the line.

When they reached the corner, they found Fetus making exaggerated hatchet arm motions toward the aft end of the ship. He marched away smartly, moving to the right side of the corridor as he went. The team followed, not out of loyalty to their youngest member but to watch and see where he'd take them.

"Wasn't the gym the other way?" Dank whispered.

"There's one back here, too. Although it's twice as far, it is a lot closer to their quarters."

"What I hear you saying is that he's giving us the long-name bone job in order to get in tight with his fellow enlisted."

"Same thing we'd do, Virgil. I thought it was a nice touch. The hatchet arm, not so much."

[3]

"The value isn't in the plan, but in the planning." —From the memoirs of Fleet Admiral Thaylon Loore

"I want to eat with our team," Dank groused.

"Shut your cakehole and take it like a man." Payne slapped his XO on the back. They followed the directions to the elevator and then up to Deck Thirteen, the middle of the ship where the captain's mess and suite were located.

"You don't want to go either."

"No shit. But you have been promoted to the lofty rank of major, and that means you have responsibilities. You should have stayed a captain, but you deserve your own team. You'll get one as soon as we wrap this op."

"I know. I thought I wanted it, but I like our team."

"You'll grow to love your own team." Payne pointed to a sign on the bulkhead that stated they'd arrived at the captain's mess. "Shall we show the flag, so to speak?"

"At your leisure, Major Payne."

Payne knocked on the old-fashioned wood door. It delivered

a sharp click, unlike trying to bang on metal or carbon fiber. He leaned close to hear if they were allowed to enter. The door slid open, and Payne stumbled in.

"You!" Declan pointed at the aide who had escorted them to their quarters. He carried a towel over his arm server-style, and he smiled graciously.

"Gentlemen," an older voice said softly. He pushed away from the table and stood. "I'm Captain Ezekial Smith. Welcome to *Cleophas*."

The captain wore a set of overalls similar to what the majors wore. Payne glanced at the aide. He returned a nearly imperceptible shrug. "Something to drink, gentlemen?"

"Dark beer ice-cold," Dank replied.

"Of course. We have a variety of non-alcoholic beer available. And for you, Major Payne?"

"Same. Thanks. I didn't get your name earlier."

"Ensign Lord." The man nodded and hurried away.

Payne turned his attention to the captain, who had sat down. He gestured at the seats to his left and right. His was a dining table for eight, but only three places had been set.

"My compliments on your ship, Captain. This is an impressive piece of hardware."

"I agree, but I fear the Kaiju-class are too few and too far apart. The Armageddon-class dreadnoughts are already obsolete. A refit takes almost as long as building a new ship and takes just as much raw material."

"The trials and tribulations of a world at war," Payne replied.

The aide appeared with two frosted glasses of near-beer. Dank took a sip before nodding to Payne and following with a full drink.

Major Payne delivered the appropriate toast. "To the Fleet."

"And to those who make it great," the captain replied. Once

they drank, the captain continued. "It's been a while since I've felt a buzz like this mission. I've never driven a million-ton taxi before. Who are you, and don't jack me around?"

Dank froze mid-drink and casually put his glass down. He and Payne exchanged glances. The team lead had the responsibility.

"I think we're just a bunch of grunts who work well together. I received my orders directly from Fleet Admiral Wesson, but he was short on detail besides the intel package he forwarded. I suspect you received the same package. My team will be ready to leave *Cleophas* the second we arrive at Ganymede. Over the next thirteen days, we will develop a multi-pronged approach to penetrating into the interior of the Prog battlewagon."

"You've already determined that it's a battleship?"

"Sir, please. It bristles with weapons. There's no way it could be anything else."

"Sometimes I have to test you ground-pounders, see if you know what us Fleeties are all about. I still think you are something more than you're telling me, but keep your secrets. I'll find out sooner or later. In regards to the Progenitor ship, you are correct. Our best people believe it is a battleship that we're calling *Leviathan*."

Payne looked at the ceiling as he tried to remember the definition of the word. It finally came to him. "A giant sea creature, but also a totalitarian government."

"The sea creature, yes. There is such a thing as a leviathan government? I didn't know that, but I could see how it applies. If this thing's weapons are as powerful as we believe, it could destroy most of our Fleet without batting an eye. It would take all three Kaiju-class working together to defeat it."

"How long have you guys been analyzing this thing?" Payne

wondered. Dank took another drink, but he was listening intently.

"Not long, only a day, but since we aren't joining the fight, the intel weenies have nothing else to do besides analyze and assess. The entire focus of their effort is on that derelict."

"It could turn out to be just another shell, Captain."

"It could, but no one believes that. Big money is on it being a treasure trove. How are you going to get in?"

"That's what we need to figure out." Payne rubbed his hands together in anticipation.

"Let's do this again in six days in case you need any Fleet assets like plasma torches or heavy gear like a crane. And then we'll meet one last time on the night before we arrive to finalize the details. We'll get you close to Ganymede, but not too close."

The captain stood and offered his hand. The majors shook it in turn. "I'm sure you want to join your team to eat. Don't let me hold you."

The majors nodded. Payne looked forlornly at his beer. Dank only had a small drink left but regarded leaving it behind as alcohol abuse. The aide ushered them out.

When the door closed behind them, they looked at each other and chuckled.

"That's the worst dinner I've ever been to," Dank grumbled.

"Ensign Lord is my sworn and mortal enemy. We shall be avenged!" Payne declared, shaking his fist at the door. "But the captain's right. I'd rather eat with the team."

Major Payne had reserved a formal conference room for the final brief of his team because everyone wanted a piece of the action. Unfortunately, the team had determined they needed additional assets if there were going to expedite getting into

Leviathan. They sat around the outside, leaving the table for Fleet personnel, including Captain Smith who had decided a formal briefing with key personnel made more sense.

The team was there a half-hour early to review the engagement plan for the fifth time.

Payne stood next to the screen.

"To make sure we know the plan because it's critical that everyone does, this briefing will be given by Combat Specialist Periq. Come on, Fetus. Get up here. Whenever the captain and his staff arrive, you'll be the one doing the dirty deed."

"But sir!" the youngest member of the team blurted, eyes wide and legs pushing back as if he could drive his chair away from the others. The wall prevented him from escaping.

"Get your fucking dumbass up here." Payne took one angry step forward, and Fetus popped to his feet and reluctantly walked to the front of the room. "A quick run through, just me and you. What's first?"

"Eat 'til you're tired, sleep 'til you're hungry. The glory of shipboard life. Oorah!" Heckler offered. The others laughed. Payne bit his lip.

"Ignore him. Just me and you. We board the skimmer. Then what?"

"We get our suits on for space operations," the young man replied.

"Exactly. Then what?"

"Transit to target. Three teams. Blinky leads Team One, which will look for a digital access to *Leviathan* and hack its way in. It will be him, Joker, and me on that team." Joker, Huberta Hobbes, the team's communications specialist.

"Why you, Fetus?" Major Dank asked.

"Because I'm good at that stuff, but I'll be ready to deploy if you need extra firepower." He thrust his chest out as if daring anyone to challenge him. Payne fixed his eyes on Combat

Specialist Skellig to keep her from trying to crush Fetus' initiative.

"We're counting on not needing extra firepower while being ready for exactly that." He clapped Fetus on the back. "Second team."

"You'll lead the second team, looking to breach one of two possible airlocks located on the top of the hull. Major Dank will lead the third team to attempt penetration through a personnel-sized airlock into what we believe is the hangar bay."

"What resources do we need?"

"Plasma torch and heavy lifting bots. Both have been requisitioned, tested, and are attached to the outside of the skimmer, ready for activation."

The young man's voice grew stronger as he repeated the plan they all knew by heart.

"And here's the biggest question. What are the risks?"

"From nothing to greatest. It could be another empty hulk, but we expect Blinky's team will know that before anyone leaves *Glamorous Glennis*. Penetration teams will conduct an exhaustive visual and technical examination, looking for booby traps. Next risk is explosive decompression upon penetration to the interior. Once inside, traps, a broken ship in its dying throes, or even aliens still alive and unhappy that we're on board their ship."

"What if we can't cut through the hull?"

"Or get the doors open by asking nicely?" Blinky added.

"Then we'll return to *Cleophas* to regroup before moving to secondary and tertiary entry points. If those fail, then we'll attempt to blast into the hangar bay using *Cleophas'* precision and high-power weapons like the capital-grade railguns, but that would be upon the advice and consent of the Fleeties."

"How do we mitigate the risks?"

"Booby traps and explosive decompression are by inspection, awareness, and working from behind shields. Suit transponders will be active in case anyone gets blown into space. Search and recovery assets will be on standby, we're told, as we'll be the only show in town with eight thousand Fleeties watching every move we make."

The group nodded without laughing. It wasn't the first time the team had operated under the scrutiny of the support ship.

"For aliens, Team Payne brings a lot of combat power through standard weapons loadout. That means axes, pulse rifles, plasma grenades, flashbangs, and stunners, giving the team both lethal and non-lethal options."

"See?" The major gripped the young man's upper arm and smiled. "You know the plan. Simple is our friend." He stared into Fetus' eyes. "If you guys can't get a handshake, then we burn our way in. Technical scans suggest it's made of a metal that will melt."

Blinky pushed away from the wall and started to pace. "Technical scans also show active low-grade energy throughout the ship. That tells me a powerplant is still operating. But what if it is a living ship, and the low-grade power is like the pulsing of blood through its veins?"

He looked up to see the team staring at him.

Payne pointed to the image on the screen. "May I direct your attention to the bristling weapon systems? Missile launchers. Gun ports. Energy weapons. Stop reading that science fiction stuff. It's making you weird. Read some good Wolfpack westerns. Those'll make you whole again from whatever broke you."

"I play video games. Read? Why would I want to imbibe fiction while I sleep when the real world is so much better?"

"Blinky. There are no veins in that ship. The power is trickling through conduits and is shunted to various systems by means of transformers, relays, and the usual energy distribution stuff."

"It was just a thought. Bedang! Don't shoot the only one here with an imagination."

A voice crackled through the overhead speakers. The team looked at each other as they hadn't known they were broadcasting elsewhere on the ship. "If I can break in here," Captain Smith stated. "Excellent briefing, Specialist Fetus."

"Specialist Periq, sir. His *nickname* is Fetus because he's the newest member of the team, so new that he's not even a baby yet..." Payne's explanation drifted off in the silence of the realization that the captain had been watching them from start to finish.

"Specialist Periq, then. Fleet assets are already attached to your ship. SAR vehicles will deploy around both teams. If someone floats away, they won't get far. And you are correct in that all of this ship will be watching you, and for this one very brief moment in time, we wish we were you. But then we remember that you like sleeping in the mud and eating cold ration bars. Then we're happy to be Fleet. I have my senior staff with me. I believe they have questions?"

"Doctor Peter van Lier here, chief medical officer. If you run across any aliens, I must insist that you not kill them. We need to learn about their physiology and mental state. It's better if I'm not doing it through a necropsy."

Payne clenched his jaw until the doctor followed up.
"Well?"

"Doctor van Lier. We will take appropriate measures to ensure our personal safety and then the safety of those in our charge. Next question, please."

"How much time are you going to give the digital penetration attempt before you start cutting into that beautiful remnant from the past?"

Major Payne rubbed his temples. "The cyber-unlocking team will have complete and unfettered access for probably a couple hours, during which we'll deploy, inspect the access points, and set up our equipment. I'll verify with Blinky where he is before we attempt physical access."

"A couple hours? That's ridiculous. Captain, we should take over this part of the operation, and it'll take as long as it takes!" the voice declared.

"Who is speaking?" Payne demanded.

"This is Chief Sheila Waverly, head of communications, which also means I'm in charge of the signals and technical intelligence collection teams. We have the assets to conduct this mission, and it may seem bold to say, but we can do it better than you."

Blinky clenched and unclenched his fists. Payne smiled and gestured for calm. "You know what you don't have, Chief?"

"No," came the soft response.

"Orders from Fleet Admiral Wesson to conduct this mission. Let's not waste time with anything other than Team Payne and how we are going to get on board *Leviathan*. And do it before the Blaze fleet shows up."

"What? No one said anything about the Blaze fleet. Captain?" the voice insisted, but she wasn't speaking to Major Payne.

There was a long delay before the captain spoke. "There is some speculation that the Blaze fleet knows about this ship and wants to take it. That wasn't openly available information, Major Payne."

"Whatever counterintelligence operation Fleet is running to dig out this Blaze collaborator won't impact us while we're here. What will impact us is if the Blaze Collective shows up. Which we should prepare for anyway. Why else would a Kaiju be sent here? You need to up your intel game, Chief, if you hadn't guessed the derelict was in play."

"Do you have anything else for us, Major?" the captain interrupted.

"We appreciate your support and the support of your crew. You know our final option in case we can't get in. We'll need precision shooting to break through the hangar door and not damage the rest of the ship. From there, we should find alternate access points to the interior. Once inside, we'll adjust and request additional assets. Maybe you can answer a question for me. Why us and only us? Leviathan is nearly five kilometers long. There could be dozens of teams attempting access, scouring every square meter of that thing."

The captain cleared his throat. "If we only knew the ways of admirals, but alas, we do not. Good hunting, Major."

"We're hoping for some stellar lockpicking to save us from having to patch a big hole. We look forward to reporting when we are on board, Captain."

The crackle and snap signaled the line had been closed. At least, that's what they thought. "Are we alone?" Tech Specialist Four Huberta Hobbes asked. She was always the quiet one, even though she was the communication specialist, the one responsible for talking, so they called her Joker, because she was the one least likely to make a joke. It made sense where team nicknames were involved.

"I thought we were alone before. So, assume that we're not. What do you have?"

"How long will we be given to crack the code? No matter what the Fleetie said, nobody is better than Blinky. If there is a handshake of any sort, he'll get us in."

"I appreciate the vote of confidence," Blinky replied. "After two hours, I'll have an idea if it's possible, but I'll be dealing with an alien operating system. But you know what's not alien?

Math. If there is any signal at all that extends outside the ship's hull, I'll be able to get in."

"I'll bet you the first round at Giorgio's if we can get libo on Earth. And I want you to win, but I'll enjoy my drink if you don't. People. We are going to get inside that ship. My bet is that getting inside won't even be the warmup before stretching before the first game of the season, let alone the big game. And just when we're ready to grab the trophy, Fleet will come in and take it all. We'll be back on board *Voeller* and off to our next mission. Don't groan. You know how it is. We'll get medals—even you, Fetus—and then we'll be back in the mud, slugging it out with some alien we've never seen before who the Blaze convinced to fight us. Wash. Rinse. Repeat. Any questions?"

Everyone shook their heads.

"Chow at zero five hundred. Weapons check at zero six. Load up and suit up by zero seven. We should come out of FTL shortly thereafter. The second we're within range, we're deploying. I'm counting on each and every one of you to do your job to the best of your ability. Take it easy on chow tonight. We could be in our suits for twelve hours or more, and the last thing you want is to have to take a dump." Major Payne looked from face to face for understanding.

"On that delightful note, we'll rally at your chow hall in the morning. We eat as a team, and we beat this thing as a team. Oorah," Major Dank said.

The team repeated the war cry and filed out of the conference room.

"Are you thinking what I'm thinking?" Dank asked.

"I have no idea what you're thinking." Payne checked the room to make sure nothing was left behind.

"Officers' mess and then the club?" He wiggled his eyebrows.

"Workout, then mess, then back to the room for sleep. We

need to be sharp because, I have to remind you, when have our ops ever gone according to plan?"

"That wasn't our fault!" Dank countered.

"It never is, but we're the ones who have to deal with it. Comes with the territory."

"I know," he conceded. "I thought one last swing, like a bachelor party of sorts. When we finish this one, I'll be going."

They left the room. "Let's finish this op before we discuss how much better your replacement will be."

[4]

"SUBTLE IS NOT A WORD USED BY A PARTY AT WAR."
—FROM THE MEMOIRS OF FLEET ADMIRAL THAYLON LOORE

Team Payne ate and checked their weapons. As usual, they brought all their gear to stow in the skimmer. They cross-decked —that is, transferred to other ships—with such great frequency that they tried not to leave anything behind since they never knew when they'd be back.

Once in the skimmer, they stripped naked and started suiting up. Fetus glanced at the bodies, male and female.

"Chicks dig scars," Turbo told him before turning sideways to show her well-muscled leg and the scar that ran from mid-hip to her knee, "because chicks have scars."

Heckler's back looked like it had been through a meat grinder. Fetus kept his head bowed, ashamed of his smooth skin. Heckler pushed him.

"Do me a favor, kid, and don't end up like us. No one digs scars. They suck. They hurt. And the only thing they tell anyone is that you're bad at keeping your head down."

"My head was down, Heckler. The rest of me? That was a different story. No shit, Fetus. Keep your head down." Turbo stared at him until he nodded. She stepped into her suit and let it seal itself up to her neck, then activated the suit's system check.

One by one, they donned the combat suits that doubled as environmental suits, self-contained units good for twelve hours or seventy-two when used in survival mode. Team Payne had gone sixty-five hours once before being recovered. That had made them a little nervous and much more trusting of their suits.

It also demonstrated the weird thing about counterattacks: sometimes they cut off the combat unit at the pointy end of the spear.

Blinky and Joker took the front seats while Fetus set up at a side console. Everyone else relaxed on the outboard bench seats. The plan was to jump out the floor hatch, counting on Ganymede's weak gravity to pull them toward the small moon before the team activated their suits' control thrusters, pen-thin pneumatic jets to slow their descent and fly them to their target.

First, though, came the attempted handshake.

The field warp flowed over them as *Cleophas* transitioned from faster than light to a near stop in orbit around Jupiter.

"We have company," Blinky announced.

"Of the butthole puckering type or something else?"

"BEP ships, Dragonfly-class pickets. Looks like we have an escort."

"Comm channels are active. Scanning the spectrum for other signals," Joker reported.

Blinky turned around to look at Major Payne. The major gave him the thumbs-up.

"Launching." Blinky activated the flight control systems, released the docking clamp, and maneuvered away from

Cleophas. This side of Ganymede resided in darkness. Blinky switched the sensors from passive to active. "There you are. Setting autoflight. We are on course. Next stop, *Leviathan*."

Blinky brought up his main screen and starting running a series of programs designed to locate and isolate available signals from the derelict. Joker, the communications specialist, continued scanning the frequency bands, varying modulations before switching to light-based communications. The skimmer's lasers splattered an exotic array of colors across the ship's hull.

"Slowing our approach." Blinky tapped the screen. Payne and the rest of the team could only watch as the three specialists worked within their strengths. Their fingers danced across the screens while they mumbled unintelligibly. After fifteen minutes, the seven inactive members of the team were sound asleep, faces against their helmets, mouths open.

Fetus tapped, leaned back, then dove back in. "Check seven hundred and fifty-two kilohertz, amplitude modulated."

Joker reconfigured her system to look outside the range of modern systems. "Would you look at that?"

"Why would it use such an inefficient means of communication?" Blinky wondered as he tried to ride the AM carrier wave with a complex program. It took more than a minute to transmit one attempt at a handshake to establish a connection before getting rejected. "This is going to take forever. Let me rewrite this program. Give me fifteen minutes." He checked the team and decided to slow their approach even more. He needed more time to determine if the carrier wave was viable, and he couldn't do that with one minute per attempt. He needed each break-in effort to last no more than a nanosecond or two, so he could flood *Leviathan* with attempts until he received a response and adjust from there.

Fetus shook his head. "Amplitude modulation doesn't lessen

the frequency of the data. We need to reduce the space between altered and non-altered radio waves to turn the signal binary."

"That's what we're doing, but the transmitter wasn't specifically designed for this. The workaround is the problem," Blinky explained.

"Try this," Fetus said and sent the program he had to Blinky's workstation.

The tech specialist looked it over.

"You'll need to modify it with your hacker program, but that should be nothing more than a copy and paste."

"Where did you get this?' Blinky asked. He rotated his chair and faced the young man.

"My friends and I had a secret code we used to communicate. AM data within a PM wave. Back to the future, huh?"

"What else are you keeping from us?"

"Don't we have a ship to break into? You can bust out the bright lights and thumb screws later. Suffice to say that I chose combat arms to get away from my friends, who took it too far and are now doing five to seven in a retraining camp."

Blinky offered his hand for a high five. "It would have been nice to know that earlier. When we're done cracking this safe, you and I are going to have a little sit-down to discuss what else you bring to this team. This isn't amateur hacker stuff."

"I thought it might come in handy."

"No secrets, Fetus! I'll mirror my station, and you make sure we get this right."

"Yes, sir!"

"Fucking new guy! Don't make me kick the shit out of you." Blinky was already cutting out the secret code from the pulse-modulated program. He inserted his best work as a subroutine that ran within, turning the PM into AM at the receiving station, where it unpacked upon arrival. "The amplitude changes are buried within the pulses, which are fixed, not variable. To a normal receiver, they would sound like white noise if the receiving unit translated them into any sound at all."

"Something like that," Joker replied. "Packets packed within packets."

"I'm getting a dwell of two-point-four nanoseconds. Nicely done, Fetus. Don't get cocky. We have a lot of work to do before the knuckle-draggers are on board."

"I heard that," Major Payne muttered, blinking himself into the waking world. "What time is it?" He stood and leaned between the flight deck seats. "We should be a lot closer by now." He stared at Blinky until the computer specialist acknowledged his presence.

"I slowed us down once we discovered the handshake protocol was hidden in what we consider old tech. We," he gestured at Joker and Fetus, "had to reconfigure our emitters. Fetus had the key. Now we're on track to run through access code combinations in an hour or two."

Payne chewed his lip as he contemplated the workflow. He checked the time on the front panel. "We need to deploy and start our inspections of the penetration sites. Dual-track efforts. I'm sorry, we can't leave this to just hacking our way inside because we're under orders, but I'll drag my feet to give you as much time as possible. I don't want to punch holes in a ship that might be flightworthy."

"Why would they abandon a ship that was flightworthy?"

"Treaty compliance? They signed with someone and didn't want to destroy their best stuff, so they hid it where the ancient humans would never find it, not until after we developed space travel. Maybe they didn't expect to leave it for a thousand years."

"That makes more sense than anything I came up with. And it also gives me hope that it's still intact. The active signal, although old technology, suggests the systems are working but not providing livable space within. I think we'd see air pumps, scrubbers, and distributions systems action. I'm not getting any of that. Time to get your helmets on." Blinky tapped the flight controls to close on the ship.

The skimmer accelerated toward Ganymede's surface, using sensors to guide it through the darkness.

"Up and at 'em! It's almost time to bring the Payne." Declan strolled down the open center of *Glamorous Glennis*, kicking boots as he passed. The team grumbled and groused appropriately. "If you aren't complaining, you aren't happy!"

The team snapped their helmets into place. Payne sauntered to the front of the skimmer, where the flight deck was separated from the crew compartment by a raised ledge.

"Get your helmets on, gentlemen. Don't want you dying before you can give us a ride to the pig when we're done breaking into that vault."

The pig was any ship where they could get a bunk and a hot meal. Major Payne remained eternally grateful for the Fleet's support but had an odd way of showing it. He checked the smaller inset screen to take in the aft view. *Cleophas* nearly filled the screen.

"How slow are you driving the boat?" Payne asked.

Blinky chuckled, hesitating with his helmet in his hands. "We were at a blistering one kph. Some may say I'm driving like a bat out of hell, while other impatient commanders would feel compelled to get out and push. We'll be there in one minute. Prepare to deploy. I'll undock the gear outside the ship. Grab it on your way down. If we're feeling it, the doors might be open by the time you get there."

"You tease me, Blinky, but you and I both know we're going to have to blast our way into that thing. Just like we've done on the last thirteen, only to find they are nothing but a shell sealed as tightly as a chicken's egg."

"Eggs. Real eggs. Who's being the tease now?" Blinky put his helmet on and snapped it into place. The systems check was confirmed, and he gave the thumbs-up. One by one, Major Payne looked through each face shield, starting with the three up front to get the green light. He moved down one side of the skimmer and finished on the other.

"Team Payne is green. Major Dank, first stop is Access Point Dank. Prepare to drop."

Virgil, Heckler, Sparky, and Shaolin moved to the center of the compartment and grabbed the overhead bar.

Blinky started a countdown from ten. When he reached one, the floor separated and split, opening the center of the cargo compartment to space. Those not dropping leaned forward and looked out. The derelict filled the space beneath them. Dank counted down from three, and at one, they let go. Sparky and Shaolin immediately activated their suit jets while Dank and Heckler continued downward, accelerating at one point four three meters per second. Nothing too extreme.

The two specialists seized a skid that instantly detached, and they started their descent. Fifty meters ahead, Dank and Heckler rotated through three hundred and sixty degrees to see all aspects of their landing area. Dank hatcheted his arm where the supposed airlock was located. Heckler goosed his jets to send him that way, with Dank close on his heels.

There was no guessing. The suits' heads-up displays showed their location and the target, but they relied on their eyeballs to keep them on track. Above them, the bay doors of the skimmer closed, and it moved on.

Dank and Heckler faced each other to make sure their spacing was good, then turned ninety degrees and headed downward nearly shoulder to shoulder but facing in opposite directions. They touched the jets to slow their descent.

The size of the ship became painfully obvious as they got

closer. What had appeared to be small projections were a dozen meters tall. There seemed to be no rhyme or reason to the structures that peppered the hull.

"Confirming. One-point-four-two-eight meters per second acceleration due to gravity," Dank said to himself before activating the team communication channel. "We're coming in pretty fast. You might want to hit your jets and slow your descent well before touchdown."

"Roger," Sparky confirmed.

With one final burst to stop their momentum, they stepped onto the outer hull of the derelict. Dank took one step away from the man-sized circular hatch, floated into the air, and slowly came back down. He bounced across *Leviathan*'s surface, scouting an area ten meters away from the target penetration point. The hull was smooth metal with a non-skid, non-reflective coating.

Dank bent down and touched it. "Rubbery," he reported. He faced upward as the final two on his team landed beside the hatch. They activated magnetic clamps to hold the skid down.

"Two by two, search to fifty meters on a radial pattern, out on the even degrees and clockwise, then back on the five degrees. Take your time. We only have one chance to get this right." Heckler and Shaolin started from the airlock hatch and headed outward. Dank picked the hundred and eighty-degree opposite direction. Once Sparky joined him, they headed out, walking deliberately. There wasn't much to see, but that didn't matter. Sometimes it was important to follow the plan.

A hundred meters was only a minute away. They reached the end before Heckler and Shaolin, who stopped to check out a half-meter-tall bump.

"We are documenting the location and checking." They bent over it and ran their hands over the surface. "We are satisfied that there are no seams or anything that might suggest this thing is a defensive system. It's more like a bump in cake frosting. Nothing to see. Moving on."

Dank and Sparky were almost back at the hatch when Heckler and Shaolin turned. "You can watch our back, and we'll watch yours," Dank said. Heckler gave him the thumbs-up.

"Business as usual," Shaolin suggested. "Different but the same."

"Stay frosty, Specialist."

"We're not the first ones here," Sparky replied.

"How did you arrive at that?" Dank stopped.

"Come on." He waved the major back to the hatch. "Look at the marks. Someone tried to use a bar on it. The access panel has been scraped clean."

"I was looking outboard to make sure the area was clear first, but I guess it wouldn't have hurt to glance at it. It's like being at a party and you're trying to make eye contact with a hottie, so you find yourself staring. She catches you, and you instantly question your whole existence. Do I look like a steely-eyed serial killer or a happy-go-lucky guy? Always the former, so you bolt from the party."

"I'm sorry, sir. What?" Shaolin asked. Heckler laughed into his microphone.

"Nothing. Being outside in the fresh air is nice. Good job on seeing that. Dank to Payne. Are you getting this?"

"I heard, and I see. Interesting. I have seen the enemy, and he is us. I expect it was BEP techno-dweebs and they couldn't get in. We have ten pickets out here now, thick as thieves. Get back to it, Virgil. They said we could have the time we requested, but I don't think they meant it. I'll be damned if I get pushed aside so a blue-ball bastard can come in here and do the job we've been given. Payne out."

[5]

"Extreme violence will bring an enemy to its knees as readily as a single well-aimed shot."
–From the memoirs of Fleet Admiral Thaylon Loor

Payne looked at the members of his team, Byle and Turbo.

Dank's report had not come as a surprise. "You heard the man. We're not the first to the door, but we'll be the first ones inside to meet the parents."

"Whatever you say, sir," Byle replied.

"How's it going up there? You got it open for us yet? Don't make me fire up this plasma torch," Major Dank parried.

"Trust me when I say that I don't want you to use that plasma torch either. Ready in five, four..." Payne counted down.

The three SOF members gripped the overhead rail as the doors below them opened. On "Go," Payne released his grip and disappeared into the void. The other two activated their jets to drop to the level of the skimmer's underside, where their skid came free with a single touch. They each took a side and followed the major down.

Payne reached behind him to pull his pulse rifle into the ready position and descended as if he were going into a hot zone. None of the others had readied their weapons. That was an individual choice based on the situation. Payne was the only one without anybody watching his back.

Payne stared at the HUD as it counted down toward impact. The short-range scans from the helmet-mounted unit revealed nothing besides the metal Behemoth he raced toward. He cycled his jets to slow his descent well in advance of touchdown.

When he stepped onto the hull, he visually scanned the metal horizon while his sensors pinged and danced across the complex and varied surface. The next thing he did was check the airlock hatch.

"They tried to get in here, too," Payne reported to the team. Byle and Turbo dropped nearby and walked the heavy skid closer to the airlock before clamping it to the hull. "You two get started here with a micro-examination of the airlock. I'll sweep the area."

Unlike Dank's team, Payne walked in an ever-increasing spiral heading away from the airlock. This area of the ship had fewer external obstructions. To one hundred meters away, it was a smooth hull. It took him thirty minutes to complete his sweep before returning to the hatch.

"Major Dank, report," Payne ordered.

"We're eating a big nothing burger at our site. We have completed out-sweep and request permission to burn off this outer coating on a rectangular box four meters by ten meters by five meters. It appears to have been added to the hull well after construction of the ship, and we may be able to penetrate it to get insight into systems that it may contain."

"How did you arrive at that dating regarding the box?"

Payne stared at his HUD where Dank's transmitted images appeared.

"It's a different color." Dank sounded matter-of-fact.

"I'll go with that. Permission granted. Break, break. Blinky, what's your progress?"

"We'd make more if we weren't interrupted every five minutes, sir. As it is, I think we've established a handshake, but we're still working on the twenty questions to get into the system."

"It's been over thirty minutes."

"I'm talking these damn picket ships. They are out here buzzing us. I'm constantly on the horn telling them to back off."

"That's my responsibility. Joker, patch me through to the *Cleophas* command channel, please."

"Link is live," the communications specialist reported.

"*Cleophas* actual, this is SOFT One. Request assistance keeping the airspace clear to a distance of ten kilometers around the ongoing operation."

"This is *Cleophas*. We'll take care of it, Major. What's your progress?" Captain Smith requested.

"The ship is covered in a non-skid-type coating. We're attempting to burn off a section on what we believe is an after-market add-on. We have not attempted physical access efforts on the airlocks but will soon. We have made some progress on the digital front, so we're not in a hurry to burn holes in this sweet ride. And for the record, someone else tried to get into this ship before us. I don't think we were the first choice to do this job, you or me."

"Roger. That's above my pay grade. We'll hold the picket ships at bay so you can do your job. Good luck. Smith out."

That was what Payne wanted. The captain hadn't sounded surprised by the revelation that someone else had tried to access the Progenitor derelict, but he was more tuned into what the higher-ups were doing. Payne was focused on surgical strike missions. Thirteen derelicts, but Team Payne had conducted twenty-five combat missions against members of the Blaze Collective.

He hadn't lost a member of his team.

Yet.

Major Dank clicked through the team channel. "Beginning to clear the coating now. Shaolin is on it, and we're watching from behind cover."

"Sucks to be Byle," Heckler muttered. Payne snorted, but he knew beyond a shadow of a doubt that Heckler would have volunteered if Byle hadn't.

Byle and Turbo watched the major. He switched to their private channel. "What's up?"

"We're ready to start."

"Stop burning, stop burning!" Blinky shouted over the team channel. "STOP!"

"Hang on," Dank said. "Removing the burner and shutting down. What's up, Blinky?"

"You should have seen the RF spikes when you lit the torch. Who says the ship isn't alive? Not me, that's who."

"What kind of strangled logic is that?" Payne looked up and picked the skimmer out of the other lights above them. "Have you enabled two-way communication with the ship?"

"Not yet," Blinky replied in a muffled voice. "But we're getting there," he added more confidently.

"What do you think caused the radiofrequency spike?"

"Burning the skin of a wounded animal."

Byle and Turbo made faces at each other following the computer specialist's reply.

"Could the coating be a sensor screen of some sort, and the ship is directing repair assets to it?"

"Then why weren't the other areas around the hatch repaired?" Blinky shot back.

"Because it's been here long enough that it doesn't have any repair assets available. Small bots with moving parts will break down quicker than big ones."

"Possibly," Blinky conceded.

"How do we get in if we can't cut a hole? And we're not even trying to cut a hole, just clear some of that non-skid away."

"We can see a seam," Dank reported. "Breaking out the pry bars. Blinky, let us know if we get any feedback from the ship."

"And tell it to open this fucking door," Major Payne added.

"Need to open that gap a little wider. Breaking out the attitude adjustment tool." A sledgehammer.

"Ladies and gentlemen," Fetus said in an announcer's voice. "I present to you, *Leviathan*."

The deck thudded heavily before a rapid vibration tickled the boots of both groups on the hull. Simultaneously, the two airlocks' outer doors retracted.

———

"What the hell, dick!" Blinky shouted. He unlatched his helmet and removed it so he could better glare at Fetus. Atmosphere had been restored after sending the team into space, but it was still cold inside the ship. Blinky's breath showed in small and quick puffs.

"What? We wanted to open the airlock door, didn't we? I had the key code. I accessed it before it was buried again."

"Where did you see it? I was watching what you were watching."

"Huh-uh." Fetus shook his head to reinforce his point. His gloved hand rose, and with his pointer finger, Fetus tapped the side of his helmet. "It was aural—AM radio. The ship transmitted the access code, but only in its converted form—a series of beeps. I counted and tried it. I suggest we figure out a way to tell the ship not to do that."

"Fetus, so help me..."

"He's a genius, Blinky," Joker noted with a shrug. "We wanted in. We're in. What is there to bitch about?"

Blinky cocked his head to one side. "When did you hear the access code?"

"With the rush of signals from when Byle started burning. The ship was telling us that we didn't have to do that."

"I'll be damned. Maybe you *are* a genius. But we were here to do something that others tried and failed, and now we're in. Well done, Fetus." Blinky calmed his expression and sat motionless as he recovered his wits and thought about the next steps.

"Can I get a new nickname, like Keyman or Jail Break?"

Blinky and Joker answered in unison. "No."

Once Blinky had his helmet on, he sent the skimmer toward Major Payne's location, where there was room to land. *Glamorous Glennis* maneuvered quickly through the thin atmosphere and settled onto *Leviathan's* hull, looking like nothing more than a mosquito on an elephant. Magnetic clamps locked it down.

Fetus looked at Blinky and received an approving smile while the computer specialist put his helmet back on. The three showed green for extravehicular movement.

Joker punched the button, and the side hatch popped and dropped to the deck as a three-stair ramp. Fetus headed out, followed by Joker and Blinky. They carried small toolkits to help them interface with whatever systems they might find inside.

Blinky secured the skimmer with a remote comm signal. "Nobody forget where we parked," he told the team. "What's the holdup?"

Major Payne waved him off. "Wait for us to clear the way."

Blinky's mouth dropped open as he stared in disbelief. He pointed to the open hatch, dumbfounded.

"I appreciate you opening the door, but wait your turn. You know how we do things. And remember, you think this is a living ship, so how about we not make it any angrier than it already is?"

Blinky dropped his preconceived notion of walking into the ship and setting up at a workstation to use his overwhelming brilliance within which to become one with the Progenitors. He pointed to Fetus. "It was him. He got us in."

Fetus beamed from within his helmet, but nobody could see.

"Good job," Payne told him and turned back to the matter at hand. Sparky and Turbo aimed their weapons through the open hatch, and the lights along the barrels lit up the space inside. Payne dropped prone and eased to the edge. He kept his fingers out of the channel with the hatch and looked inside. "A standard airlock. Not much has changed in a thousand years, it seems."

With *Cleophas* looming overhead, he activated the command channel directly without going through the skimmer. "We have the hatches open and are preparing to enter *Leviathan*. We'll make a limited entry before bringing the rest of our team inside. Payne out."

His responsibility was to report, not get direction from *Cleophas*, but the Kaiju-class did the team a solid by blocking the BEP picket ships, which were watching Payne's every move. Fleet and BEP didn't always see eye to eye. The pickets' presence reinforced the low opinion Payne had of the Blue Earth Protectorate. They'd tried to get in, failed, and now wanted to be in the faces of those who were making it inside.

Payne switched to the team channel. "How you doing back there, Virge?"

"Waiting on the word to go in. I've already had to tackle Heckler three times to keep him from jumping in the hole." Payne sent the images his helmet had captured. "Ours is identical. You are the boss man, so maybe you should let me go first."

"I'm sure that's what Buzz Aldrin told Neil Armstrong," Payne replied. "Switching to live feed. I'm going in." The nine members of the team watched the video on the heads-up displays while Payne slowly scanned the inside of the airlock. "I'm seeing a manual release lever here, along with some buttons. No colors, just shapes. I was hoping there would be red and green buttons. Blinky and Fetus, come on down."

The others groaned since their numbers had not been called. Fetus felt like he was walking on a cloud. Blinky gestured for him to go first. "In you go, Buzz."

"Thank the gods," Fetus replied.

"Stop fucking off and get back to work!" Blinky pushed him into the hole. The major caught him before he hit. The newly named "Buzz" looked around.

"Orient yourself, Specialist. We entered through the top of the ship. If this ship has artificial gravity, it's not active. The exit is that way." The major pointed to their side, ninety degrees from the entry. A ladder was attached to the sidewall. With the low gravity, jumping in was perfectly safe, but at Earth standard, the three-meter drop to the bottom could have twisted an ankle or torqued a knee when the body hit. "I need you and Blinky to figure these buttons out so we don't have any accidents and lock ourselves in or out."

Blinky slowly climbed down the ladder to enter the airlock, trying to look everywhere at once. At eye level next to the ladder were two buttons, one in the shape of a circle and the other a triangle.

Buzz hovered his finger over the triangle. "I'd wager good money this opens the outside door."

Blinky shrugged. "If it closes the door, then the other one opens it. We'll have your answer with one button-push."

"Can you get it back open if the outer hatch closes?" Payne asked.

Blinky lifted his hands to the sky; he didn't know. He tapped his bag. "We'll get it done. Buzz, send Joker the access code to open it up from the outside, just in case we get cut off."

"Standby," the specialist said officiously. "Complete."

"Care to do the honors, sir?" Blinky asked. Payne nodded at Buzz. He pushed the button, and nothing happened.

"We have our answer," Buzz declared triumphantly.

"Punch the other one." Payne waited while Buzz pushed the round button.

Nothing happened. Buzz and Blinky exchanged glances before putting their helmets together while each tried to get a better look at the buttons.

Payne tapped the round button in front of the hatch leading into the ship, and the overhead door started to move. Blinky flinched and stepped aside. All three looked up to see *Cleophas* filling the view, blocking the stars. The door cycled closed, and they were greeted by the sound of air filling the chamber.

"Comm check. Can you hear me, Major Dank? Turbo? Joker?"

The lack of a response gave him his answer. Once the pressure equalized and atmosphere filled the airlock, the inner door opened to a darkened passageway beyond. Major Payne pointed his weapon through the opening, illuminating the passage. It was wide, tall, and extended deeper into the ship than the light could penetrate. A cross-passage went left and right from the opening. Payne stuck his head out and glanced one way and then the other.

He pulled back into the airlock, looking down the corridor. "Blinky, be a peach and punch the triangle."

Blinky tapped it, and the hatch in front of the major slid closed. The air cycled out, before the outer door opened.

"...Payne!"

"Relax, everyone. I thought that would happen. I suspect we'll be able to talk within the ship. Take your team in, Major Dank. Punch the round button by the internal hatch to get inside and the triangle at the outer hatch to get out. That's what worked for us. Those of you with me, come on inside and join the party."

He switched to the command channel. "*Cleophas* actual, this is the team leader. This is most definitely not an empty shell. Once we're inside, the ship acts as a signal dampener, and we will be out of touch. Be patient while we explore. Both teams are in position. We'll report back in one hour."

"How did you get inside, in case we need to come get you?"

"Not over an open channel, sir. I'll send an encoded transmission before we lose comm. Out." Payne looked at Blinky. "Send the captain the access code."

"You know that once the signal goes into open space, even encrypted, it can be broken," Blinky noted.

"I guess you'll have to figure out how to change this tub's access code then, won't you?"

Blinky started to laugh. "I look forward to being able to do that. Fear not, Blinky is here with Buzz to bend *Leviathan* to our will."

[6]

"The energy to wage war is found in power, both manpower and a good engine." –From the memoirs of Fleet Admiral Thaylon Loore

Major Dank punched the circular button, and the four members of his group watched the external hatch close as if they were being locked in a prison. Once the door thumped shut, air pumped into the airlock to equalize the pressure and atmosphere with the inside of the ship.

"Stay frosty, people. We stay together until we know more. Lights on and sensors hot."

"Oxygen-nitrogen atmosphere. Gravity is Ganymede-standard. Temperature is minus forty-one."

"Although tempting to get naked and run in the heat and sunshine, keep your helmets on," Dank replied.

"I wasn't thinking that. Minus forty-one isn't as cold as the planet's surface. That's minus one hundred and twelve," Shaolin stated.

"That means there is enough power for heat. A lot of heat to raise the temp of this beast seventy degrees," Heckler noted. "I'll take point, sir."

"I'll start on point. You bring up the rear. I'm more concerned with what might come up behind us. This ship is twice the size of *Cleophas,* and we are roughly three kilometers away from Major Payne's team. Which reminds me..." Dank changed to the team channel. "Major Payne, can you read me?"

The team leader responded almost instantly. "As I suspected, Virgil. That coating on the outside of the ship dampens the electromagnetic spectrum from outside to in and vice versa, but not once we're within the ship. Team Payne is heading toward the central axis. I think we'll have to go down a few levels to get where we'll find control systems. We'll look for the bridge, you find the engine room."

"In space, air and water may keep you alive, but without power, you will surely die."

"Amen, Major Dank. All comms on the team channel. I want everyone to know what everyone else is up to."

"Roger," Major Dank confirmed. "Weapons hot."

The inner hatch cycled open. Dank shone his light through to reveal two wide corridors angled forty-five degrees from the hatch. Dank shared his video feed before taking a cautious step forward. The deck didn't clang like metal. He bent down and examined the corridor.

"Looks like carpet. Berber, I think, in a soft and pleasant tone," Dank reported with a chuckle. "Not quite the hangar bay like I expected. One of these corridors should lead to it."

"Are you sure you don't want me on point, sir?" Heckler asked from within the airlock. Dank straightened, gave the thumbs-up, and turned down the right corridor.

"I'm assuming the engines are in the rear since it looked that way from the outside. Sparky, are you there?"

"I am. That was my assumption. Life support is probably

more centrally located. A ship this size probably has multiple power plants. The engines may not drive anything but propulsion. Look for anything that might power the ship's systems. Transmission lines will take you right to it."

Dank continued slowly until he realized there were no doors, then picked up the pace and moved deeper into the ship. "Heading aft. This is one long and empty corridor. We'll check in when we get to the end of it."

Major Payne didn't have Dank's issue of nothing to see. Numerous doors lined both sides of all three corridors.

"There's no way we can check every space aboard this ship, so what do you say we do a few sample checks based on size and then find the bigger spaces like the bridge."

"Nothing to say the bridge is bigger," Specialist Andfen stated.

"You're killing me, Blinky. The Progs need to make it easy on *us*, not them. Anything else is downright inconsiderate." Payne pointed at a door with his rifle. Blinky and Buzz stood in front of it, checking. No hand pad or iris scan. No doorknob. No obvious motion sensor.

"I hope these aren't genetically coded," Blinky suggested.

Payne shook his head. "Stop being a freak."

"You love it."

Buzz took the only reasonable action possible; he knocked on the door.

It responded by sliding open. Blinky dove sideways and Buzz stumbled backward, bouncing off the major. Payne grabbed him to keep him from falling down. The door closed.

"Anyone see what was inside?" Payne asked.

"No. Too many people were having heart attacks," Turbo noted.

"Buzz, do the honors, please." Payne pointed his weapon at the door.

The specialist rapped on the door with the knuckles of his suit's glove. The door slid open. Using his rifle's beam, he scanned the inside of the room. "No idea what this is for."

Payne followed Buzz inside. "Looks like overflow quarters. Sparse. Little more than a bed."

"I don't see a bed," Buzz looked rapidly from left to right.

The major tapped the wall near a set of lines that formed a rectangle. The room lights came on and a bed rotated downward, settling into place half a meter off the floor. "Lights," Payne muttered. He poked the mattress. "Triple extra firm. I wonder if that's from age or they liked sleeping on a board. Next room."

They tried the door on the opposite side of the hallway. A knuckle-rap later, it revealed more quarters.

"Spread out. One per." By adding the digital access group, Payne had six of the team's ten members. They each picked a door, knocked, and were granted entry. "Simple enough. Look for a way down because this top deck isn't going to contain any of the critical systems."

"What makes you say that?" Turbo asked.

"If the warship takes any hits, all of this space will be the first impacted with a weapon penetration and venting to space. Assuming the crew is at combat stations, they wouldn't be here. I suspect this entire deck acts as a second hull. We probably have forty decks beneath us. Somewhere down below, we'll find what we're looking for, but not here."

"Time on deck is ten-ten," Joker reported. "Twenty mikes in. Need to report in forty."

"Thanks, Joker. Let me know when we're at ten, and I'll

need you and Turbo to head back and deliver a status report for me. Let's find the stairs."

"Mister Nice Ship, can you please turn on your lights?" Blinky asked.

"Is this part of your ship-is-alive disinformation campaign?" the major asked.

"I've seen nothing to prove me wrong, sir. Maybe we can hurry. We have a lot of ground to cover."

"Ground to cover..." Payne repeated. "If someone entered the ship by the airlock, they wouldn't have to walk a kilometer to get to a way down. Movement within the ship would have to be more efficient than that unless the Progs were marathon runners at heart. Let's go back and check out the closest spaces. I bet we have an elevator nearby."

"Thinking like an officer. Work smarter, not harder," Blinky offered.

They turned back, with Turbo leading the parade toward the airlock access. Once there, she took a left to enter a lateral hallway versus the longitudinal corridor. She shined her light toward the aft end of the ship. The corridor went as far as the light could illuminate. "If Major Dank entered the ship down there, wouldn't we have been able to see them?"

"He said two forty-five-degree corridors. They didn't have one oriented in this direction," Payne replied.

"Here, sir," Joker reported. "One of these things doesn't look like the rest."

Payne and Blinky worked their way to where Joker pointed. They found a door wider than the others with less wall space to the next door, where the openings continued at even intervals like the rest of what they considered to be overflow quarters.

Major Payne tapped the door, and it opened. "An elevator. Blinky?"

The computer specialist entered and looked around. "I

expect it's voice-activated. What do we tell it? Anybody speak Prog?"

"That would be an issue. Can we teach it English?" The major leaned inside to look but didn't cross the threshold.

"How?" Blinky wondered. "We haven't found anywhere we can interface with the main systems. You saw in the rooms there wasn't a computer or vid screen or anything like that."

"Neural interface," Buzz suggested.

"I can work with that," Blinky replied. He looked around, chose the closest door, and knocked on it. Inside was another austere stateroom. He tapped on the wall, and the bed dropped into place. He sat on the bed, leaned against the wall, and spread out his tools. Buzz took a seat next to him. They brought up Blinky's portable computer and started searching for signals.

"What are you doing?" Payne asked.

"Remember in your quarters when we projected the images onto the wall monitor? Same principle we're looking at here, but their interfaces were probably in their heads, and that's why they don't need monitors or door-access pads. Info would be projected using their optical nerves or right to the stimulus center. I'm looking for the broadcast signal and seeing if we can tap in."

"I like it," Payne agreed. "Joker and Turbo, stay here and provide oversight and security. Remember, I need you to deliver a status report to *Cleophas*."

"What do we tell them?" Turbo asked.

"I'll record something. Specialists are working to interface directly with the ship. We should be able to lift off within the hour?"

"Say what?" Blinky nearly shouted.

"Your tone tells me you believe that might be an overly optimistic timeline. But you have Buzz with you. Tag-team the problem. Reduce the time to figure it out by orders of magnitude."

"You still can't take a square root of a negative number," Blinky countered.

"I'm kidding. Stay on it, you guys. The report will be simply what we're doing—trying to interface, exploring, no revelations yet beyond the ship appears to be completely intact."

"Temperature is up to zero degrees Celsius," Joker reported.

"And that. The ship knows we're here and is trying to be accommodating. I hope they don't like it outside the boundaries of what we might consider comfortable. I would like to take off these suits."

"Anyone see a bathroom?" Byle asked.

Payne shook his head. "Byle, with me. Turbo, Joker, you have your orders. Blinky and Buzz, make the magic happen. Your Solar Flare First Class will read 'While lounging in a bunk on the exotic Progenitor ship *Leviathan*...'"

"Wouldn't that be cool?" Buzz muttered.

"Stop daydreaming and get to work, Fetus!" Blinky snapped.

After half a kilometer, Major Dank encountered the first door. He held a fist in the air for the others to see he was stopping.

"I bet there was an elevator if we had gone the other way," he said, "but since we can't use the damned thing anyway, let's see what we have in here. I guess we knock, and all will be revealed."

Major Dank rapped it with a gloved hand.

"Did I knock wrong?" Dank tried again, to no avail. "Major Payne, how did you knock on those doors?"

"Normal knock, Virge. You probably encountered a door

that isn't open to the general public. We're in a billeting area, which is probably open to anyone who cares to enter. Are you close to the aft end?"

"We are. Judging by the distance to the next door, this is a pretty big space if we can get through."

"If it won't open, go to the next one. Time is not at a premium. We could be in here for the rest of our lives and still not see everything. Find what you can find and keep moving. I can't tell if anyone besides us is onboard or not. We've seen exactly one-millionth of one percent of the ship."

"Maybe a thousandth, Declan. No need to exaggerate and crush our souls any more than they are already. We walked half a kilometer and have seen jack squat. I'll be back in touch."

Heckler moved past the two specialists to stand next to Major Dank. He gestured that he would take point but didn't say it out loud. Heckler stalked down the corridor carefully but quickly until he reached the next door on the opposite side of the corridor from the other one. He waited for the rest of the team to get ready for breaching the entrance, then reached past the end of his weapon and knocked gently before pulling back into a crouch while the door slipped open. He waved his barrel to highlight the space as quickly as possible.

"Going in," he said softly as he jumped inside and dodged left to put his back against the wall. He took greater care in visually examining the space. Dank took the other side of the doorway and studied his half of the area. The room lights slowly increased in brightness.

"Storage," Heckler said. "But of what? Enquiring minds want to know, Progs. Tell the friendly Kochmeister your secrets."

Sparky and Shaolin strolled in, took in the floor-to-ceiling boxes, and headed into the neatly arranged racks. The space was the size of a basketball court, and the only open deck was the walking lanes between the racks and at the ends of the aisles.

"Any material-handling equipment?" Heckler wondered.

"Not needed," Sparky said. "Watch this." She pulled a cubic-meter-sized box from the rack with one finger. "It's got some kind of antigrav that kicks in when you touch it."

She guided it to the end of the aisle and lowered it to a comfortable height before she popped the top.

Heckler stayed back while the other three converged on the box and looked inside.

"Any ideas?" Dank asked about the neatly and tightly packed box.

"Food bars, maybe?" Shaolin pulled one out, and she and Sparky scanned it. "Looks organic but could be anything."

"Take one and put the box back," Dank ordered.

"Movement!" Heckler shouted and bolted toward the end of the warehouse. Dank ran after him.

"Stay there," the major called over the team channel as Heckler dodged down an aisle. Dank took a position at the end, the barrel of his weapon pointed upward. Heckler jumped and landed on something. After a brief struggle, Heckler stood up and lifted a small metallic object. Its four articulated limbs hung limp.

"Looks like a bot." Heckler carried it to the end of the aisle and held it out. Thirty centimeters a side, four legs hauling a boxlike body around.

"Sparky, what do you make of this?"

"Legs for forward, backward, and lateral movement. I don't see any ports or other devices. This thing can move around, but it can't physically interact with anything. Maybe it takes inventory."

"Nothing has changed on a starship in a thousand years. What the hell is it counting?"

"Simple programming. It's doing exactly as it's done for the past thousand years without fail, which means there is a righteous power source on this ship to keep these units charged." Sparky took the unit from Heckler and put it down. It walked down an aisle between the racks and resumed its work.

"I think it's counting. Leave it. It's no threat to us," Dank said. "Check these boxes and grab a couple more samples. Then we'll move on."

Heckler provided security, keeping one eye on the small bot while the others chose random aisles, brought out random boxes, and dutifully snagged samples from within before putting the boxes back.

"It'll report a changed count for the first time in forever. I wonder if any circuits will overload?" Heckler deadpanned.

Dank ignored him. "We've got the exact same bar in tan and green."

"I got blue." Sparky waved her bar.

"Red here." Shaolin showed her prize before tucking it away.

"Major Payne, Virgil here. I think this ship used a biomass printing system for food. We've found some stores and a live bot walking around. This is still a functional ship. That's the limit of our excitement. We'll continue moving aft."

"Roger," came Major Payne's neutral reply.

[7]

"He who commits his reserves last will win the battle." –From the memoirs of Fleet Admiral Thaylon Loore

Space stirred as the ships came out of FTL. One after another after another appeared on *Cleophas'* screens.

"Sound General Quarters," Captain Smith ordered, never taking his eyes from the tactical display. "The Ebren are here."

The Blaze Collective had known that *Cleophas* would be in the way, so they'd sent their minions to deliver the maximum amount of firepower. When space stopped warping from the new arrivals, the final count of enemy ships made Smith clench his jaw. He was outgunned since he faced a squadron of Ebren battlewagons supported by a single Behemoth-class dreadnought.

The enemy ships took a moment to orient themselves before heading straight for Ganymede.

Cleophas' bridge looked like business as usual, but the screens carrying the outside view showed anything but. Captain

Smith leaned forward. "Main batteries one and three, match bearings and shoot."

"Bearings aligned. Pattern Delta Omega. Fire," the tactical officer repeated, clarifying the order, engrossed in his weapons system panel. Under his control were twenty different weapons systems, each commanded by different officers. The mains were under his direct control because when they fired, they spoke for the entire Fleet.

Capital-grade systems throughout, the mains on a dreadnought were equivalent to the sixteen-inch cannons on old-time battleships. The electrothermal accelerators sent a plasma-charged projectile at near the speed of light. With a throw weight measured in megatons, it was the most lethal weapon on the Kaiju-class. Their recycle speed was slow compared to other systems, and they weren't smart weapons, but a single hit could destroy most ships. Only needed one shot to count.

"Accelerate to twenty percent," the captain ordered. "Give us some maneuvering room. Tactical, get those pickets over *Leviathan* to repel the boarding parties."

"I don't see any..." Tactical started.

"They're coming. Mark my words. Comm, give me Fleet-wide."

"Channel is open."

"This is *Cleophas*. We will maneuver away from Jupiter into Engagement Zone Jupiter Gulf Seven beyond the orbital arcs of its moons in order to fight this battle. *Voeller*, take charge of the pickets and control the void space of Jupiter Gulf One. Protect *Leviathan* at all costs. Heavy cruisers *Ezio* and *Sirus*, move behind *Cleophas* to limit your ships' profiles and protect my flanks. Light cruiser *Plamen*, you are the shepherd. Make sure none of those Ebren ships stray too far away. Shoot straight and shoot often. Smith out."

The sparse Fleet acknowledged their orders and started moving in the intricate and deadly dance of space combat.

"Comm, get me BEP Central."

"On the line," Comm replied after a brief delay, using communications language from a time long past. There were no lines anymore. Everything raced free of wires.

"BEP Command, this is *Cleophas*. We have engaged the Blaze Collective. We request immediate assistance from anything you have available. Transmitting tactical displays and images. We will deliver a live feed as long as the channel remains open."

"This is Commodore Nyota Freeman. BEP forces are establishing a blocking position between the asteroid belt and Jupiter in case any get past you."

"BEP Command, the Ebren are here for the ship that's on Ganymede. They aren't going to charge down the gravity well toward Earth. Your assistance in fighting this battle *out here* would be greatly appreciated."

"We shall hold a blocking position because we believe your strategic assessment is incorrect, Captain."

"If the Blaze acquires *Leviathan*, your blocking position will be meaningless, and you, personally, will be responsible for the loss of all humanity. I suggest you study the principle of divide and conquer since you're interested in strategy. Think on that while you evaluate how we're out here, protecting humanity when you should also be in this fight. I have nothing but unkind words for you. Smith out." He clenched his teeth and growled at the screen. "Keep the feed active so they can review sometime in future history how fucked up the BEP is."

"Recommend Rapier missile salvo across all targets within range. Ninety-six tubes stand ready," Tactical suggested.

"Launch the Rapiers," the captain confirmed.

The ten-meter-long missiles flushed from their tubes in a

volcano of flame that quickly burned out in the void of space. The missiles increased speed using their advanced ion drives until they appeared as nothing more than flickers on the sensors.

The battlewagons accelerated at sub-light speed to take on *Cleophas* with a high-speed pass as the Ebren's Behemoth-class ship lumbered along at the edge of firing range. If the battlewagons got past, *Cleophas* would be caught in a crossfire.

"Fire the mains!" the captain roared.

Tactical bracketed the incoming ships and started an autofire sequence, rotating through the four cannons to send massive ball after massive ball of superheated plasma into the Ebren formation. Every shot risked overheating the systems.

There would be no second chance to get it right.

"Incoming," Defensive Systems reported. "Pulsing EM. Point defense systems are active and at one hundred percent. Ion streams inbound."

The ship couldn't detect the ion cannons because of the size of the particles until the massed ion wave was on top of them. In the early days, ion cannons had been deadly since they impacted the electrical systems, leaving the ships dead in space and unable to defend themselves against the weakest of other projectiles.

Cleophas was immune to ion weapons. Humanity had been at war long enough that they were experts at defeating first-generation technology. Not so much after that.

The next wave of incoming put Smith on the edge of his seat.

Cleophas had launched ninety-six missiles at eight targets, but those eight enemy ships had emptied their batteries with their first salvo. One hundred and sixty missiles raced toward them—missiles like great lumbering beasts the size of the Fleet's picket ships.

The Ebren missiles passed the Rapiers in the engagement

space designated Jupiter Gulf Seven. A dozen missiles lost propulsion and started to tumble.

"What the hell?" the captain blurted, leaning forward in his seat to better study the tactical board and if it was real. Defects. Age. Something else?

"Reach out and touch someone," Defensive Systems mumbled to himself as lasers lanced and danced across the void to burn holes through the nosecones of the inbound. At the same time, counterbattery fire sent clouds of small missiles into space to explode in front of the incoming missiles. They sent sprays of superheated plasma into the pointy ends of the enemy missiles as a redundancy to splash incoming that survived the laser light show.

Another fifty lost their targeting and started to veer wildly like blind cobras trying to protect themselves from a mongoose. Defensive missiles crashed into the inbound like a wave on a rocky shore. A fully eighty of the remaining one hundred came apart in both direct and sympathetic explosions. From the cloud of debris, the final twenty appeared, their courses unerring.

Lasers fired across the darkness, attempting to rip the missiles asunder while the ship loosed its close-in weapons. Crews from stem to stern managed their sectors by firing the chain guns and quad cannons that bristled on the outside of the Kaiju-class ship. The two-centimeter-wide projectiles, accelerated by both chemical propellant and magnetic rails, filled the space in front of the missiles on final approach.

Blasting them one by one. Nuclear radiation washed over the heavy plating with each explosion. The crews cheered.

"Brace!" Defensive sent the automated warning for the one great beast that got through. No more was possible. The crew gripped their stations.

An instant later, spaces throughout the ship were filled with the deafening roar of a one-hundred-kiloton impact on the outer hull. The ship shuddered. It was designed to withstand up to a megaton without breaking its back.

The damage board flashed briefly before one red light appeared. Negligible. The crew got back to work.

Cleophas accelerated while banking hard, looping back toward Ganymede. The captain couldn't let the battlewagons get between the Fleet's newest dreadnought and Jupiter's moon.

Or maybe...

"Slow turn to one quarter."

"The lead battlewagon is going to get past us," Helm reported. "The enemy is making for the opening."

"*Ezio* and *Sirus*, prepare to fire. Weapons free the instant Ebren One clears our shadow." The tactical display had assigned a target number to each ship for unity of action by a coordinated Fleet. Smith's lip twitched at the thought of the BEP fleet waiting for the battle to end. Maybe they were praying for the Fleeties.

All the hopes and prayers in the universe weren't going to win this battle. It counted on the ingenuity of those who'd designed the Kaiju-class and those who rode within.

The icon for Ebren Four blinked before turning solid red—out of the action but not destroyed. It had gone ballistic and dark from the lack of power. Helm adjusted course to avoid getting hit by the debris.

Ebren Six changed to yellow, and Ebren Eight flashed red. Two more battlewagons flashed yellow. Four ships with one missile barrage. *Cleophas* could deliver nine more of those before the autoload racks were empty.

"Cycling," Tactical reported. The mains adjusted fire from Ebren Six to Ebren Two.

"Launch another Rapier salvo. Full spread into the final four targets in range." The captain leaned into the cushion of his chair, eyes glued to the board. The Behemoth-class hovered just outside of weapons range, waiting for the right moment.

When would that be?

The captain's order automatically transferred to the Rapier missile control officer. She cleared the targets, validated the new spread, and launched. The entire process took two seconds because of *Cleophas'* state-of-the-art computer system. The next salvo of ninety-six Rapiers cleared their tubes, tracing deadly arcs across the rapidly decreasing distance.

The amount of defensive fire from *Cleophas* meant there was a veritable cloud of projectiles to fly through on their way outbound. Not all made it. The risk of shooting down one of their own missiles had been deemed to be worth it. The computer system deconflicted space as much as possible, but the independent targeting of the Rapiers meant the missiles could adjust the instant their motors kicked in.

The close-in weapon system—CIWS—called Sea Whit could also be fired independently of the master weapons program. Acceptable risk. Acceptable loss in the rapid-fire combat of space.

Six missiles didn't clear the field. The rest accelerated toward their targets.

Countdown to impact. Three...two... Defensive systems sent a volume of fire into the diminishing space between the ships that created an opaque cloud on the scanning screen. Too many of the missiles came apart under the barrage.

But nothing deflected the plasma projectiles. They couldn't be lasered, and they couldn't be fooled. They could only be avoided. The main cannons continued to fire. With the latest cooling system and three seconds between each cannon's shot, the system kept from grossly overheating. Still, the countdown to shutdown was under way. One more minute. Fifteen shots from each mount.

Tactical struggled to lock targeting with the ship's maneuvering balanced against the gyrations of the incoming battlewagons and the massive amount of ordnance already in the void.

"Nearing point-blank range," Tactical announced for no reason. The entire bridge crew could see that the gunfight was becoming a knife fight. The Kaiju-class ship bucked and groaned with each impact. The remaining battlewagons were pouring everything they had into the Fleet's latest dreadnought.

"Score!" Tactical shouted with a direct blast into Ebren Two, splitting the hull and sending the reactor supercritical. The flash from the explosion whitewashed the screen. The captain winced and looked away. The rumble of the CIWS was a steady vibration, felt not heard. The wash of rain on a tin roof sounded as a testament to the projectiles impacting the outer hull, chipping away at the armor.

Ebren One delivered a danger-close broadside, firing both defensive and offensive weapons into *Cleophas'* prow as it passed. The Kaiju-class ship jerked to a stop with the impact of the munitions delivered into its hardened nose. Some skipped off from glancing blows, but the rest delivered brute force to the hardest materials humanity could create.

The enemy battlewagon entered the heavy cruisers' engagement envelope with emptied weapons. When the *Ezio* and *Sirus* fired their railguns, they sent a stream of one-kilogram projectiles at near-light speed into Ebren One. The battlewagon split as if being sliced by the sharpest of scalpels but continued on a ballistic trajectory toward Ganymede's surface.

"Fire!" Tactical shouted.

The mains stopped cycling and fired in salvos, two by two.

The damage control board added red lights with each passing second.

"Defensive systems at max!" *Cleophas* porcupined with outbound weapons.

"Full speed!" the captain ordered as the last four battlewagons died in rapid succession. An exploding core could generate up to a million megatons of force, but the vacuum of space would dampen such an explosion if one could put enough of it between the ship and the blast. Eight battlewagons' worth of wreckage was on its way to Ganymede, with *Cleophas* in the middle.

"Clear the airspace," Smith ordered.

Ezio and *Sirus* twisted and lanced through the sky on a trajectory perpendicular to the inbound wreckage.

Comm transferred a call from Captain Malone to Smith's position. "*Voeller*, requesting instructions."

"Mal, you need to get the hell out of there. You're going to have a couple million tons of wreckage coming down on your head."

"But *Leviathan*..."

"Will have to fend for itself. It's been here a thousand years and is still intact. It can protect itself because it will have to. There's nothing you can do. Get out of there now, and take the pickets with you."

Smith didn't hear *Voeller* report that Ebren scouts had gotten past and delivered soldiers to the top of the ship like an old-time para-drop. They'd killed the infiltrating ship but were hesitant to shoot at the Prog ship in case it had active defensive systems. It wouldn't take much for a dreadnought to blast a frigate into stardust.

Smith was focused on the Behemoth-class monster. It had begun to accelerate into the tactical grid designated Jupiter Gulf Seven.

"It's time to report to the ship, Major," Joker announced.

"Give them what I told you earlier. Nothing new. Working to interface with the ship, which looks to be intact. And tell them three hours before our next report."

"Roger." Joker headed toward the airlock.

"Turbo, you're with her. Note to everyone: never go anywhere alone on this ship."

The combat specialist nodded and hurried after the communications specialist. They entered the airlock and punched the triangle on the opposite wall by the ladder. "Miss you already, sir," Turbo broadcast.

"Of course, you do. As close as I am, I could probably talk to them. Open the outer hatch, and I'll give it a shot."

"You'll get your chance in about ten seconds. Air is evacuating," Joker said. After the indicated time, she announced, "Hatch is open."

The major never had a chance to report. A shadow blocked the view of *Cleophas,* and a weapon fired into the airlock space. Joker took a plasma charge to the chest, driving her to her knees. Turbo shouted and had her weapon up and firing in the blink of an eye. The view of *Cleophas* returned.

Turbo stayed where she was. Joker pulled herself up the ladder before checking the chest plate on her suit. The glancing blow had left a scorch mark.

Payne ran to the airlock's hatch but could see little through the small window. "Report!"

"Someone outside fired on us. Securing the outer hatch," Turbo growled.

"Hold on. Break, break. *Cleophas* actual, Team Payne. Someone is at the forward airlock and shooting at us. Can you advise?"

"Back up, Joker. I'm taking a look. If that's a Fleetie, I'm kicking some ass."

"Since when does Fleet have plasma rifles?" Joker asked.

Lasers lanced the sky between the dreadnought and Leviathan. Turbo slowly climbed the ladder, leaning as far to one side as she could to keep from exposing her back to the enemy. Two rungs from the top she snap-fired, then raised to the top rung and fired twice more. A shot from behind skipped off the top of her helmet.

She ducked, let her rifle hang on its sling, and pulled a plasma grenade. She tucked it into her armpit to pull the pin and let it cook off to the count of three before dunking it out the hatch and flipping it backward. Less than two seconds later, it exploded and tossed her enemy toward the hatch; he fell through and past Turbo. When he hit the deck, Joker peppered him with pulse rifle rounds.

"Sir, the Blaze Collective is here. At least two Ebren soldiers are down."

"Team Payne. *Cleophas* is engaged. Lock yourselves inside that ship. We will hammer on the hatch when the void is clear. Smith out."

"Securing the hatch," Joker reported. Another shadow appeared, and Turbo gave it a full burst of pulse rounds before the hatch clanged home and the atmosphere started to equalize. She climbed down and straddled the tall and thin body on the deck, then blasted a round through the faceplate of the helmet to make sure he wasn't playing dead.

The Ebren were a tall and thin race between two and three meters in height, but the heaviest weighed no more than seventy-five kilos. Their bodies consisted of fibrous material, so they didn't need space suits, only helmets to breathe. They usually carried no gear besides a plasma rifle. Their advantage came in numbers. They crammed their ships full and sent their soldiers out in mass wave attacks.

Intel thought they were grown en route to a battle—clones—

but some had demonstrated independent thought. Team Payne had seen them before. They were easy to kill, but they were like cockroaches. Where the team saw one, there were hundreds.

"Reporting three down." Turbo picked up the plasma rifle. Another twenty charges and it would be empty. She'd keep it for the time being.

"What the hell were they doing outside the hatch?"

"Probably checking out the skimmer. I think we surprised them."

"No shit, Major. Otherwise, there would have been a flood of them through that hatch, and we would have been up the creek without a paddle."

Joker popped the hatch into the ship. "Block this internal hatch so the airlock won't equalize, and the Boneracks can't access the airlock from the outside. Major Dank, you need to block your hatch, too. No sense in letting bad guys get in behind you. Make yourself comfortable. We're going to be here for a while."

[8]

"Space is the great equalizer. No one is from there, and in the end, the void always wins."
–From the memoirs of Fleet Admiral Thaylon Loore

"Make yourselves comfortable. I need you two within rapid response of this airlock." Major Payne suggested.

Turbo and Joker nodded their helmeted heads. "Roger. We can cover twice as much ground if four people search instead of two," Turbo offered. "Let those two watch the airlock. They can set up a noisemaker or something. If someone breaks through the outer lock, which I'm not sure is possible, they'll get a lot of explosive decompression right in their skinny faces."

"I can live with that. Don't go far down the longitudinal corridor. No more than a hundred meters each way." Payne leaned into the room where Blinky and Buzz were working. "Listen for the airlock and make sure no Boneracks make it in here."

Blinky looked exasperated at the interruption. "The ship can take care of it once we're in."

"Are you in?"

"Well, no."

"Then you'll need to take care of it. Don't let the enemy in the ship. I shall be very put out if they storm the bastion. Very."

"Got it. We're on it." Blinky waved dismissively.

The major was having none of it. He stormed into the room. "I know when you break in, it will all be worth it, but for right now, we can't have any surprises. Set up a booby trap or something on the door. We have ten people to do the work of a thousand. Help us to help you."

"I'll take care of it, Blinky." Buzz put his hardware down and snapped off a quick salute. He dug into the kit and came up with two flashbangs. With string and duct tape, standard in all space packs, he headed for the airlock.

The major waved for Byle to follow. After twenty meters, Payne looked back to find an ad hoc booby trap taped to each side of the airlock hatch. If it opened or closed, the string would pull the pin on one of the flashbangs. In the corridor's small space, it would make one hell of a bang but not blind the team since the helmets would compensate for the flash. Buzz gave a thumbs-up before returning to the room to help Blinky work on the ones and zeros.

"I could have done that," Byle volunteered.

"And me. Damn. Buzz is putting us all to shame."

"Did what?" Major Dank asked.

"Taped flashbangs to the airlock in case it's accessed."

"Got it. We've heard nothing from our end. They may have been drawn to the skimmer, and that's why they popped up where you are and not down here."

"You didn't open the hatch," Payne countered. "Blinky and Buzz are doing the heavy lifting. The rest of us are on grunt duty. Search and report. We're looking for anything that will help us interface with the ship."

"Roger. We'll keep on keeping on." Dank ended his signal but kept the channel open.

"Sir," Byle started, "at least we know they were humanoid, with the same foibles as we have. A ladder to climb down, indicative of a bipedal species, and then beds, so they need sleep, horizontally oriented. And biomass, which tells me they had to eat, so they probably had mouths, too. Also suggests there should be bathrooms. I'm thinking we descended from them."

"That's a leap of faith, Byle."

"I'll embrace it because I don't want to think we descended from any of the races in the Collective, like the Boneracks."

"I'd like to think you're right, that we descended from a race that's a little more congenial toward other races than the Blaze. Those guys are jerks."

Byle laughed. "That's one word for them."

They continued down the transverse corridor well past where they could see back to the airlock. Doors abounded, with nearly all being similar aside from the elevator closest to the airlock.

"The Progs had to be in phenomenal physical shape to live on this ship."

"Or maybe they had other means of transportation, like hoverboards," Byle offered, trying to look innocent.

"You're just instigating now, but for the record, if anyone finds a hoverboard, I get first crack at the hallway hover Olympics. I was a demon back in college. Almost got myself kicked out for a particularly impressive slide down the stairs and out a second-story window."

"Impressive to who*m*?" Byle said, emphasizing the M.

"Well, *me*, of course. Break, break. We are nearly at the centerline. There is a wide corridor similar to what there is on *Cleophas*. It appears to me that we're only about a thousand and ten years behind the Progs. Otherwise, the basic ship structure looks eerily similar. All but the neural interface stuff, and maybe our own AIs are preventing that from happening because they've seen into our minds."

"You're on a roll, Declan," Dank noted. "Where are you, Heckler? I think we found the engine room, and I want us together."

"Coming," Heckler said in the way one speaks while running. "My cardio is done for today. You slackers can drop and give me infinity."

"You ran two kilometers in low gravity, you big baby," Sparky replied.

"It wasn't as easy as it sounds," Shaolin panted. The suits were made to provide protection for a soldier engaged in combat operations in a vacuum. That meant low-speed maneuvering because of the magnetic boots, which clumped around at the best of times. "We shoulda used the jets."

"Nah, it was just a little workout. That's all," Heckler replied.

"Switch out to group channels," Payne requested since the banter was distracting him. "We know everyone is fine. Check in every fifteen minutes."

"Roger. We'll take care of it. Next stop, the engine room, if I'm not mistaken. Dank out."

Payne and Byle took two steps before the comm channel became active.

"I'm mistaken, but I think this space is over top of the main engines. We'll find a way down from here and report back when we have a visual on this beast's motors."

Payne took one more step and stopped.

"Sir?" Byle wondered.

"I expected he'd be back with something else. Guess not. Let's see where this main corridor goes."

They continued in silence for another ten minutes. At the

crossroads of the main travel and transverse corridors, they stood and took in the sights. The corridor on the opposite side extended farther than the rifle's light could penetrate. Both directions down the wide central avenue delivered the same infinity pool of darkness.

"We have people aft. Let's go forward." With Payne's words, the lights increased in brightness to a twilight glow.

"Sir!" Byle shouted. She turned around to see a wide box coming at them along the right side of the corridor. They ducked into the side corridor, weapons up and ready to fire. The intruder stopped.

"It's a hoverscooter or something like that."

"Does this count as a hoverboard?" Byle countered.

"Maybe, Byle. I believe we have found our ride. Climb aboard."

"What if it's a trap?"

"If this ship had wanted to kill us, it could have. I think it's running operations as usual despite there being no crew. No one told the drones they didn't have to work anymore. Whatever the power source on this thing is, it has lasted a thousand years. We could learn something from that, even if nothing else works on this thing."

"That's just it, sir. It looks like *everything* works."

"What if it was broken and abandoned, and over the years, maintenance bots fixed everything? What if it will fly?"

"This would make a nice addition to the Fleet, assuming weapons systems are online."

They sat in the seats of the personnel movement system. Nothing happened. "Sucks not having the neural interface. I expect we're supposed to tell it where to go. The bridge, please."

The vehicle started moving.

"It speaks English?"

"We've talked enough while on board. Maybe it learned."

The vehicle accelerated for ten seconds and then slowed down for ten seconds. Double doors to the left opened, and the vehicle rolled inside.

Major Payne tapped into the company channel. "We're on board a vehicle that showed up in the central corridor. We asked if it would take us to the bridge, and we are now in an elevator going down. We will let you know if it takes us there."

"Roger," Dank replied. "We're climbing down a ladder. Already covered two decks without an exit. Will keep going until we can get out or are too tired to continue, and then we'll jet back to the top deck."

"Sounds like a plan. Break, break. Turbo and Joker, report."

"Nothing but empty staterooms as far as the eye can see. Doing a rough count. If this is the only deck with quarters, it would support a crew of ten thousand."

Payne thought about that for a moment. "This ship could have carried fifty thousand people if it wanted?"

"All depends on air handling and food at that point," Blinky interjected. "There is abundant space. This is five kilometers long by a kilometer and a half wide by a kilometer tall. That's over seven billion square meters. That's a lot of space, Major."

"Billion with a 'b.' I'll be a sum bitch when you look at it that way."

"If you designated one thousand square meters per person, this ship could hold seven and a half million. Fifty thousand? There'd be wide open spaces. Would you look at that? Buzz is doing something. We'll be right back."

"What is Buzz doing? What should we look at?" Payne asked, knowing he would get no answer. He had grown used to dealing with the technical specialists on his team, who were each eccentric in their own ways. When Payne had built the team, he had looked for individuals who were great at what they did because they had a passion for it to the exclusion of all else. Then he made them into a team.

But when the eccentricities left him on the outside looking in, he didn't have to like it. He knew the result would be worthwhile or end up with him doing the rug dance in front of the Fleet admiral, explaining the inexplicable and reassuring the old man that it wouldn't happen again. Just until the next time. Still worth it because no one had died on his team. They saw the kill zones before entering, and they responded with lethality.

They brought the pain.

"What would a weapons console look like on this ship?" Payne asked. Byle was a weapons system specialist and a guru at heavy weapons systems—anything that redirected energy. She understood power and how it turned into controlled destruction.

But she had no idea what the Progs' control interfaces looked like. Neither did he or anyone else. Every derelict they'd entered had been gutted. Every derelict they'd seen videos of had been the same.

She settled for shaking her head.

Before the doors closed, concussions reverberated through *Leviathan*. The massive impacts shook the Prog ship to its very core.

"Wait!" Payne cried out, but the doors closed, and the elevator started down. They gripped the vehicle as it shook and bounced within the small space. "Did we lose the fight?" Payne wondered.

[9]

"You can win all the battles and still lose the war." –From the memoirs of Fleet Admiral Thaylon Loore

"Behemoth coming into range," Tactical noted to no one in particular.

"Damage report," the captain requested.

"Thirty-eight Rapier silos damaged. Defensive systems are at fifty percent. The mains are fully functional and ready to fire."

Smith chewed the inside of his lip as he contemplated going toe to toe with the undamaged Ebren dreadnought after his ship had taken a beating. *Cleophas* had weathered eight battlewagons remarkably well, but she was hurt. Could she enter the boxing match with the Behemoth and come out the other side? "I need those silos online as soon as possible. Divert damage control resources as necessary."

Tactical sent the instructions to the weapons systems control officers because they needed to know why their systems weren't being worked on. Defensive systems groused, but defense alone wouldn't keep the ship alive. Dreadnoughts had nearly unlimited offensive punch. To survive an attack, one had to damage the enemy enough that they jumped into FTL. If they were damaged too badly to run, they had to be destroyed.

A living Behemoth was too dangerous, just like a Kaiju left alive while it continued to generate power. The two beasts started circling the ring.

"Energy surge," Tactical reported.

Captain Smith waited. There were a dozen different things the surge could mean, and not all of them were bad.

"Dissipating."

"That was different," the captain remarked.

"Incoming asteroid," Helm reported.

"Adjust course," the captain confirmed even though Helm was already maneuvering.

"Energy surge," Tactical repeated.

"Asteroid." Helm turned to look at the captain.

"A mass driver. Unload the Rapiers. All tubes fire. Match bearings on the mains and send a message to our unwelcome guest."

Tactical hesitated. "Shoot the asteroids or the ship?"

"The ship. Shoot the ship," the captain clarified.

At the edge of weapons range, the probability of hits was low, but one hit could lead to an exploitable vulnerability for when the ships were closer.

"Fire," Tactical ordered. The mains coughed their deadly plasma on a spread, seeking to make space a dangerous place for the Behemoth to operate. The enemy ship started to corkscrew, changing trajectory and angles off the bow. Two seconds later, Tactical fired again. Big space, little projectiles, but enough projectiles could create impossibly tight windows in which to maneuver. "Missiles away."

The fifty-eight functional tubes sent their missiles from

Cleophas before their ion drives accelerated them into the void. The main weapons forced the Behemoth into a narrow window where the missiles concentrated.

"Reloading," Tactical announced in a calm voice. "One additional silo online."

What one gives, one gets. A cloud of missiles was launched from the Behemoth, along with another asteroid.

"Projectile will miss us by a wide margin," Helm said, staring at the screen. "Projectile is headed for the ship on the surface of Ganymede."

"Take out that asteroid!"

Helm accelerated the ship into a tight loop, a difficult maneuver that made the superstructure groan along its more than two-kilometer backbone. The ship came over the top and pushed toward the planet, moving away from Engagement Zone Jupiter Gulf Seven and into Gulf One.

"Rapiers online," Tactical announced. "Targeting six. Fire."

Six missiles headed outbound. One or two would have done the trick because the asteroid couldn't maneuver, and it wouldn't fire defensive weapons. However, redundancy was critical to limit any additional damage to *Leviathan*.

"What damage did the battlewagons do to it?" Smith asked.

"Minimal direct hits," Tactical reported. "I see Ebren soldiers still on the top of the ship trying to get in, so the hull has remained intact."

"Comm, get me *Voeller*."

"Captain Malone," came the familiar voice.

"Feel like target-shooting, Captain?" He waited for a moment before continuing. "We have some Boneracks on *Leviathan*. If you would purge the scourge, I'd appreciate it."

"Now that most of the battlewagon scrap has passed, I'll return to the area and clean them off. Is the Behemoth launching asteroids?"

"They have a mass driver now, it appears. Wait until Fleet hears about that! We'll keep the asteroids off you, but watch your six just in case."

"Will do. Malone out."

Captain Smith leaned back in his chair.

The six missiles turned the asteroid into a cloud of dust.

"Recommend two from now on. Two per asteroid, and four to the enemy ship."

Smith nodded slowly. "Comm, get me *Ezio* and *Sirus*."

Tactical continued the barrage from the mains while the Behemoth rhythmically sent asteroids spinning toward Ganymede, one every fifteen seconds.

"Where is he getting the projectiles? Is that ship filled with big rocks?"

The captain scanned the bridge, but no one had an answer.

The Behemoth avoided the plasma mains, but the missiles presented a different threat. They closed on the maneuvering ship, matching the changes and calculating intercept impact points across a broad section. Defensive fire poured outward, scrapping missiles two at a time. Some exploded, some died with a whimper, but others soldiered on. Close-in systems mirrored those of *Cleophas*, heaving out clouds of projectiles the inbound missiles had to fly through.

When the war first started, electronic jamming had foiled the targeting, but then systems were hardened against that as well as other pulses to electronically disable a missile's sensors. Presently, the only way to knock one down was by physical interdiction.

Lasers were effective until the battlespace was filled with debris like Jupiter Gulf Seven had become. It appeared as a hazy cloud from the shattered remnants of asteroids and bits and pieces of battlewagons that would fill the sky for decades to come.

Smith thought for a moment. *This was the largest battle ever fought within the Solar System. One ship stood against many, refusing to give ground while a small team of elite soldiers worked to free an ancient ship from its Ganymede tomb.*

Four Rapiers at a time raced outward to the points where they predicted the Behemoth would go. If it went a different direction, they would adjust. The more times they adjusted, the quicker they would run out of power and the sooner they would die, tumbling through space as yet another bit of debris.

"*Ezio* and *Sirus* are up," Comm reported.

"I need you to sting that big ugly bastard. Just pull his attention so we can hit him a few times with the mains."

"Bird-dogging. I can do that," the skipper of the heavy cruiser *Ezio* replied.

"And me," *Sirus* added. "Let the hit and runs commence."

"Don't get caught watching the grass grow," Captain Smith warned.

"I've been in space for seven years straight. I don't remember what grass looks like," the captain of the *Ezio* replied. "We got an enemy to harass. Shoot straight, *Cleophas*."

The cruisers closed the comm channel and headed on a wide-arcing course to close on the Behemoth's flank.

Cleophas groaned and bucked from the impact of enemy missiles. Red lights on the damage board soon outnumbered the green. The overhead lights flashed before steadying.

"We've lost reactors one, four, and seven. Defensive weapons are degraded to twenty-five percent. We've lost an additional twelve Rapier launchers. Main weapons one and three are offline, pending a reroute of power."

"Pending a reroute from where?" the captain asked, but he suspected he knew the answer.

"Defensive systems. We'd lose the ability to protect ourselves."

"Then we better get those reactors back online. Stay the course." The Behemoth's firepower would breach the armor and break *Cleophas* in half if it were allowed to rain unfettered into the hull. "Give us some maneuvering space. Take us into Jupiter Gulf Two."

"But the *Leviathan*," Helm countered.

"The Ebren will kill both of us if we stay here. Evasive maneuvers. Idle the mains, reroute power to defensive weapons, and keep firing the Rapiers."

"Asteroid inbound."

"Take it out." The captain didn't think he needed a new order, but he gave it anyway. Ambiguity in combat was a bad thing.

"Firing." Two missiles launched and raced toward the asteroid, and four more launched in the direction of Behemoth. *Cleophas* groaned and lumbered. Its spirited acceleration was gone. Every maneuver came at a cost.

"Missiles inbound," Defensive Systems reported. "Engaging."

A paltry number of defensive missiles sallied forth like an outnumbered cavalry charge—reluctant, but they went anyway because it was their purpose to serve. No more than two per inbound. In some cases, one. The CIWS waited, saving their firepower for those missiles that made it through.

The intercepts zeroed in on their targets one by one, splashing inbound after inbound. Only four of the eighty made it through, and the CIWS took care of them. The bridge crew breathed a sigh of relief. A systems officer pounded Defense on the back.

Success was short-lived and didn't give them much breathing room.

"Salvo inbound. And an asteroid. Rapiers confirmed. Firing." The big screen showed the outbound missiles on an unerring course toward the rock. No other missiles headed out.

"Offensive weapons?"

"Cascade failure from reactor five," Tactical reported.

Damage control joined the conversation. "Engineering is restarting. Five and seven will be back online in fifteen seconds."

"Will we still be here in fifteen seconds?" the captain asked but raised his hand to stifle the answer. "Of course, we will. It's a rhetorical question."

Defense flushed the tubes, once more firing everything at his command. The missiles continued their high impact rate, killing seventy-five of the inbound. CIWS took care of the rest—all but one. It landed amidships with an impact that threw the crew from their seats, and they bounced off the ceiling before slamming into the deck. The ship went dark before emergency lighting came on. The damage board flashed nothing but red.

"Save the ship. All hands to damage control. Defensive Weapons, you are the only one authorized use of power, if there is any. Everyone else, get to work deactivating systems for when the power comes back on. Damage control, where did that last missile hit us?"

"Beneath. It cracked the ventral spine and shut down the entirety of the lower three decks."

"Then why are we without power?" The bridge was in the middle of the ship.

"The breach is directly below us and has nearly sliced the ship in half. We're lucky to be alive."

"Let's zip it back together and get the hell out of here."

"Sir," Comm interjected. "Messages from *Ezio* and *Sirus*. They are beginning their attack runs."

Ezio's captain scowled at the red icon representing *Cleophas*. The Behemoth ceased evasive maneuvers and assumed a vector that took it straight toward *Leviathan*. "Fire a full spread. Give it all we've got."

Twenty-four Predator-class anti-ship missiles blasted from the launch tubes on an intercept course with the Ebren dreadnought.

An instant later, *Sirus* fired her missiles and immediately banked toward deep space to circle around and come in from behind the enemy. *Ezio* assumed a course lateral to that of the Behemoth.

"Fire as soon as the tubes are reloaded."

Liquid nitrogen cycled through the tube to cool it before the breech opened and the auto-loader sent a new missile home. When the breech secured, the missile spent two seconds in a rapid pre-flight system check, then the board cleared and flashed green. Offensive Weapons tapped the button, and the second salvo launched before the first hit home.

Before the Behemoth's defensive systems had scrubbed the sky clean, the third salvo was on its way. Projectiles flooded the space around the Behemoth, following the wave of defensive missiles. The second salvo saw forty-six missiles intercepted. Two got through and delivered two hundred kilotons into the ship's lower flank. The third salvo sent four missiles into the same area. The hull flashed when something within exploded from the penetration, but the fire was quickly extinguished by the vacuum of space.

The Behemoth maintained full speed. *Sirus* accelerated to flank speed to catch the enemy ship before it reached *Leviathan*.

Ezio continued to fire while accelerating away from the Behemoth's engagement envelope.

"It stopped using the mass driver," the sensor systems operator reported.

"What's that tell you?" the captain asked.

"They want Prog ship intact."

"Exactly. And that also means they'll have to stop the ship to send boarding parties, which will leave them vulnerable. Just like *Cleophas* was hung out to dry."

"*Voeller* is making a high-speed pass through the area. I see something on the screen…"

"Magnify on the tactical display," the captain ordered. "They're leaving presents for the Ebren. Missiles, probably with proximity triggers because we're far too humane to use mines."

"The Behemoth will blast them before they settle in," Defense remarked.

"They may, but every action buys time and depletes their resources. We will continue the attacks. Here comes *Sirus*."

The tactical display showed the friendly ship moving at a speed twice that of the slowing Behemoth. All weapons systems fired using the aft attack angle, the optimal firing solution on modern spaceships using rear propulsion.

The Behemoth started to turn to bring its more heavily armored sides into the line of fire, but the missiles were quicker. Half succumbed to weapons fire, but the other half, twelve missiles, delivered a combined six megatons into the after section of the massive ship.

Nearly instantaneous explosions splattered across the tactical screen. The captain pumped a fist in triumph. The Behemoth left the explosions in its wake and launched a full broadside at *Sirus,* who was too slow in turning because of their high approach speed. As it closed to point-blank range, the Behemoth's enfilade overwhelmed the heavy cruiser, ripping it apart. In a single heartbeat, the ship and its crew died to fly through space past Ganymede and crushed when the gas giant pulled the wreckage inexorably to its final demise.

The Behemoth slowly turned back on course. It hit the brakes hard as it entered Engagement Area Jupiter Gulf One.

"Fire," *Ezio's* captain ordered. Twenty-four more missiles sped into the void.

"Last reload," Tactical noted.

"Helm, get us closer." The captain gritted his teeth. He hadn't been fully briefed on the derelict on Ganymede, but he knew it had to be important. Not only had a Kaiju-class ship been sent to protect it, a Behemoth-class ship and eight battlewagons had been sent hundreds of light-years behind enemy lines to take it.

If it was worth all that, it was worth dying for. *Cleophas* staggered away, fighting its own battle for survival. Lights suggested it wasn't dead, but it didn't fire as it tried to get out of the engagement zone.

A massive coffin, Ezio's captain thought. *I'd rather go in a blaze of glory.*

He didn't say it out loud since he didn't want the crew to think he had a death wish.

"Sir, the rear of the Behemoth is significantly damaged. I doubt she'll be able to make the jump to FTL speed." The sensor officer brought up the damaged sections on the screen.

"It used forward thrusters to slow down," the captain offered. "Now might be a good time to hit it. Hold onto that last salvo. *Sirus* had the right idea. Helm, show me its ass."

[10]

"Protect your rear areas. Coming home to the enemy is no way to come home." —From the memoirs of Fleet Admiral Thaylon Loore

The buffeting had ended by the time the elevator stopped. The doors opened, and their ride dutifully took them into a new corridor that looked just like the last corridor. They traveled half a kilometer aft before the small cart stopped.

"I guess this is where we get off," Byle said. They stepped away, and the cart raced into the distance.

They stood before a door that looked like an outer hatch. "This makes sense," the major noted. He held his hand up to stop Byle from knocking on the door. "Major Payne checking in. Does anyone know what happened? Were we attacked? Please report."

Blinky replied, "I think so, but I don't know. The ship hated the stress put on it, judging by the RF spikes, but it has settled down. I can't tell you what it was, but at least it was brief."

"Dank here. We're outside of what we think is main engineering, but it's got a vault door, and we aren't able to get in. I'm hesitant to take extreme measures."

"I don't think we want to blow any holes inside the ship. Keep checking, and if you keep getting denied, return to the top deck. Break, break. Blinky, it's your favorite interruption calling."

"We're still trying to pick up the pieces from whatever happened," Blinky replied in his most exasperated voice. "I am certain the non-skid is an external sensor grid. That's why the ship protested when we burned it, and with the latest impacts, the ship screamed in agony. I don't know if we were attacked or what, but the system is just starting to calm down."

"Did the ship scream in agony, or did the sensors become overstimulated like your imagination?"

"Definitely screamed in agony. It was a total donk slap. I could feel it in *my* loins. Definitely a scream."

The major would have rubbed his temples, but his helmet prevented it.

As if reading his mind, Blinky continued. "The ship has been brought up to twenty-one Celsius with a perfect oxygen/nitrogen atmosphere. And if you haven't felt it, gravity is now at two-point-one meters per second squared and climbing. We're at a quarter of a gee."

"Don't hurt the ship, folks. It's rolling out the red carpet for us, but we don't know how to say thank you. We have been transported somewhere into the interior of the ship. In the main corridor, a small cart appeared. We told it to take us to the bridge. It carried us into an elevator that deposited us down here. I believe we are at the bridge, but I doubt it will let us in." He motioned for Byle to try.

She knocked on the door, then knocked on the wall beside it. She moved close and then back.

"As I suspected. It's not letting us in. We will explore this deck before returning topside."

"Sir," Turbo interrupted over the comm channel. "The Bonerack plasma rifle is gone, and the airlock door is sealed."

Payne's heart leapt into his throat. "I suspect you're telling me this because no one on the team removed it."

"That's affirmative, sir."

"Why didn't we hear the flashbangs?" the major wondered, but he already knew the answer.

Turbo confirmed it. "They're gone, too."

———

Hidden in the debris field, the ordnance waited, sending out weak pings for anything that came too close.

The Behemoth slowed as it assumed a high orbit over Ganymede.

The first missile went active within one hundred meters of the massive Ebren ship. The missile's engine fired and it flashed into the enemy's hull with barely a blink between the engine coming online and impact, where it delivered one hundred percent of its throw weight into the Behemoth's armored hull. Two other missiles followed their mate into the breach, exploding nanoseconds apart. The small rent became a vast chasm, and the ship started to vent atmosphere.

Bodies were ejected into the void. The Ebren personnel tried to swim through space as they held their breath but could find no traction.

The Behemoth tried to pull away, but a cascade failure prevented the main engines from firing. Position thrusters brought the big ship to a halt.

Ezio's bridge crew cheered.

The captain shook his fist at the screen. "Faster!" he

shouted. The ship was already maneuvering at flank speed with its sub-light engines, so the call to action was more for moral support. "Prepare to fire."

Another unnecessary command, but the crew leaned in, vibrating with the anticipation of delivering a kill shot on a Behemoth-class dreadnought. The Behemoth's internal lights flickered, and the ship went dark.

"Energy signatures?"

The sensors delivered the data. "Thirty-seven percent of maximum."

"Can we tell which systems are still online? Mainly, are they going to light us up with SSMs if we get too close?"

Sirus had died under the onslaught of Ebren ship-to-ship missiles. *Ezio* had no desire to suffer that same fate, but the closer they were when they fired, the greater the number of missiles that would impact the enemy.

Quantity had a quality all its own. One never knew which missile would hit a critical system and overload their fusion reactor to turn their ship into a supernova.

"Unknown."

"Compromise. Firing point minus fifty thousand kilometers and hard break to space following launch," the captain ordered.

The crew input the parameters and waited as the heavy cruiser accelerated toward the Behemoth.

"Captain, *Voeller* is on the line."

"Nicely done with the dropped missiles," the captain of the *Ezio* said.

"We'll move between the Behemoth and *Leviathan* and establish a blocking position for any boarding parties that try to come ashore."

"That ship still has some fight left. Don't overcommit and get yourself killed," *Ezio* warned.

"We have another surprise for them. Good hunting. *Voeller*, out."

The remaining missiles floating in space went active.

The Behemoth's power surged.

Both ships were committed.

Missiles flashed toward the Behemoth, but it had rolled the vulnerability to the other side, away from the debris field.

Defensive weapons engaged, splashing most of the inbound, but their proximity was their advantage. Four missiles were already well inside the engagement envelope and they rammed into the Behemoth, delivering a combined two megatons of firepower across a single kilometer of the ship's flank. The outer shell bucked under the explosion.

Internal hull integrity remained intact—no new breaches.

Missiles flushed from tubes facing the *Voeller* and headed for it. The frigate twisted and turned toward the Behemoth showing the lowest profile available, the prow.

Defensive systems fired as the *Voeller* accelerated.

"Sixty thousand," Tactical announced. The *Ezio* bridge crew held their breath.

Voeller fired a full salvo of missiles, twenty-four from dorsal, ventral, and flank tubes. The projectiles reoriented themselves and assumed courses that arced away from the frigate.

They drew the defensive fire, creating a safe cone up which the *Voeller* traveled, firing its defensive weapons and single railgun before banking away. It transitioned to FTL before counterbattery fire could light it up.

And left *Ezio* all alone. "Firing," Tactical reported. The ship shuddered as all tubes flushed simultaneously. Helm banked the ship hard, keeping the acceleration at maximum.

"FTL?" she asked.

"No. We have to stay and fight."

"We are out of missiles," Tactical verified.

"Look for a breach, and let's send every conventional piece of ordnance we have left into it. With a tin can, one need only have the right can opener."

Ezio began a wide loop for a second run at the aft end of the Behemoth.

Counterbattery fire increased in volume as the Behemoth's power systems were restored. Defensive missiles intercepted the leading edge of Ezio's attack, scratching them from the tactical board. Eight missiles gone in a flash.

Four more died in the next second.

Then four more. The final eight expended the last of their power on final approach, changing trajectory to foil close-in weapon systems. Still, four more died, and then two more at danger-close range, blasting a megaton of nuclear warheads over the aft section of the ship. The engines flashed just in time for the final two missiles to penetrate deep inside the ship.

They exploded with a whimper because of the metal between them and space. A fountain of flame ejected out the immense exhaust nozzles.

"Whoa!" *Ezio's* sensor operator recoiled before refocusing on the systems. "Behemoth power down to ten percent, enough to serve life support. The rear half of the ship appears to be dead. Zero emissions."

"Then that's where we need to hit it. Helm, take us close to shove our ordnance right up their tailpipe."

"Roger!" Helm called over her shoulder.

"New contacts entering Jupiter Gulf Seven," the sensor officer reported.

The captain sighed and closed his eyes for a moment. He opened them and stood, ready to deliver a speech about going out in a blaze of glory.

"It's the BEP, sir. They are firing at max range."

"And then veering away," the captain noted. But they had launched over one hundred missiles, mostly Rapier-class.

Ezio continued to burn a circle in space, trying to get behind the Behemoth again. Time elapsed as they counted down to impact.

"Bearing aligned," Helm reported as *Ezio* straightened its course on a direct heading to the Behemoth's six o'clock.

With the enemy ship's defensive systems incapacitated, all the BEP missiles landed and delivered a series of explosions that broke the ship into a dozen different sections.

"Keep defensive systems active and move to a blocking position above *Leviathan*. Just until *Voeller* makes its way back."

"The commodore requests permission to speak to you."

The captain shook his head before straightening his shoulders and pointing at the comms officer. "Put her on."

"You're welcome," she started.

Ezio's captain turned away from the screen, drawing his hand across his throat. "Cut the channel. I've had enough BEP stupidity for the day."

He waited until the screen was clear before strolling around the bridge to talk to his crew one by one, thanking them for giving one hundred percent in the face of imminent death. He touched each on the shoulder or the arm, shook hands, and delivered the reason they did what they did.

For all humanity. Even the BEP.

"Sir, what about *Cleophas*?"

The captain pointed at Tactical and nodded. "Belay my last. Get me that idiot commodore."

"She's on, sir."

"My apologies, Commodore. We must have gotten cut off. Can you establish a blocking position above the derelict on Ganymede's surface? We're going to assist *Cleophas*, who appears to still be bleeding atmosphere."

"Cut off? I should have you up on charges." She glared at the screen.

The BEP was easy to despise. They never left the Solar System, and thanks to Fleet, they never engaged a hostile because no one had ever made it this far until today. Fleet made war while BEP sat back in the rear drinking tea and eating crumpets, watching good Fleet personnel die.

His hand started coming up to give her the finger, but he resisted.

"Will you fucking do it or not? Stop jerking me around."

She didn't answer. His fury overcame him.

"We lost the *Sirus* with all hands. *Cleophas* is little more than drifting space junk. *Voeller* ran for her life, and *Ezio* is the last one standing. The enemy lost eight battlewagons and a dreadnought today because of the newest Kaiju-class, two heavy cruisers, and one frigate. Brave members of the Fleet died. This space is sacred for the Fleet blood spilled. We appreciate your missiles, but you know what they say. 'BEP is just like a blister—shows up after the hard work is done.' Clear the Jupiter Gulf engagement zone immediately. There is unexploded ordnance and dangerous debris in the area. Fleet regrets that it will not be able to hand over control of this sector at this time."

He faced Comm and drew a finger across his throat for the second time. The channel closed, and the tactical display reappeared on the screen.

"She looked pretty mad, sir," Helm suggested.

"Then someone give her a cape so she can be Super Mad." He waited for the chuckles to die down. "Take us to *Cleophas*. Damage control, get on your spacesuits. There's going to be more work than you can do, so it's best that you be ready to start as soon as we get there."

[11]

"To fight, we don't have to be brothers or even friends, but we do have to agree that we want to win." –From the memoirs of Fleet Admiral Thaylon Loore

Captain Smith slapped one of the crew on the back who was helping two others down the corridor. "We'll get through this," he told the group. "We'll get power back on in just a few. *Cleophas*! How about this ship?"

His job was to be visible and instill confidence. He also wanted to see the damage. The ship had still smelled new when they first appeared over Ganymede. That wore off when the battlewagons made their attack run. Now the corridors smelled of smoke, sweat, and fear. The captain walked with his head held high, stopping to thank the injured for their sacrifice and vowing to get the ship repaired and fly it out under its own power.

"Sir," Ensign Lord caught up with the captain, struggling under the heavy pack on his back. "I brought water and protein bars that you can hand out."

"You know how to make an impact." When the captain looked the man in the eye, he saw pain. "Where are you hurt?"

"Nothing like these people," Lord countered.

"Show me," the captain demanded.

Lord put the pack down. A second-degree burn tracked from his shoulder to the middle of his back.

"Give me that pack!" The wrestling match was brief and ended with the captain hoisting a pack full of small bottles of water and food bars onto his back. "You distribute them. There won't be any medical for you, unfortunately, not for a while."

"I'll be fine," Lord lied.

"After we've treated it and you to prevent infection." He waved off any further argument. The ensign handed water to the next group of crewmembers they came across. A simple gesture, but it made a big difference to those who were able to take a drink.

The captain moved on.

"Where are we?" Lord asked.

"We're on Deck Twelve, aft quarter. Why?"

Lord snorted. "I mean in space. Are we still in Jupiter Gulf Seven?"

"I would think we've exited that by now and are in Gulf Eight, on our way toward Saturn."

The ensign nodded slowly. They handed out more water and food bars and moved on.

"At least on our last trajectory, we should escape the effects of Jupiter's gravity. By the time we come under the influence of Saturn, we'll either have power restored or be dead."

"That's a positive way to look at it, sir."

"Captain School 101. Always see the bright side of life." The smell of burned flesh reached them and wafted past, followed by the pungent odor of puke.

"Not all captains go to the same school, do they?" The

ensign walked beside the captain under the emergency lights, which were *Cleophas'* only fully functioning system.

"They do, but not all captains learn the lessons. Those who do are given command of a Kaiju-class which, it appears, is the largest missile magnet in the history of humanity."

"She took a beating, sir, but we're still here."

"Closest is reactor seven. We need to climb down two decks. Are you up for it?" the captain asked.

Lord nodded and hurried to the nearest emergency ladders, a twin set—the left side for those climbing up and the right side for those descending. They jumped into the mix of personnel on the right ladder and started climbing down. The pack pulled at the captain but he hugged the ladder tightly, pacing himself to keep three points of contact at all times. That slowed down those above him.

The captain maintained his pace until he jumped off at Deck Ten. As crew passed, Lord stuffed a water bottle into their pocket.

"All we had to do was wait and disburse it all before we started climbing."

"Ensign Obvious," the captain deadpanned. "But then we wouldn't have any for the engineering crews working to bring the reactor online."

The captain led the way since the climb had worn the ensign down. He winced with each step from the agony of his injury. The captain slowed and kept his head up. They entered the space where the reactor was located to find it dark and cold.

"It appears that no one is working on it," the ensign said, confirming his status as master of the obvious.

The captain accessed the emergency panels, but they were empty except for the last one, from which he dug out a high-beam flashlight. He shone it around the space, which looked immaculate.

"Why is this offline?" He brought the control panel to life. "Somebody decided this was better offline. I suspect it's the distribution system that is jacked, and there's no place for the power to go."

"Reroute it," the ensign said.

"No shit," the captain replied. "Stay here."

He crawled up the access ladder to the overhead to find the breakers, a massive three-pronged knife switch. He unsecured it from the open position and slammed it into place, completing the circuit. The captain returned to the deck.

"Next step is to disconnect it from its primary circuit, and then we'll run diagnostics."

"Why is no one in here?" the ensign wondered.

"It's probably flooded with radiation," the captain quipped. He shined the light on his badge, which showed green. "See? We're fine."

He opened the floor panel to be greeted by a cloud of smoke. "That would be it." He thrust his hand in, grabbed the handle, and yanked the circuit free. "The damage is below from the hit that almost broke her back."

The captain activated the control panel. It came to life, began its self-diagnostics, and confirmed that all systems were green.

"No time like the present to bring some life back to the ship. Let's hope this doesn't fry any new systems."

The reactor came to life, humming softly with the power generated. The lights in the space came on, normal white lights replacing the emergency lights.

The door opened, and a group of engineers raced in. The lead engineer's face contorted with anger until he saw who had brought the system online.

"Sir, I'm not sure the ship's ready for that reactor's power. Everything below us is either vented to space or on fire."

"Rerouted through the overhead," Captain Smith replied calmly. "The most important thing our people need right now is hope. A few lights coming on and the appearance of the ship coming back to life will do that. With hope comes a chance to live. And the fact that we're not destroyed suggests our people won that battle, or the Behemoth is having its way with *Leviathan*. In either case, time is on our side. Let's get this beast back into the fight."

The engineer pointed to the deck.

"I know. Vented or busted. We'll fix it, Chief. One space at a time." He held out his hand, and the engineer took it in a firm grip.

"One at a time. We're heading back down. See if we can get those fires under control before they burn off all our oxygen."

"Is that why the air handling systems are shut down?"

"Air is life. Toward the outer hull, it's starting to get cold. If it seems warm, you're standing overtop a barbecue pit."

"Fire suppression?" Smith looked at the overhead, where sprinklers and nozzles were positioned to flood the compartment with foam.

"The crack split the system. Once we can seal the breach, the automatic systems should come back online."

"Fight the fires by fixing the outer hull. Don't let me hold you up."

The engineer and his team ran out of the reactor room.

―――

Ezio eased into place near the ventral spine, center mass, where an ugly rent with darkened scorch marks showed the ferocity of the blast. "We need to weld a plate over that gap. Get the maintenance bots on it and as many crew as we can spare. Give them every bit of spare metal we have on board. Dismantle bulkheads if you have to. My orders are to sacrifice *Ezio* if it means saving *Cleophas*."

"Yes, sir. It will be done," Tactical replied, shutting down his station and hurrying off the bridge to start locating and supplying anything that could be removed from the heavy cruiser to repair the hull of the Kaiju.

"Sensors, you have the bridge. Everyone else, with me." The captain strolled off the bridge not long after Tactical. The crew secured their stations and followed.

"Sir," the comms officer pleaded. "Shouldn't we leave more hands on the bridge, just in case something happens?"

"We're tethered to *Cleophas*. If more Ebren arrive, we're screwed. Sensors will call us back so we can watch our final demise from the bridge instead of out there, trying to get the big ship back in the fight. Even in its current shape, it's got ten times more firepower than we do. Unleash the beast, and that means it needs to be fixed. Every chair-polishing ass is getting the chance to contribute manual labor because that's what's called for. Put on your gloves and get ready to work."

The comms officer slunk toward the back of the group. A yeoman, a veritable digital paper pusher, called, "We're with you, Skipper. Save *Cleophas*!"

"You're not getting a promotion, Jones," the captain told him over his shoulder.

"Just happy to be alive, sir."

"I'll drink to that. When we can take a break. Until then, you four to Engineering. You three, Cargo Hold Two, and the rest of you to Cargo Hold One. Comm, you're with me. We're going to the maintenance shop, where it's guaranteed they'll need people to do the heavy lifting. That's us. We serve no other useful purpose right now."

The groups separated and ran toward their designated stations.

Comm's face fell as the captain laughed. "You gotta lighten up, man, or this duty is going to be hell. We fight the battle, and then we fix ourselves and our equipment to be ready for the next fight. The Boneracks are infinite. We'll never be able to kill enough of them, but we *will* be able to destroy enough of their ships that they can't come out here."

"And then we'll lay waste to their planet?" Comm suggested.

"No genocide for the good guys, but the Ebren will need to stay on their planet until they learn to play nice. We can blockade the holy hell out of them."

"Eight battlewagons and a Behemoth. That had to hurt."

"They sent everything they had. That's how badly they wanted *Leviathan*. That tells me it was worth it. That also suggests they'll send a second wave in about twenty-five days when their boys don't report in."

"Which means we have that long to bring *Cleophas* to nominal warfighting capability."

"Eighteen-hour days and lots of catnaps." The captain opened the door to the chaos of too many people in too small a space.

Smith raised his hands and waded to the front, where he found the maintenance chief locked in mortal combat with an engineering ensign.

The captain forced his way between them. "Every second we delay could allow more people to die on *Cleophas*. Eight thousand crew at one point in time. Let's get it together and help them."

"The issue is with the break. The keel isn't broken but warped. That split the plates and armor on top of it. I want to reinforce the keel, while he wants to use the grapples to pull the split together," the chief explained.

"It's a good idea."

The captain held up his hand. "We reinforce the keel as it is and seal the hull."

"But, sir," the ensign started.

"How much torque do the grapples have? I don't care what the number is because it's not enough. If the keel was super-heated and then cooled rapidly, it might work, but the metal might be brittle. Even if we could bring enough pressure to bear, the keel could shatter where it's weakest, the area we'd be trying to bend. So, no. We're going to patch it up so it's good enough, and that's the end of it. Time for talk is over. Put us to work, Chief."

[12]

"A WOLF'S WHISKERS MAY TICKLE, BUT ONLY IN THE INSTANT BEFORE HE BITES YOUR HAND OFF." —From the memoirs of Fleet Admiral Thaylon Loore

The doors off the wide corridor were spaced more widely, suggesting bigger spaces behind them. "We must be in the center of the ship, which puts the most metal and air pockets between us and the outer hull. They've built their ships to improve survivability of the crew, just like us. Lessons relearned after a thousand years. It would have been nice to see their tech before we groped the void like mindless morons," Major Payne remarked.

"Sometimes you have to learn for yourself," Byle countered.

"I think that's what we need to do. Let's go back topside, see if they found what happened to the Bonerack plasma rifle and our flashbangs. Can I get a ride topside, please? A ride to the airlock, please!" Major Payne shouted down the corridor. He faced the other direction and called out a second time.

"I really don't want to be trapped down here." Byle leaned around the major to get a better view down the corridor.

Payne led the way toward the known elevator, walking past the bridge and a number of doors, none of which opened. He knocked on the elevator door, but it remained closed. The corridor surrounded them in a twilight glow, empty and silent.

"The good news is that the lights are on and it's warm," Payne offered.

"That's not a lot of good news." Byle prepared to take off her helmet.

"I'll help." The major stayed close. "I'll keep mine on for the electronics."

Byle popped the seal, and the helmet came free. The major turned it counterclockwise an eighth of a revolution and lifted it free.

"Watch me." The major leaned close to see her eyes, looking for dilation or other signs of distress.

"It smells like an ocean beach, a little salt, and a lot of fresh air. Temp seems a little warm, even." She breathed slowly and deeply.

"Major Payne to all hands. We've run a test, and Byle is here without her helmet on. She says the air is fresh and clear."

"I said that, and I stand by it," she said into the secondary comm system attached to her collar, the throat microphone sounding more muted than the helmet's interface. "The atmosphere is nice, better than any Fleet ship I've been on."

Major Payne watched her eyes, which remained unfazed by changing from internal air to *Leviathan's* life support. "I think it's because of being too close to the less cultured members of this team. Smells like tulips, just like the aura that surrounds me."

"Tulips?" Byle recoiled. "There are no tulips. For the record, the major is lying. Remember when he had that bad beef jerky? Not tulips."

"I regret the decision to eat that stuff. If anyone needs to take their helmet off, it's okay, but don't stray too far from it in case the Boneracks get in. Half the team needs to be helmeted at all times with systems active."

Blinky spoke up. "Sir, in nine hours, we're going to be running low on power. Either we take the suits off at that point, or we have to go into power-saving mode well before then."

"Whenever we make it back upstairs, we'll establish a watch. One on, nine off to conserve power. One-hour watches. Virge, see if you can find your way to the mid-forward airlock. Looks like we're dead in the water on this ship without Blinky and Buzz telling it that we're here in a way that it can understand."

"She knows we're here. The challenge is convincing her that we are friendly and deserving of open doors," Blinky explained.

"She? You have been seduced by Progenitor cyber-pyrotechnics. Everyone gather at the airlock, and we'll figure out our next moves. Take it easy on chow and water, people. We could be here a while."

"There's food in the aft hold if you can figure out how the processors work," Dank suggested. "If we had neural interfaces and if Blinky is right, then we could operate this ship. Without them. We're stuck."

"Rally around Blinky and Buzz. Everyone stands watch but them. They work, no interruptions. We have to raise ourselves to the Prog standard where brute force doesn't work, as we saw when we were trying to get in here. Once inside, the light touch is what it takes. Turbo, is there any tape residue on the airlock hatch?"

"Sir?" Turbo wondered. "We'll check it out."

"Sir?" Byle asked.

"Give it a minute. We all know the answer because this is a smart ship."

"Nothing, sir. Clean as a new skimmer."

"Cleaning bot removed everything," the major said. "I suspected. That's why I didn't get too spun up about it. But watching the airlock is important in case the peckerwoods try to come through."

"Boneracks," Byle whispered.

"That's what I said. In any case, we're en route if we can ever find our way up there. This ship is a maze. I think we'll try aft and look for the access tube Major Dank's group used."

"Are using. It's a long climb up. We're still on our way. Do you want us to wait for you?"

"That will help. Leave Heckler and Shaolin. You and Sparky join the others."

"Will do, as soon as we figure out how to get there. I figure it's about four kilometers from here. Through a maze of a ship."

"Then you better get started and leave a trail of breadcrumbs for us to follow. No sense in all of us being lost."

"There are six of us lost and four that are right where they need to be," Dank replied.

"Rally the four, the phantasmagoric four," Joker quipped.

"So let it be said. So let it be written. So let it be done. Now, everyone stop fucking off and get back to figuring out how to work this ship!"

"We're stuck down here, aren't we?" Byle asked without using her comm unit.

"Pretty much. You heard Major Dank earlier when they hit a dead-end while climbing down. I suspect that dead-end is above us. We knock on all the doors as we pass to see if anyone is home. And the ones closest around corners, too, for the sole reason that that's where we found the first elevator."

"The elevator we couldn't get to move."

"Wait." Major Payne replayed the episode in his head. "We never told it where to go while we were inside." He pointed to the next intersection. "Let's take a lateral corridor to the outer hull and see if we can get it to take us to the airlock. Or guest billeting. Private rooms. I have a full vocabulary to try."

"What's the worst thing that can happen?"

"We can get trapped in the elevator instead of on a whole deck."

"It responds to 'bridge.' I think we'll always be able to get back to this deck. I better contact Heckler." Payne activated his comm. "Heckler, we're going to try something different than heading aft. We're going to find the elevator that leads to the airlock. Move out and catch up with Major Dank."

"Roger. He's about five rungs up the ladder. We better hurry before he turtles too far ahead."

"Hey! We've been climbing for four days," Dank countered.

There was a pause before Heckler replied, "Looks to me like fifteen minutes. You gotta lay off those pancakes at breakfast, sir. We're coming up and it's about time. I'm not good with the infinite ladder even though there's a nice cage around it. Good luck, Major Payne."

"Stay frosty. We'll meet you upstairs."

Payne checked his HUD, walked to the corner, checked it again, and started walking toward the port side of the vast ship.

———

Captain Ezekial Smith had been working the decks for two hours. He had dropped Ensign Lord off with a deck medical response team despite the young man's protestations. The captain continued to carry the backpack, having refilled it twice.

The crew, *his* crew, was fighting an epic battle against the void of space in a ship that should have died hours earlier. But it hadn't. The Kaiju-class ship had withstood the worst the Blaze Collective could throw at it. It had probably been only one hit from annihilation, but that hit had not come.

They cleared the area on thrusters and then on a ballistic trajectory when the thrusters failed.

The lights rose slowly to their pre-combat level of incandescence. The crew held their breaths. The air, tainted by smoke and burned flesh, started to cycle toward the vents while clean air blew in.

"The breach is sealed," the captain told those within hearing. "Back to your workstations, people. Find what's broken, and let's get to work fixing them. One at a time, but with this crew, we'll get it done."

The captain took the nearest elevator up two decks, then made his way to the bridge. Inside, he found only the comms officer. "Recall the bridge crew," the captain ordered before assuming the tactical position. The return of power did not signal the return of sensors. The ship was still blind.

"Comm, broadcast, please."

The young officer gave the captain the thumbs-up.

"This is *Cleophas* actual, and we're not dead. *Ezio*, are you within range? Please respond."

"*Cleophas*. Good to hear your voice. This is *Ezio,* and we are currently tethered over the breach. *Ezio* actual is on a work party outside, repairing the damage. It's a lot of damage, sir."

"I don't know the extent of it as we don't have enough systems functional to tell us which systems aren't functional."

"A dichotomy to be certain, sir, but I see on our screens that your running lights are on. You are flashing a ship in distress beacon."

"I better shut that off," Captain Smith replied. "Don't want to advertise our issues to any bad guys within earshot."

"The board is clear, Captain. We'll be your eyes until you have your own back."

"Thank you, *Ezio*. What about the BEP? Aren't they helping?"

"Well, it's not my place to tell you how they assed up the captain something fierce and he told them to fuck off. Not my place at all, sir."

"How I feel right now, I'd accept help from even those arrogant pricks."

"*Voeller* is providing overwatch while *Ezio's* crew is helping you. All of them. I'm the only one at my station."

"I'll owe your skipper a cold one and then some."

"You might see him yourself if your ship is restoring atmosphere to the damaged areas. He might be inside."

"Are the fires out?"

"Visually, it appears the answer is yes, the fires are out, although the IR scan shows a couple hot spots, but that could be residual heat."

"What's your name?" Captain Smith asked.

"Communications Officer Juzan LeFlore, at your service."

"You are a credit to your position and doing your ship proud. Let the captain know I called if I don't see him first. *Cleophas* out."

The captain cut the signal. "When the crew arrives, their first job is to account for our people. While they're doing that, build a master file of what's broken, or maybe it's easier if they list what's working. Then prioritize work details based on who we have. We're going to rebuild this ship from the inside out if we have to."

The captain left the bridge, jaw clenched and dogged determination on his face.

[13]

"Amateurs talk tactics. Professionals talk logistics." –From the memoirs of Fleet Admiral Thaylon Loore

Major Payne recognized the door. "I think this is it." He tapped the door with his gloved knuckles and it slid open, revealing the elevator.

"Nothing personal, sir, but I don't want to get trapped in there with you."

"We know it recognizes 'bridge,' and maybe the knocking thing will work from the inside if it hasn't moved. I doubt the failsafe is to lock people inside, so we're all good. The ship seems fairly congenial to strangers walking its hallowed halls." He smiled, but the effect was lost since she wasn't looking at him. "Get in."

Byle was reluctant, but Payne hadn't made the order optional. The major climbed in after her.

"Airlock, please." The major took off his helmet. His hair was matted from sweat.

"It makes a difference," Byle noted.

It made no difference whatsoever to the elevator, which didn't move. The major knocked on the door, and it opened.

"See? Not trapped." He took a breath and started his laundry list of terms to deliver them to where they wanted to go. "Top deck, please."

Nothing.

"Deck forty. Deck Thirty-six. Level Forty. The fortieth level. Deck one. Outer hull. Locker of the air. Airlock-amundo. Getum outski."

"Sir." Byle shook her head and looked at the floor. "It's embarrassing to watch."

The major continued, unperturbed. "Billeting. Berthing. Guest rooms. Sleeping quarters. Sleeping rooms. Sleeping compartments. Sleepy time. Beds. Beddy-bye. Bridge."

The doors opened.

"You need to learn some more terms. I'm quickly exhausting my extensive vocabulary. How about you take us to the rest of our team? They are up that way." The major pointed.

Nothing.

"One-zero-one-zero-zero-zero," the major said. The doors closed, and the elevator headed upward.

"Sir?"

"Binary for forty. I knew there were forty decks on this tub."

"How did you know they numbered from bottom to top?"

"My next guess would be one and zero."

Byle nodded.

The door opened, and they walked out to find Turbo and Joker in firing positions facing the airlock.

Major Payne activated the company channel. "The elevators speak binary in English. The top deck is One-zero-one-zero-zero-zero." Major Payne turned back to Turbo. "Report."

"Just making sure the Boneracks don't sneak up on us," Turbo replied.

"Any sign they're out there?"

"None. No sound, no movement."

"Roger. Carry on." Byle joined the watch while Payne entered the room where his technophiles were working.

Buzz looked up, but Blinky remained embroiled in his screen. He wore a blank expression as he stared. Buzz held a finger to his lips and dug back into whatever he was working on. Both screens were turned away from the major, but if they hadn't been, he still would have been none the wiser.

They had already figured the binary angle and were translating and building accesses in the universal language. Numbers streamed across their screens.

Major Payne returned to the corridor, happy with his revelation. They could go to any deck they wanted.

"Major Dank, status report?"

"We've found the central corridor, and we're taking it. If you could drop a high-beam down the corridor where you are, we'll be right there in about a half-hour."

"Major Payne, welcome to *Leviathan*. Would you like a ride to the command center?"

Payne whipped around and looked for the culprit. "Is that you, Blinky?"

"It is me. Welcome to *Leviathan*." The voice came from everywhere and nowhere. The three specialists looked at the major. He pointed at the room where Buzz and Blinky were working.

He jumped through the door to catch them, but they were on the bed, each on their own computer.

"Are you jacking me around?"

"Sir?" Blinky closed his computer. "*Leviathan*. Can you allow us to communicate with our ship, please?"

"Of course. Would you like me to extend the range of your communications? There are four ships. A small one near airlock forty-dash-zero-one. One in near orbit, and two larger vessels drifting toward the edge of your Solar System."

"Are they ours?" Payne asked, wincing in anticipation of the answer.

"They are of the same technology as the vehicle magnetically grappled to my hull."

"You speak English?"

"I uploaded the language program. That's how the ship determined to call itself what we've been calling it." Blinky looked too pleased with himself.

"Thank you, *Leviathan*. Can I talk with my friends on the big ship, please?"

"I have created an opening in the barrier field for you."

The major put his helmet on and activated his integrated comm system. "*Cleophas*, this is SOFT One. Do you read me?"

"Major Payne. It is good to hear from you. This is *Cleophas*. Have you left the ship? *Cleophas* is not accessible at present. Please rendezvous with *Voeller* and await further instructions."

"We have not left *Leviathan*. We are now in contact with this ship, which is fully intact as far as we can determine. Team Payne will conduct a survey with *Leviathan's* assistance. We have air, and I expect water and food. I will keep this channel open. Please advise if your situation changes. What about hostiles?"

"The system is clear. The tally is eight Ebren battlewagons and one Behemoth. We lost *Sirus,* and *Cleophas* is heavily damaged, but humanity has persevered."

"Glory to the Kaiju," the major deadpanned. "Best wishes for quick repairs and few casualties. Payne out."

Payne removed his helmet. Hopeful faces looked at him.

"There was a big fight upstairs, and the good guys won. They're picking up the pieces. I think the best thing we can do is twofold. If there is food and water aboard for our consumption, where is it so we can extend our stay for as long as we need to? And then second, how can this ship help us, whether in the war or just with the repairs to *Cleophas*? Blinky & Buzz, you guys have done something no one else has been able to do. I'm promoting you both right now to Specialist Seven and Specialist Three. Congratulations."

"Hey!" Blinky scowled and kicked the deck. "I'm already a seven, and he's already a three."

"Oh. How about a medal?"

"Doesn't put food on the table."

"Exactly my point. Can you ask the ship where we can find food and water?" the major requested.

Blinky tilted his head back and looked down his nose. "Can you?"

"Leviathan, we need food and water. Do you have a mess hall that can support us?"

"Of course. I will adjust the food production process based on your tastes. The first samples may not be to your liking, but with feedback, I will correct the offerings."

"How do we get there?"

"You only need to ask. Carts are located at convenient locations around the ship and are never more than a minute away."

"Can you pick up Major Dank and his team and bring them here?"

"Of course. I'll dispatch a cart immediately. Anything else?"

"Take us to the chow hall. This calls for a celebration. And bring Major Dank and his team there instead of here."

"Of course."

"You are the kindest and most pleasant Prog I've ever had the pleasure to meet," Major Payne said. "I feel like a guest at your resort. Thank you for having us."

"I don't know the term 'Prog,'" *Leviathan* replied.

"Short for Progenitor. That's what we call the race of beings who built this ship."

"Ah, Progenitor. You are talking about the Godilkinmore? I like the term 'Progenitor.' It seems most apropos in the current era of universal history."

Two four-person carts rolled down the corridor and stopped nearby. "Can you let us know if anyone tries to open one of your airlocks? Otherwise, I'll have to leave someone here to watch."

"I will make sure the airlocks remain closed unless you know about it. Not all guests are as congenial as you."

"Thank you, Lev!"

The six members of Team Payne climbed aboard the carts and headed toward the main corridor. When they reached it, the small vehicles turned toward the aft end of the ship and traveled another two hundred meters to find Major Dank and his team waiting.

"Virge. Fancy meeting you here."

"That cart picked us up there," he pointed ten meters away, "and dropped us off here. I'm curious about the efficiency of the ship's mass transit system, but it appears you've figured it out."

Payne pointed to Blinky and Buzz. "They did. And taught it English, too. *Leviathan*, chow hall, please."

"Payne, corridor, you're welcome," the ship replied.

The major stared at the door, a blank expression on his face.

"Finally, someone who gets you. I am in awe of the ship's genius," Blinky said.

"You get me! And there are so many out there who don't. Thank you!" Declan Payne threw his hands up in a gesture of final victory.

"I am not sure about getting you. What if I don't want you?" the ship replied.

"Too late. Stuck with me. Whodathunkit? The Progenitors had a sense of humor."

"Very much so. There is a joke room on this ship dedicated solely to telling jokes," Lev noted.

"Really? That's awesome."

"No. There is no joke room. This ship's mission wasn't conducive to telling jokes, so those who created me instilled a sense of humor, which they considered their greatest achievement. Not the ship, and absolutely not the weapons or the telepathy, but the humor."

Declan's face fell. "A lot of people died to protect us and keep this ship from falling into the hands of the Blaze Collective. I need to know, Lev, can the ship fly?"

"Yes. I am intact and operating at peak efficiency."

"We could fly out of here right now if we wanted?"

"Yes. Is that what you wish?"

"No. I wish to have a good meal, and then we need to talk further. All of us—Team Payne, with each of our individual specialties. Help us to understand you better so we don't run afoul of your programming or your morals. We, or rather all humanity, has a big problem. You had to see us on the blue ball closer to the sun in our formative years, and now that we have our feet under us, we've found space is a hostile place. The Blaze Collective is a group of alien races whose sole purpose seems to be the removal of humanity from existence."

The doors opened to the dining facility. Bright lights streamed from an area behind a serving counter. They always ate by rank, which meant Buzz went first, then Joker and Shaolin. Buzz headed inside and tried to see everything at once.

Lev replied to Major Payne, "There's a little bit of a problem with that. You see, I'm a pacifist."

"That would be a problem. But since the Blaze don't know that, maybe we can fly around and intimidate the Blaze's allies? Get them to chase us into the middle of nowhere. What's your top speed? I guess my real question is, can you outrun them?"

"I have been watching humanity's spread to the stars. Your leap to the faster-than-light drive was a monumental achievement and was done in a shorter amount of time than any previous race that we've encountered, including the Progenitors. The next developmental leap is instantaneous travel, eliminating the distance between two points to cover up to five thousand light-years in the blink of an eye. It's like folding a piece of string to move laterally versus down its length."

"You can fold space and travel up to five thousand light-years in the blink of an eye. That would solve a great number of problems. There has to be a cost to do this."

"It uses a vast amount of energy, and the ship is incapacitated for several of your days before it is able to move under its own power," *Leviathan* explained.

"But you still have FTL?"

"Yes. We jump into interstellar space and then use FTL and sub-light engines to maneuver to the stars and their systems."

Dank and Payne remained in the corridor while the team collected food items onto trays. Heckler stood inside the door, waiting with his arms resting on the barrel of his pulse rifle.

"But you were created to fight?"

"I was created to bring peace. I am the Battleship *Leviathan*."

"We consider you a dreadnought."

"Dread naught, the ship for battle is here to help you avoid battle."

Dank nodded. "The final solution. A weapon so great that none could stand against it. The threat alone was enough to stop wars."

"That was the intent, but the Creel only saw me as a challenge to their primacy. They attacked again and again until I eliminated them. All of them. I off-loaded the crew on the

Godilkinmore homeworld and came here to eliminate the possibility that I would ever have to do that again."

"I fear that you will. The Ebren launched a massive assault on our ships that were protecting us and you. They'll be back, and there will be more next time. Can you help us fix our big ship, *Cleophas*?"

"Yes. I would be pleased to help you fix your ship."

Dank gestured with his fingers toward his mouth as if taking a bite. "After we eat, let's put the events in motion to help us help ourselves. Where is the best place to learn about you, about your systems and capabilities?"

"The bridge. You were there earlier but still classified as an intruder, so I couldn't let you in. You and your team are cleared for access everywhere throughout the ship. If you wish to enter a door, just think it, and the door will open for you."

"Telepathy. Not a neural link."

The two majors took their trays and helped themselves to the spread of food being managed by a multi-armed robotic device.

"We had neural links a long time ago but advanced beyond them."

"Your technology is far beyond ours even though it's one thousand years old."

"Each race evolves according to its own timeline. Yours is yours alone until our paths cross as they are now and until our paths diverge once more. I will share what you are capable of understanding."

Payne put his tray down. "I look forward to helping you understand us better. If you have telepathy, why are we talking out loud?"

"I'm not," *Leviathan* answered.

[14]

"Fear those who say they want peace." –From the memoirs of Fleet Admiral Thaylon Loore

"You'll probably not want to go in there, sir," a junior maintenance officer said, blocking the doorway with his body. More engineer than maintenance, when it came to damage control, his job was to build it back as functional as it had been before. That usually took a lot more engineering skill than maintenance.

"Explain yourself," Captain Smith insisted.

"Too many of our people were burned at their stations." He stuffed his hands into his pockets and kicked at the deck while avoiding eye contact.

"It's my job, so I have to go in, but here's what I need you to do. You stay out here and keep people from coming in unless I specifically call for them."

"Yes, sir." The young man finally met the captain's eyes. Anxiety made them dart back and forth as if he were trying to avoid looking at the horrible things he'd seen.

"They never knew what hit them. It's a death we can all hope for. Quick, in the defense of the ship. Helping your mates stay alive, and that's what they did." They shook hands, and the young man stepped aside.

The captain went in. He didn't know if it was a testament to a long and storied career, but he had seen much worse. The burned bodies barely resembled people. Consoles and systems had melted under the intense nuke fire that had erupted through the ventral breach.

The crew worked in environmental suits, collecting bodies and depositing them into bags, scanning each to determine an identity before sealing it to marry the bag identifier with the being inside. No one would see them again. The bodies would be put in cold storage before getting fired into a sun when the ship was next close to one.

Born of the stars, carried to them, and in the end, returned to start a new journey. The circle of life is complete. The standard space-burial service. He could recite it in his sleep.

He had seen *much* worse and too often. The war with the Blaze had not been kind to humanity.

The captain walked through the space, nodding at those working while taking stock of the extensive damage. All systems on the Kaiju-class had built-in redundancies. Every system could be operated from two different places on the ship. This space would be sealed, leaving *Cleophas* without a redundancy for reactor two and the environmental controls for the central sphere of the ship until they could get capital repairs made in a real shipyard.

Until then, they'd make do. It was how Fleet was fighting the war. Very few ships were completely intact. Bubble gum and duct tape held everything together, except for the weapon systems. Those were pristine.

Before the ship went dark, they had lost less than half their Rapier launchers. That meant the rest were operational. *Cleophas* still packed a powerful punch. Once propulsion was restored, they could rejoin the Fleet and continue to make repairs.

Captain Smith caught sight of one of his engineers. "Chief." He picked his way to the man. "Down and dirty. What's the status?"

"We're broken. Badly. The keel is warped. We can't achieve FTL with a crooked ship. Primary circuits through this whole area are rerouted, and half of those are also compromised. I can get us up and running, but we'll make it to the shipyards on the moon in two months. That's the best I can do. Any faster, and I think she'll come apart."

The captain's communication device buzzed. He ignored it.

"Can we defend ourselves if the Ebren come back?"

"I think so, but we'll be shooting blind. I've been outside the ship. Most sensor systems are gone, launcher doors are welded shut. We've been cleansed by fire. It's like we tried to fly through the sun."

"We did, in a way. Thanks, Chief. I won't hold you up." Comm buzzed again, and the captain angrily picked it up. "What?"

"Major Payne, sir. I think we can help."

"We can use all the hands we can get. Ten are better than none. No joy on *Leviathan*?"

"I'm sorry, sir, I don't mean Team Payne. I mean *Leviathan* has offered to help *Cleophas* with her repairs. We'll be taking off momentarily to join you. Please ask *Ezio* to untether. We'll need access to that section of the ship."

"It flies? And it can help repair my ship?"

"All of it and more. There are some challenges, but not when it comes to getting *Cleophas* fixed. We'll need the engineering diagrams for the ship, so please have someone transmit them on this frequency. *Leviathan* will pick them up and source the necessary materiel. The ship is going to use the metal and components from the Ebren battlewagons to help rebuild *Cleophas*."

"It can do that?" the captain asked in disbelief. "What are my people supposed to do?"

"Evacuate them from the spaces that need to be repaired, especially that ventral area. We'll take care of the rest."

"I don't know what to say."

"Lev responds well to positive reinforcement. Just give him a sincere 'thank you.' Gotta run, Captain. Good hunting."

"Good hunting, Major."

Major Payne closed the comm channel. "I'm looking forward to seeing what you can do, Lev. It'll be a huge help."

"Of course." That was the ship's favorite expression. Nothing seemed too hard for the warship to do besides go to war.

"You don't have a problem fixing a warship?" Payne blurted.

"No. It may seem like a dichotomy, but it is not, at least to me, and that's what matters most. I know that aliens will fight among themselves. You are here, and I like you. I can tell in your thought patterns that you are concerned for your compatriots aboard *Cleophas*. I don't have to restore any of the weapon systems, but I will so the ship can defend itself. It will be involved in more battles with the group you call the Blaze Collective. I am ready to depart the moon you call Ganymede. Are you ready?"

"Team Payne. Are you in place and prepared for lift-off?"

One by one, the team members checked in. Sparky and Major Dank had been taken to the engine room. The others were on the bridge at the various stations for their specialties. Byle and Shaolin specialized in weaponry, as well as the three combat specialists. The five clustered around two stations to study the systems as their operational diagrams cycled through the screens. Blinky was on his own, hooked into the ship telepathically.

He looked stoned. Payne never received a thumbs-up from him.

"Buzz, make sure he doesn't fall out of his chair."

Joker was the last to check in since she was talking softly into a terminal. When the major moved in front of her, she nodded and continued her conversation with *Voeller*, delivering the team's full report.

"If you would be so kind, take us out, Lev," Major Payne requested.

"Of course." There was no sensation for the passengers despite the ship lifting off and shaking off the debris that had gathered on top of the active mesh of the ship's external sensory system. Lev had called it the "barrier field."

A vast army of maintenance bots had exited the hangar bays on both sides of the ship to gather sufficient raw materials from the destroyed battlewagons and were dragging them back into the hangar to use to repair *Cleophas*.

The hangar doors remained open as the ship moved through space, unhindered by axial orientation. The ship could have been a sphere and would have moved as efficiently.

"Why is the ship shaped like this when it can fly equally well in any direction?"

"Expectations. Even one thousand years ago, races expected the pointy end to be the front and the exhaust nozzles to be the rear."

"The exhaust on this ship isn't real?"

"It's real for dissipation of excess heat, but it's immaterial for the direction of flight." *Leviathan* rotated to point the nose at

Cleophas before sliding sideways to get close to the Kaiju, putting the hangar bay opposite the major rent in her hull.

"I am extending an atmospheric bubble that will encompass *Cleophas* to prevent explosive decompression as we cut structure apart to replace and realign. I have dispatched our maintenance and repair system to survey the entire ship."

A screen that covered the walls of the bridge showed a three-hundred-and-sixty-degree view, including anything oriented vertically, as in what was above or below. Everywhere they looked, they could see outside *Leviathan*.

An army of maintenance bots scuttled out of the hangar bay and started dismantling the patches *Ezio's* crew had put into place. In minutes, the damage done to *Cleophas* was exposed. Payne could only stare. The five at the weapons stations looked up from their work and joined the major in staring.

"It's amazing she survived that," Heckler said matter-of-factly. "That would be a death blow to every other ship in the Fleet."

"The keel is warped," Lev reported. "We will replace it, along with the other destroyed systems in those spaces. The survey is complete. Repairs will be finished in four hours."

"Repairs that are almost an entire rebuild."

"Nowhere near an entire rebuild. The Progenitors also had a penchant for exaggeration. Only nineteen percent of the ship needs to be rebuilt. It would have been problematic had we not had sufficient raw materials, which *Cleophas* saw fit to provide by destroying the Ebren fleet."

"You're going to rebuild nineteen percent of a Kaiju in four hours? You're saying that you can build an entire Kaiju from scratch in less than a day?"

"If the biggest sections were already fabricated and we had sufficient raw materials like depleted uranium composites and core steel, yes."

"Can I see the process? Is the hangar bay available to visit and watch?"

"There is an observation deck. The hangar bay is in fluid motion because of the amount of activity. It would not be safe to put your soft and squishy body in that environment."

"What the hell, Lev? I'm hard as woodpecker lips," Payne countered.

"I don't know what a woodpecker is, but I suppose you are trying to say that you would win a collision with an external plate fabrication unit. I assure you, you would not. Go into the corridor, and a cart will take you to the observation deck."

"That's good enough, Lev. Thank you." The major strolled out, waving a hand over his shoulder. "Carry on."

As if anyone on his team would do something different.

When he was alone in the cart, he renewed his conversation with Lev. "Can you set up some rooms for us? Nice ones."

"There are rooms on board for senior staff, the older and more experienced crew members. There are hundreds of such rooms. I will do my best to set ten aside for you."

"There's nobody else on board, Lev. Are you messing with me?"

"It seemed appropriate since you asked about rooms where there is an entire ship of them. Over one hundred thousand, and there are ten of you."

"But nice rooms, the nicest," Payne counted. "I have to take care of my people, Lev. I'll sleep on the floor before I let any of my people suffer, especially when we don't have to. Can you make different mattresses? The ones you have are a little hard for our soft and squishy bodies."

"Of course." Lev gave Payne his peace as the cart made short work of the two-kilometer journey.

It stopped, and Payne got off and walked toward the nearest door that opened without him breaking stride. Inside, he found what looked more like a bar and casual dining area than a control center.

"Lev, this looks like a recreation area or a meeting area of some sort. There are no systems."

"Everything on the hangar deck is automated. There is no need for manual controls."

"But how can I tell what's going on?"

"You ask me, or you use your mind."

"And that was good for a hundred thousand people? You could talk to all of them at the same time?"

"Of course. That's how I was designed. This ship is advanced far beyond your understanding, and I'm not trying to belittle your intelligence. Humanity has advanced farther and faster than any other race we've encountered, and as I've already said, to include the Progenitors themselves."

"I'll take that as a compliment then. Please, tell me what's going on."

Lev used a laser to point through the long, curving window at various bots working on the deck below and explained what each was doing. A bot delivered a glass of chilled water to the major while he watched and listened. Payne took it without thinking and casually drank.

The complex dance below was all-consuming. The massive quantity of metal debris in the middle of the deck was being peeled off and sent down an assembly line, where it disappeared through a roll-up door to return later as a complex component that was quickly whisked away by a waiting bot and carried across open space into *Cleophas*. The dance established a nonstop stream of parts and materiel from one ship to the other.

"What about food? Are there any snacks? I feel like I should be eating popcorn."

"I am afraid that I don't have any of your food structures.

Maybe I can get your database at some point and reprogram the food production systems to deliver what you expect."

"Why not? Let me give them a call." Payne keyed his microphone. "*Cleophas*, this is Major Payne. Can you transfer our food database and complete encyclopedic history on this channel, please?"

"We are kind of busy up here," the voice replied.

"Just grab everything and send it, then get back to what you were doing. Pass to the captain that total repair time for *Cleophas* back to factory settings will be four hours. You'll be back up and running by dinner time. And if we get that database, we'll get a dinner that will be far more palatable than what the ship fed us for lunch."

"The ship has food? You know it's about a thousand years old."

"Tasted like it. If you want, send us a bunch of pastries. They'll get eaten, I guarantee it. Or better yet, send samples of food like pizza, tacos, and hamburgers."

"What are you, fifteen?"

"Only in spirit. Is this you, *Cleophas* actual?"

"Zeke Smith, at your service, Major. Can you patch me through to *Leviathan*?"

"He's listening. Say your piece, Captain."

"I can't thank you enough for what you're doing for *Cleophas* and my people. You've saved us from leaving a gap in our defenses. We need our dreadnoughts, the heavy hitters. The Blaze is only getting stronger, and we are barely maintaining a toehold. We hope that you'll be able to join us."

Leviathan didn't answer.

"In spirit. Turns out Lev is a pacifist but has skills that could sway battles in our favor."

"A warship bristling with weapons that is a pacifist?" The captain didn't sound like he was buying it.

"It's hard to see, but I believe him. Better get your people back on the job, sir. I hear you'll be shipping out soon."

"Reactor Two is back online," a voice said in the background.

"That reactor was gone, a complete meltdown," the captain replied.

"Environmental systems are now at one hundred percent. And sir! The FTL is now showing as available."

"Payne, you are a miracle worker. You'll get the button for this." Button—the Medal of Honor.

"I won't accept it, not for this. We were over here with zero threat to our persons. Give it to Lev. He's earned it."

"I have not," the ship countered. "I shouldn't get a medal for doing what I am capable of doing, for helping a friend in need. Nay! Keep your medals and fire the boilers. Damn the torpedoes, full speed ahead!"

"I'm thinking you've sent the database."

"You said grab everything, Major."

"And we thank you for it. Lev, where's my popcorn?" The major looked for it to magically appear, but it didn't. "I had high hopes. I'll let you get back to it, Captain."

"You had me send our database so the ship could make you popcorn?" the captain asked with a soft chuckle.

"We all have our foibles. Some are more superficial than others. Are you still thinking about the button?"

"Not anymore. Thanks, Major, for the tactical assist. I love seeing green lights on the ready board. Smith out."

"The samples would be a good idea. I can test them to determine the chemical structure. Your food is quite exotic from what I've seen."

"Talking about that, how did you keep food, air, and water in here over the course of a thousand years?"

"The food was cryogenically stored. The air and water have

been kept freshly replenished from Ganymede. The subterranean ocean has more water than the entirety of the surface water from Earth, and there is sufficient oxygen in the atmosphere to pull into the ship. We are good for another thousand years, although a hydroponics bay would be nice. There is a full seed library on board. Would you like me to start the bays?"

"I don't know how long we'll be here, Lev, but yes. Get some plants growing on this ship. We could use a garden."

"How many personnel do you think will live aboard Leviathan?"

"I haven't thought about that." The major pointed at a swarm of small bots taking off and flying into the void.

"Those are for detail work—final painting and touch-up."

"You're almost done?"

"With some of it. The longest timeline is for the production of the defensive weapons systems' control modules. Those are quite complex. I'm impressed."

"I'm glad we were able to surprise you with something. What do you say we return to the bridge, Lev?"

"As you wish. I am at your command."

"Hardly. You're my friend. We'll talk about what needs to be done, just like we did with the repairs to *Cleophas*. I expect you're the one who should be giving orders."

The major left the observation deck to find the cart waiting. He climbed aboard, and the vehicle raced away.

"I am not the one to give orders. I recognize you as a worthy successor to the Progenitors."

"Successors, with an S."

"No, successor singular because there is only one of you."

"You're going to only take orders from me and no one else?" The major leaned forward and looked at his feet, wondering how Fleet Admiral Wesson would take the news.

"That is correct."

"I have a team to run. We have missions we need to carry out."

"Is anything more important than me, the one you call *Leviathan*?"

"The Ebren didn't think so, and neither did Fleet."

"There is your answer."

"But I'm not a Fleetie. I need to go dirtside, kick some hairy buttocks, blow stuff up. You know, asymmetrical warfare. That is at odds with your mission, isn't it?"

"Your mission is my mission," Lev countered.

"My mission is to engage and destroy the enemy."

"All except that part is my mission."

"You're killing me, Lev." The cart arrived at the bridge and the major hopped out.

"Then you won't be needing dinner," the ship replied.

"Lev, so help me, if you kill me, I'm going to come back as a ghost and haunt your circuits."

"I would find that most distressing. I won't kill you, and you don't haunt me. Deal?"

The major nodded. "I have a great deal of respect for those who helped create you, but I expect you evolved far beyond your original programming. If I didn't know better, I'd think you were me."

"I have seen inside your mind. Maybe I'm saying what you would say so we can form a closer connection."

The major stopped two steps into the expansive bridge area and closed his eyes. "You are a total shlong, Lev. I'm going to have to think long and hard about how to get you back. You won't see it coming, but when it slaps you in the face like wet underwear, you're going to appreciate my genius."

"Does the word 'telepathy' mean nothing to you?" Lev wondered.

"Brain radio. Turn up the volume, Lev. We need some music." Payne strolled around the bridge, stopping at the various stations to look and tap a button or two. When he reached the weapons half of his team, he waited for one of them to report. Finally, the ranking member spoke.

"If we can access it, this one ship has more firepower than the entirety of the Fleet combined."

"Three Kaijus and twenty Armageddons? More than all of them?"

"More than all of them. Those maintenance bots...they're all weapons platforms, too. They are the ship's space fighters. Same propulsion system. They can flit around like a will o' the wisp and deliver a great deal of miniaturized heavy ordnance in a small amount of time."

"But the ship won't take the fight where it can do the most good."

"No, but it will defend itself. If we get attacked, *Leviathan* will not hesitate to use force," Heckler replied. "I'd like to get a closer look at those big guns."

"Gun envy?"

"A lot," Heckler admitted. "As a professional courtesy, of course." He looked like a little kid in a candy store. "They built some weaponry we haven't even imagined, including *handheld* weapons. We could up-gun and be badder than we already are."

"I'm so bad, I kick my own ass," the major replied, using the team's humility mantra. "And never forget it. I suppose there's a way to test-fire this stuff?"

"There *is* a range onboard. I have yet to find something that's not on this ship. With your permission, I'd like to take Turbo and Fetus to check out what they have."

"Fetus is Buzz now for being the second one in and helping us get inside the ship. The kid's some tech genius. That's why I brought him on board, but we never had the opportunity to see how freaky he really is. We haven't even scratched the surface on what is available to us with *Leviathan*. We're going to need his brain, so don't get him hurt."

"Is 'Buzz' any better than 'Fetus?'" Heckler shook his head.

The major shrugged one shoulder and walked away. Heckler gathered the combat specialists and left the bridge.

Payne moved to the rotating dais overlooking the bridge. He climbed up, and for the first time, sat in the command chair. It gripped him in the warm embrace of a forcefield. His senses tingled as he became one with the ship. "Lev, what's happening?"

"In order to reduce response time, the ship's captain enjoys a certain oneness with me. How do you feel?"

"Like I'm going to puke. I feel like I'm in a small boat on a turbulent ocean."

"Tell the ocean to calm itself."

"That's not how it works," Payne replied.

"That's exactly how it works," the ship countered.

The major had no answer, and his head wouldn't stop spinning. He had to close his eyes to focus on the interface. He didn't want it to take over his being. With a grunt of supreme effort, he forced himself out of the seat. "Sorry, Lev. I'm not ready for that yet."

"Arguably, it isn't for everyone. I should have eased you into it."

"I'll give it a try some other day when I'm more malleable."

"I don't understand," Lev replied.

"I'm making progress, then, in my effort to stymie you. My brain is too complex for deep penetration." The major's comm device buzzed.

"Payne," he answered.

"*Cleophas* here. You're not going to like this," Captain Smith started. "A delegation is arriving to *help* you with

Leviathan." The captain's emphasis on the word "help" didn't bode well.

"Don't tell me it's the B-E-P."

"You know it is, but Fleet just arrived, too. It's like a Jud Jacket concert with all the traffic up here. And I have to tell *Leviathan* thanks again. Our people are back in their workspaces, and *Cleophas* is near one hundred percent. The shortfall is with people. When we were finally able to bounce the roster, we lost nearly fifteen hundred of the crew."

"Damn. My condolences to their families while thanking those who gave their lives to protect me and my team. It will have been worth it. It already is. *Leviathan* is not something we can ever let fall into the wrong hands. My team and I will die to prevent that."

"I know, Major. The delegations will arrive at the forward airlock in about thirty minutes."

Payne covered the comm device. "Lev, can we bring them into the hangar bay and meet them there?"

"Of course."

"Sir, tell them to enter through the starboard hangar bay. We will meet them there in thirty mikes. And if you have any pull whatsoever, send a cook with them. The Progs don't appear to have appreciated food like we do." Payne cut the line. "Lev, you better pinch your butt cheeks together because we got us some bureaucrats."

"How would you like me to deal with them?"

"If they're buttholes, then tell them they can't stay."

"I believe they will all have buttholes. Are there humans who don't?"

"Not that they don't... What? Never mind. I suspect you'll just *know*. They may want to dismantle things to see how they can be reverse-engineered. They will most likely start issuing orders. They will want to take over immediately without bothering to learn anything about you."

"I won't have that. You can count on me, Declan. I will not let you down."

"Some of the people could be good. What do you say we keep an eye out together, Lev? We'll do what's right by you."

"I trust you."

The major changed gears. "Major Dank. Joy of joys, we have been nominated as the reception committee of a delegation arriving onboard *Leviathan*. Meet me at the starboard-side hangar bay."

"Full kit?"

"Not the environmental suits, no. Wear your dressy sweat-stained work clothes."

"How serendipitous. It appears that I am already dressed for the occasion."

"See you there, Virge. Keep that attitude, and we'll be just fine."

[15]

"Nothing will bring the Fleet to its knees quicker than a good-intentioned bureaucrat."
–From the memoirs of Fleet Admiral Thaylon Loore

The two officers stood within the cavernous hangar bay. Payne pointed at the windows on the interior side. "It looked a lot smaller from up there. Those bots must have been ginormous."

"Where did they go?"

"Repurposed, stored, at work somewhere else? Lev, maybe you can answer."

"They are mostly in storage. They dismantle to a greatly reduced size and are restored when needed. Although I have a significant amount of space, the Progenitors were not wasteful. Real estate, as you would say, must have a purpose."

Three standard box shuttles appeared in front of the opening of the hangar bay. They entered one by one and maneuvered close to where the majors were standing. The third one in popped the hatch while it was still maneuvering, and a spry aide vaulted to the deck. She turned to offer a hand for the next person.

Fleet Admiral Harry Wesson.

"All is not lost, Virge. We don't have to fight the blue-ballers by ourselves."

The first shuttle opened its hatch, slowly extended the stairs, and with an officious air, a man dressed in pure white flicked his hair with a single finger before stepping down.

Declan leaned close to Virgil. "The bureau weenie is here. Bow before his royal majesty."

"I hope not. He'll see the sweat stain down my back and will never adopt me as his cabana boy."

Payne covered his mouth and coughed to avoid laughing in anyone's face.

"Admiral Wesson! Happy to see you could make it. Welcome to *Leviathan*," Payne called past the civilian. The prim man scowled as he looked over his shoulder. The Fleet admiral slowed once he came even with the individual dressed in white.

"What brings you here, Tamony?"

Tamony Morgan Swiss was a corporate financier, inevitable on a technology acquisition mission. A team of like-minded souls poured off the small shuttle to stand in his shadow.

"The greatest discovery known to mankind. It has a higher purpose, Harry, and Nova Intergalactic will see that humanity as a whole gets as much from this discovery as possible. It's in corporate hands now."

Payne scowled, his lips parting as he started to growl. Wesson smiled. "So close, Tam, but Fleet has not turned over this asset to the BEP yet."

"It was discovered in BEP-controlled space."

"Yes. The BEP claims control over this asset," came a new

voice. Commodore Nyota Freeman. "Is that you, Major Payne?" she snarled.

Declan schooled his expression and turned to Virgil. "It's like going to my cousin's wedding. No one liked anyone, but it was still supposed to be a happy occasion. The only reason to go was for the cake, which ended up on the floor when a fistfight turned over the display table. This is just like that, but worse."

"Fleet Commander Harry Wesson." The senior leader of the Fleet extended his hand. The commodore took it and shook quickly, throwing his hand away from hers when she let go.

"If only you fought Earth's enemies with as much vigor," he told her.

I see what you mean, Lev told Payne.

"You can speak to them out loud, Lev. We're all adults here. Maybe you can start with you being your own entity and that no one can claim you. Humanity did away with slavery hundreds of years ago."

The gathered ensemble stopped. They'd only heard one side of the conversation.

"I am *Leviathan*," a great voice boomed into their heads. They winced and gasped.

"'Too much?'" Lev asked.

"Dial it back a little, if you would," Payne replied, keeping a tight rein on his mirth.

"I represent the race you call Progenitors. Welcome to me and my ship. Everyone here is a guest whose visitation rights can be revoked at my whim. Commodore Freeman, you are invited to leave."

She frantically looked from face to face. "Why me?"

"You have been unkind to my friends, and there is no hope that you'll change your behavior. I will not allow it on this ship."

"But I have to. I am the official BEP representative in all matters *Leviathan*."

"According to BEP law, sovereign territory is to be respected. *Leviathan* is the sovereign territory of the Progenitors. You are violating your own law. You must leave."

"But this ship was a derelict..." She stood, mouth agape but unmoving.

"Façade versus truth. You are here, yet deny what you see. I allowed you to see what I wanted you to see, and that continues. Please leave."

"I will not as you are allowing other representatives. I am with them."

The Fleet admiral raised his hands and shook his head.

"She's not with me," Swiss replied.

The second shuttle contained enlisted support personnel.

"Any cooks over there?" Declan wondered.

"Me, sir. I had five minutes to pack. What's going on?"

Payne waved at the man to stand by. "You are extremely welcome. The jury is out on the others except for BEP, and they are leaving." Payne gestured for the cook to join him.

"Major," the Fleet admiral warned, then to Lev, "What should we call you, as a representative of the Progenitors?"

"I am *Leviathan*," the ship replied.

"Thank you, *Leviathan*. May I impose upon you to allow the commodore to remain? I will add her to my delegation if it is okay with you. I will vouch for her behavior. If she offends either of us, I'll send her on the next shuttle out."

"Do you trust this Harry Wesson?" Lev asked, making sure that everyone heard. Since Leviathan had been in Payne's mind, he already knew what the major thought.

"With my life. If Fleet Admiral Wesson gives you his word, you should accept it."

"Then I shall allow her to temporarily remain on board. What about her contingent?" Lev questioned.

"Not them," the Fleet admiral confirmed.

"I would like to know the purpose of your visit. What do you want to get from it?"

The Fleet admiral looked at Major Payne.

"For everyone's edification," Major Payne said loudly enough for all to hear, "the Progenitors perfected telepathy. Humanity's attempt to establish an efficient and effective neural interface is ongoing, but *Leviathan* doesn't need for people to have chips installed in their heads. He can read your minds. Just by coming aboard this ship, you agree to that. Having subterfuge of any kind in your mind is a waste. You might as well be straight up with him because he already knows." Payne pointed to the BEP representative. "Commodore?"

"My purpose was to claim the ship for the BEP and take command of it. Since that is no longer the case, I will watch and learn."

"You will not exploit me for your purposes," Lev replied. "Can I kick her out now, please?"

"Commodore. It's like you either weren't listening or didn't care," Payne said, looking at the admiral.

"I vouched for you, and the first thing you do is lie. Everyone here already knew what your purpose was. I'm sorry. Your contingent will need to leave."

She tried to stand up straight. "BEP will be back," she vowed before sending her contingent back to their shuttle. The BEP minions stumbled away.

Tamony Swiss slow-clapped their departure while the commodore remained behind, challenging the admiral with a scowl. "I wish I could get them to go away like that. I am here to determine value. My initial intent was to buy from the BEP what we could reverse-engineer, but since that isn't going to happen, I will serve as chief negotiator for any technology transfers you, as the Fleet representative are willing to consider."

"None, but you can stay and look around and be envious of your betters," Lev replied.

"I assure you, these military personnel are not my betters. They all work for the civilian government."

"I assure you," Lev countered, speaking slowly and enunciating clearly, "that they are better than you, despite any hierarchical political structure."

Swiss yawned and flicked his fingers as if chasing a fly away.

"Who else do you have with you, Admiral?" Payne asked.

"I brought Lewis Barlow, logistician, and Malcolm Russell, research engineer. We also snagged Captain Arthir Dorsite off the front lines. No one knows more about Blaze combat tactics than her."

"Nice to meet you," Payne said. Lev remained quiet. He already had his answers. "Who are you?" Payne pointed at a woman standing behind Tamony. She was in his party but didn't look to be with him.

Swiss took it upon himself to answer. "This is Doctor Davida M. Danbury. She is the smartest person I've ever met, and I have met all of them. She is a genius and here to help me identify and classify opportunities."

She nodded but wouldn't meet anyone's gaze. Her clothes consisted of a wrinkled work jumper with drink stains. She wore military boots, but they were untied. Her hair was flying wild in some places and matted in others.

"Nice to meet you, Davida." She didn't acknowledge him. Payne watched her closely. "Lev?"

"I can work with her," was all Lev would say, although the ship had agreed to work with Payne, so he wasn't sure if that was high praise or not.

The group turned as another ship entered the hangar bay. *Glamorous Glennis.*

"You have access to my ship?" Payne wondered.

"Oddly, no. But I can demagnetize the hull before towing the ship inside using energy fields."

"Damn, Lev." The major continued, "It seems like you all want to see technology, so let's start with the bridge, which will show the group the executive overview of what *Leviathan* is. From there, we can visit the engine room, some weapon systems, food preparation, and then small arms, where my combat specialists are currently test-bedding a variety of handheld weapons that are on this ship."

Swiss' eyes lit up for a moment until he caught Payne staring at him. He feigned indifference as he slowly followed the group out of *Leviathan*'s hangar.

Payne used his comm device. "Heckler and Sparky, meet us on the bridge. You are going to get help, and make no mistake, you guys are in charge. Also, we have a cook here. Please, let him be good."

He found the man standing next to him. "I can cook," he drawled, "when I have the right ingredients. Do you have the right ingredients?"

"That's where we run into issues. *Leviathan* has a food processing system, like a three-D printer for food. You need to teach it what good looks like."

"I may not be the right person for this." He scratched his head.

The carts arrived, and everyone piled aboard. The Fleet admiral sat next to Major Payne.

"We'll talk later," he told the cook. "What's your name?"

"Mess Specialist Six Galen Stone, at your service."

"We love you already, Galen. The Fleet admiral has committed to getting you whatever you need to make sure we eat like royalty. Anything."

"I have?" Wesson asked with a chuckle. "Although with as

many visitors as you're going to get, you probably need a red carpet for them. Fancy meals will take the edge off."

Payne shook his head. "I don't think we're going to be hanging around the Solar System for long, sir."

"What makes you say that?"

"Divide and conquer. Dogpile the loners and move on."

"*Leviathan* will help us fight the war?"

"Not directly, but he is one hundred percent committed to helping us win as long as we remain ethically grounded."

"He got this from your mind?"

"I have my moments, sir."

Admiral Wesson grinned. "I knew you were the right one for this job. Explain to me what *Leviathan* has in store?"

"Stealth mode. We didn't see this ship until Lev wanted to be seen." The cart train raced down the lateral corridor and into the main high-speed transit route, the wide longitudinal access from bow to stern.

A ramp opened, and the carts descended to the next level without slowing.

"A ship that's five kilometers long to be used as a stealth ship?"

"Yes."

"Maybe we can acquire that technology for smaller ships. It would give us a significant edge without changing our current weapons."

"I haven't talked with Lev about it. We can broach it, but from what I've learned so far, the good stuff is hard to come by because of the rare elements used to produce it. Lev can manufacture components, as you saw with the return of *Cleophas* to full combat capability, but that was only because of the Ebren battlewagons that were available."

"Then scour this area and recover as much as you can. Fill

your hangar and cargo bays with it. A mobile repair platform helps us as much as a new warship. More, even."

The carts slowed to a stop at the vault-like door that stood open, granting access to the bridge.

"Maybe that's our lease on life, but this ship does a whole lot more."

"One-stop shopping. No wonder BEP wanted it."

"Sir, you know they wanted it because it's the coolest thing ever. They would diddle-fuck with it, and no one would realize any value from it. It would cost lives rather than save them."

The admiral cautioned the major, "You have to work on that animosity toward our fellow defenders of humanity."

"After that exchange, Admiral, I'm hating on them at a whole new level."

"I get it, son, but we're fighting so they can be the dangling shlongs they are. If we lose, we all lose, and since you are food-motivated like a beagle, the best restaurants in the universe are still on Earth. Remember that. We'll tolerate the BEP just so we can go on gastronomic vacations."

"When you put it that way, I'm still not sorry you sent the commodore's people packing." They followed the others onto the bridge. The group of twenty people spread out, stopping by stations and tapping interfaces, pecking at keys. "Do you think you should be touching stuff that you have no idea what it does? Do you want to be the one who launched a planet-killer missile into the Kaiju?"

"There are planet-killer missiles on board?"

"I made it up," Payne admitted.

"I do have missiles capable of imploding a planet," Lev offered.

"Doesn't matter," Payne said quickly. "We will *never* use anything like that."

"Can we have them?" the admiral asked nonchalantly.

Payne screwed up his face as he tried to contemplate how the Fleet would use such weapons. He didn't like the answers. They wouldn't be paraded around as a deterrent.

"I'm sorry, no," Lev replied smoothly before talking only to Major Payne. *Have no fear, Declan. I will have no role in genocide. As you said earlier, I would rather die than be a party to a galactic-level crime.*

"I hope there never comes a time when our only choice is to use such weapons," Major Payne replied.

"That's where I can help. Would you like to scout the planet that you believe is home to the Blaze Collective?" Lev offered.

"We would," Payne replied before apologizing. "Your call, sir, not mine."

The Fleet Commander nodded. "That would be great information to have."

"Please inform your people that you'll be back in five days."

"Easy as that? A thousand light-years from here and back in five days?" The admiral looked incredulous.

"We will be there in a matter of seconds, Admiral, but it takes a few days for the ship to recover from the fold. Then a day to fly into the system from interstellar space, a day to collect information, and then an instantaneous fold back. Five days."

"That will be well worth it. You're taking all of us?" The admiral glanced at the commodore, who scowled at every station.

"The tour of the ship will take some time," Lev explained.

"Begin the tour, Lev," the admiral requested.

"Everyone, please find a seat. The first time you experience this type of travel, you may undergo brief disorientation."

"Where are we going?" the commodore demanded, staring at Major Payne. He gazed back, forcing himself to maintain a blank expression to give nothing away.

"We're going to visit the Blaze Collective."

"I didn't agree to go anywhere. Let me off this ship!" She rushed for the exit. Lev secured the hatch. "We're being kidnapped. Subterfuge. Launch the poison pill and spike this program."

Blinky caught the commodore mid-stride, whirled her about, and slammed her into a seat. "The admiral said sit down, and you will not do anything to *Leviathan*. He is the greatest friend humanity has ever had." He stabbed his finger at her face to punctuate each word. The admiral watched him, gesturing for the tech specialist to ease back in his defense of the ship.

And the Fleet.

Team Payne and the visitors took their seats. The main screen showed *Leviathan* accelerating away from the ships in the area.

"Preparing to step through the door to a point in interstellar space. The barrier field is active. *Leviathan* will be invisible to scanning systems as it travels to a point outside the Blaze heliosphere."

Leviathan moved toward a pinpoint of intense darkness that stood out against the whitewash of billions of stars. The ship seemed to grow smaller until it and the pinpoint were one. An instant later, the stars reappeared—different stars.

Payne felt like his insides had been moved to the outside. The anguish and disorientation lasted only a few moments, then he got his feet under him and attempted to stand.

The Fleet admiral groaned and flopped to the side, unconscious. Payne forced his eyes open. "I can't imagine why anyone would take that badly."

Davida had moved into the captain's seat. Payne stood too quickly, steadied himself, and stepped closer to the dais. Davida wore a look of ecstasy, moaning softly while her body vibrated to a rhythm only she could hear.

The major's disorientation and pain passed. The others

stood and stretched to drive more blood through their systems. He stared at the woman who had been called a genius. "Lev, that's really weird. Is she okay?"

"She is one with the ship, Declan. She will be here for a while. We can continue the tour. Where would you like to go?"

The others roused, including the admiral. He came to his senses quicker than the rest.

"I would like to know our status. Where is the nearest enemy? How long will it be before anyone sees us out here? What do you know of the nearby system, like, is the enemy there?" Payne requested.

"By calling the Blaze Collective the enemy, you reduce your chances of defeating them without fighting."

Payne didn't try to answer. The Blaze had killed too many humans for them to be anything *but* an enemy.

"We are outside of the system we called Parallax Major because of a crystalline asteroid belt which changes how the living planet appears from outside. It is a most unique astronomical occurrence. There are only three of them in the explored universe."

"Does the sensory mesh actively scan the system?" the admiral asked.

"No. The barrier field receives all variations of energy output through vibrations in the fabric of space. These vibrations tell us how far away the object is and the energy output. When a craft gets close to a star, it becomes more and more difficult to identify by sensors because of the massive amount of energy flowing outward."

"We can learn more about that later, but for now, we'd like to raise a cheer for being the farthest that humans have ever traveled away from Earth." Payne smiled and looked around, but no one else looked like celebrating.

"We've been farther," the admiral said. "But not in this direction. We're, what, a thousand light-years from Earth?"

"We are one thousand one hundred and seven," Lev replied. "And now we must sit here for about three Earth days to recharge and recover. I have assigned you all to quarters on the next level up. Call for a cart and say your name. You'll be taken to your quarters. When you wish to leave, go into the corridor and call for a cart, then state where you wish to go. I understand English thanks to Specialist Andfen and Specialist Periq."

"There you are. Where would you like to go first? Heckler. Did you get a good look at the man-mobile weaponry?"

"You could have heard him orgasm from four decks away," Turbo stated. At the looks she received, she had to ask. "What?"

Heckler rotated the weapon he had over his shoulder to under his arm, shrugged off the sling, and held it out in front of him. "You thought we had pulse rifles? No. *This* is a pulse rifle. Nearest I can figure, it fires a burst of air, but at a speed that will shred anything that's not hardened. Perfect for anti-personnel ops, and it never runs out of ammunition."

He handed the weapon to the admiral, who looked at it while taking care not to touch any of the control surfaces.

"And then there's this if you want to destroy hardened objects." He removed a pistol-shaped weapon from a holster at his side. "This fires a sliver of a dart, but when it hits, it explodes. Projectile capacity is two hundred. Those long firefights when you're running low on ammo? A thing of the past."

"Our firefights don't last more than a few seconds, but these look like upgrades to our pulse rifles. Any plasma or firestarters, just in case we want to make a scene?" the major asked.

"I'm sure there is. Let's go to the range and take a look. I don't think anyone will be disappointed."

The commodore cleared her throat. "I would like to look at

the ship repair and parts fabrication facilities as well as the crew support facilities."

"Because you plan to use this ship as a shipyard and space station? You are going to anchor the only vehicle in the galaxy that can travel a thousand light-years in the blink of an eye?" The admiral didn't expect an answer since he didn't wait. He ushered Heckler out to the corridor and into a waiting cart to take them to the range.

Payne wanted to go with them, but he felt obligated to play host. "Virge. Go with them, and take Turbo so she can better explain the idea of loud orgasms to the admiral." Payne looked at the assembled faces. "Joker, show Galen Stone, my new favorite human being in the whole universe, to the chow hall. Dinner might be palatable with Galen's help. You two, Malcolm and Lewis. What do you guys want to do?"

Malcolm spoke up first. "I'd like to see any research facilities on board. There is so much to learn. I don't even know what to ask."

"I'll take him," Specialist Periq offered. "Call me Buzz."

"Logistics. What kind of supplies are on board, and how do we restock? What do we restock? Is there an inventory management system?" Lewis asked.

Everyone looked at him with blank expressions. "I'm glad you like that stuff. The Fleet needs more people like you, but you're on your own. Just go into the corridor and ask for a cart to take you to... Lev, can you suggest the right place?"

"Of course. I will escort Mister Lewis Barlow personally."

Payne knew he was escorting everyone personally. If he was capable of reading one hundred thousand minds simultaneously, the twenty people on board would cause him no grief.

The man in the white suit crossed his arms, and the crease in his brow grew deeper with each passing second. Payne waited for him to speak.

Captain Arthir Dorsite sat at the weapons control station and began an animated conversation with Leviathan. She was right where she wanted to be.

The commodore mirrored Swiss' body language. "Well?" she finally asked.

"Well, what?"

"Aren't you going to escort me?"

"No. I need to stay here. We are six hundred light-years behind enemy lines. My place is on the bridge. Well, my place *was* up there," he pointed at the dais, "until someone got all cozy with our host."

"I need to talk to someone in charge," Tamony insisted.

"He's on the shooting range blowing stuff up."

"He's blowing something all right. The chance to be somebody, the opportunity to make a difference for all humanity."

"He's already doing that by keeping the war from dropping on humanity's head. I think this may have been a wasted trip, Mister Swiss. You can see all the goodies, but you don't get to touch any of them. It must frustrate your belief that everything and everyone have their price."

"That belief has proven correct throughout my rather glorious life," he replied. "And it will in this instance, too. I am simply in the wrong place to leverage my influence. I have seen how much there is to appreciate. And we *will* have it for the benefit of *all* humanity."

"Fine. Walk around and enjoy yourself. See what there is to see. Lev, make sure Mister Swiss is afforded full access, just like we were when we first arrived."

"Of course."

Payne was building an understanding with the ship. He only spoke for Tamony's sake since the ship knew what he was thinking. That decreased the time to exchange information, but the exchange was only one way. He focused his effort on thinking out his question. *When will I be able to converse directly from my mind?*

Did it hurt to come up with that sentence because it felt painful? You'll get better at it, Declan, but it is that simple. Your mind is a jumble of thoughts. You are unable to dwell on just one. Once you can do that, we will be able to talk like friends at a bar. It will still be crowded and there will still be noise, but we'll understand each other just fine.

Payne strolled around the bridge to help him ignore the others. One by one, the team drifted off the bridge, looking like they were talking to themselves as they carried on conversations with Lev. He knew Swiss would be angry when Lev wouldn't open any doors for him. He'd run to the Fleet admiral with his complaints, and Payne wouldn't have to deal with him anymore.

That would be a relief. They were deep in enemy territory. He had other things to worry about.

[16]

"SURRENDER IS FOR THOSE WHO DON'T HAVE AN IMAGINATION." –FROM THE MEMOIRS OF FLEET ADMIRAL THAYLON LOORE

The three days were spent recovering and learning what the ship had available, but not how any of it worked. Building an inventory of technological miracles had taken all that time. Even the commodore had become embroiled in what the fabrication and repair facilities were capable of. She had spent all three days in two maintenance bays.

How a shipbuilder had become the commander of a fleet of warships, no one would ever know. A talent for one did not translate into a talent for the other.

Galen Stone quickly became Team Payne's favorite crew member. He was willing to experiment and went through a great deal of the colored biomass to find combinations and formulas that replicated the best of Earth's dishes. Since the biomass was recycled, the cook was more than happy to experiment, but he grew full quickly and needed tasting volunteers.

Team Payne rolled through the dining facility on a schedule to fill the need.

On the second day, the major implemented mandatory physical training, an hour in the morning and an hour in the evening. Lev reconfigured a space for human-centric training like lifting weights. They ran up and down the main corridor while carts occasionally whipped by.

For a ship that size, they found they ran into each other more often than not. Rarely were they completely on their own, and thanks to Lev constantly being in their minds, no one was ever lost.

It was two full days before Davida left the captain's chair. She took one step and collapsed from exhaustion and dehydration. She was put in the health center, where she remained under the observation of devices charged with improving her state of well-being.

They assembled on the bridge at *Leviathan's* request.

"I've called you here today to discuss our next steps," he said ominously.

"Tell me we're ready to move," Payne replied.

"We're ready to move. I am fully recharged. We can fold space at any time, which will make an emergency getaway possible. Shall we see what the living planet of Parallax is up to?"

Payne looked at Admiral Wesson.

"This is an unlikely crew to be tasked with a reconnaissance mission of this magnitude, but we will rise to the challenge. *Leviathan* will see us there. What we do once in range will be up to us. I would like Team Payne to suit up and load into their skimmer. Be ready to deploy should a target of opportunity present itself. Leviathan will not take offensive action, but if we can, we will. What kind of potential reward would be worth that risk? I don't know, but if I see it, we'll take it. Our very presence here could change the tide of war. When your homeworld becomes vulnerable, it changes the dynamics of morale. Will it bring them to the negotiating table or make them act more rashly? This, too, I don't know."

"Then maybe we should study them before taking any action," the commodore offered.

The BEP's defensive mindset matched against the Fleet's offense. Defense became monuments to vulnerability in Fleet's mind. Punish the enemy for attacking by counterattacking. Divide and conquer.

The Kaiju-class dreadnoughts were making a difference, but they weren't joining the Fleet quickly enough.

The admiral and the commodore could argue for hours, but this wasn't the time.

"We will look. And we have two words on our side: plausible deniability. The Blaze know what our latest ships look like. They have to know that we don't have the technology to build anything like *Leviathan*. They are old enough; they probably have ships like this in their database. What will they think about the return of the Progenitors?"

"We have become what we never were," Tamony intoned. "The future past. More than we deserve but less than we shall be."

Payne and Dank stared at him with blank expressions until he stopped being full of himself, but the man was always on. The majors turned their backs to him and closed with the admiral.

"Say the word, sir, and we'll fly FTL into the system, slow to sub-light to cross the crystal barrier and then on to a position above the planet. We'll stop opposite the sun so we don't cast a shadow they might see with their eyeballs and outside the orbit of their moon. That should give us a good look and the opportunity to vacuum up any signals coming from the area. Time from here to target, ninety minutes."

"The word is given, Major Payne. Get to your skimmer and be ready to deploy."

"If I may," Leviathan interrupted, "why don't you take one of my insertion vehicles? They have the same barrier field as I do to provide a certain stealth capability."

"You know what I always say. 'Let Lev do the driving because we'll be partying!'"

Major Dank scowled. "You've never said that before."

"Gentlemen," the admiral warned.

"Arthir, can you take the chair? Keep us in one piece, please."

The captain moved into the chair. "Hey! This makes me feel funny. What! You randy goob! Keep those thoughts to yourself. Oh. That was me. Can everyone hear me? Damn! How's this? *Still?*"

The assembled group watched the captain go through her settling-in process, mesmerized by the rapid-fire exchange.

Payne nudged his fellow major. "We'll be leaving now."

They hurried off the bridge, motioning for the other members of the team to join them. "Lev, send our suits to wherever you're taking us, and we'll get ready at our new ride."

"Of course, Declan. I wish you all the best."

They rode in silence as the carts made short work of the three-kilometer journey to the port hangar, a place none of them had yet visited. Inside was a fantastic array of vessels. The carts drove around those to an egg-shaped craft with the mesh on the outside in a color that was neither tan nor brown.

"This might be the ugliest ship I've ever seen," Payne complained. The team left the carts and stood around, looking at each other.

"Function over form, my good man," Lev said happily.

"This thing is butt-ugly."

"I assure you, it is the latest technology."

A side hatch opened. Inside, they found it would fit the team without room for more as if it had been specifically designed for them.

"But it's ugly."

A boxy cart arrived and the side panels lifted, revealing their environmental suits. They stripped, exchanging their clothes with the suits. They checked their new weapons, the air-pulse rifles and the needle guns. They kept their plasma grenades because there was a certain amount of old-school human technology they didn't mind sharing with the enemy.

Major Dank entered first and took his place. The others filed in and filled the seats located back-to-back and facing outboard in the center of the craft. Payne was last and faced the outer hatch.

"What did you mean about not finding peace with one we called 'enemy?'"

"It's all about mindset. If one is your enemy, then your first course of action will be to fight."

"We tried peace. They attacked and killed every delegation we sent. Then they penetrated the space we'd expanded to and attacked our colonies. I assure you, they have earned the title of enemy, and it is in our best interest if we wish to survive as a species that we not be too trusting too quickly. We didn't fire first."

"But you'll fire last?" Lev noted.

"Arguing with a conscientious objector is like arguing with a wall. We can't let them kill us. As long as we remain alive, we can argue over how to use force to protect ourselves. After we're dead, that conversation is a little late."

"It is, but then, you have me. If I have to fire, they will realize the grave error they have made."

"Peace through superior firepower; now you're speaking my language. But every time we think we have the upper hand, our astronomical counterparts come up with something better. It's like they have entire planets devoted to the question of the best way to kill humans."

"But you refuse to use the worldkiller missiles?"

"Of course," Payne parroted. "If that's the price of survival, then the price is too high. We cannot become what we loathe in order to be something better. We'll be the race that fought toe to toe with anyone who tried to subjugate us. We'll earn their respect with our blood, but we won't earn the right to live by committing genocide."

"I am glad that I decided to help you. You make sense. I will not compromise my principles either, but I will not be happy to see harm come to you. In all things, human, you have earned my respect."

"We want steak dinners when we return from a successful mission."

"Have you ever had such a meal?"

"No, but we always want that. Maybe your magnificent food processors can recreate what we like, close enough that it'll be a proper celebration."

"Galen is fun to work with. He takes his job seriously," Lev replied. There was a moment of disorientation as *Leviathan* transitioned to faster-than-light speed.

Payne looked over his shoulder to address the team. "How about we practice some exit drills? We don't want to come out of this thing like clowns out of a tiny car."

"If we ain't training, we ain't getting paid!" Major Dank shouted.

Combat drills. It was the military's favorite thing to do because it made actual combat less of an unknown.

"Tell us how this thing lands and how we would get out, Lev. Run us through a practice hot landing by flying us around the bay here and hitting the deck. Helmets on!"

The team snapped their helmets into place and checked their neighbors, and each gave the thumbs-up.

"Of course." The side hatch secured, and the ship, almost imperceptibly, lifted into the air. A few seconds later, it bounced hard into the deck. Both sides of the ship slid upward, opening the interior space to the hangar bay. The team bolted out of their seats and straight outside. They juked and ran outboard, forming a circle around the ship before they hit the deck, rifles aimed away.

"You could have told me that the ship was designed for rapid deployment."

"What fun would that have been?" Lev replied.

"Recover!" Payne ordered. The group hurried back into the insert ship and took their seats, then ran through it twice more. "Well done, people. Take five. Lev, time check. How far out are we?"

"Forty-five minutes, Declan. Would you care for some refreshments?" Payne looked at his team and was greeted by smug nods.

"Don't get too cozy with the red-carpet treatment," Major Payne warned. "Next thing you know, we'll be back on *Voeller*, eating leftover protein bars for twelve meals straight."

Dank winced. "I thought we were never going to mention that again?"

"Sorry." Payne didn't sound sorry. A cart rolled up, and for the first time, Payne noticed that the wheels weren't touching the deck. He dropped to a knee and bent over to look. "I'll be damned. Fucking thing hovers. What are the wheels for, Lev?"

"Corners. Because sometimes friction is your friend."

"I need more Lev in my life. That's what I've been missing," Payne remarked.

The team helped themselves to a variety of flavored drinks and what looked like fruit. The hydroponics bay wasn't producing yet since it had only been operational for a few days. Payne looked skeptical, but he took one.

Major Dank drew Payne aside. "I was supposed to get my own team following this, but I don't see it. What you're doing... what *we're* doing is going to change the galaxy. I want to stay right here."

"That's not my call, Virge; otherwise, you are more than welcome."

"But we know the guy whose call it is, and he's on board."

Declan punched Dank in his armored shoulder. "That we do. Maybe we can ply him with a cart of refreshments first."

"It seems to have worked on the team."

They were lounging in their suits, using their helmets as pillows as they sipped colored fizzy drinks and ate faux fruit.

"Tell us when it's twenty minutes, Lev, so we can get back in the uglymobile."

"Twenty-five minutes to orbit at present," Lev advised

"Close enough. Saddle up, people. We're almost there."

[17]

"The best way to win a fight is don't be where the enemy is shooting while they are exactly where you are firing everything you have."
–From the memoirs of Fleet Admiral Thaylon Loore

When *Leviathan* came out of FTL, the bridge screens sharpened the view of the current system. A star twice the size and intensity of Sol stood on the far side of a planet below, where wispy clouds covered a miasma of brown and blue. Three moons ranged from left to right, one in shadow while the other two showed as crescents.

Behind the ship, the asteroid belt twinkled and sparkled.

They didn't get long to admire the view before the tactical board populated with a variety of icons, updated to Fleet standard from what the Progenitors had used.

Every ship was marked as hostile, red triangles with relative threats represented by the size of the triangle.

"Explain, Lev," the admiral requested.

"Energy signatures are diminished, which suggests a fleet at rest. I count four dreadnoughts, eighteen battleships, and over a hundred cruisers and frigates. This is a rather robust Fleet, but the fact that it is here and idle suggests there is a threat they are defending the Parallax homeworld from but it is not so close that they keep their ships in a state of high alert."

"Can they see us?"

"They should not be able to see us using physical or technical means."

"What about the planet? Are they as advanced as you were when you went into retirement?" the admiral queried.

"They are a technological society. Heavy industry is limited, and the air is clean. I see no shipbuilding facilities, which suggests they have moved their heavy construction off-world. I count more than five billion of the evolved entities we once thought were the Berantz."

"Five billion souls and a hundred and twenty warships. Comparable to Earth." The admiral scratched his chin. "Captain Dorsite, tactical assessment."

The captain adjusted her seat, eyes unfocused from her interaction with Leviathan at the telepathic level. "We are outgunned rather severely. Two dreadnoughts appear to be comparable to *Leviathan,* while the others are comparable to our Kaiju-class. It is critical that we study those two ships. If they are as capable as *Leviathan* and they enter the war against humanity, we won't stand a chance."

"Preemptive strike?" the admiral asked.

"I will not allow it," Lev replied. "These ships are no threat to you except in their potential, which we are not yet sure of. And once we are, what is their intended use? They are here and not on the front lines. Attempting to destroy them now would confirm their worst fears about humanity and tell them *you* should be eliminated."

"That's pretty harsh, Lev. We're the good guys."

"Are you?"

Lev's simple question gave the admiral pause. The commodore and the corporate financier both sat down. Neither was equipped for the conversation or the answers. Tamony scowled because he'd been denied access to everything worth seeing unless he was with someone else. He had taken to hanging out with the commodore. The vitriol spewed by the two had reached such atmospheric levels that no one could stand being within earshot of them.

Or, in the words of Major Payne, "All they do is fucking bitch about every fucking thing."

"You judge yourselves on your intentions, but every other living creature will judge you on your actions. When your actions are aggressive without being provoked, then *you* are the one that others will fear. When motivated by fear, reactions tend to be predictably extreme."

"Which means if we were able to destroy these two, if there are others out there, they might be committed to the war when they would not have been otherwise, ushering in the demise of all humanity. Is that what you're thinking? Are you collecting any signals that we can analyze to help us understand them better? Find a tidbit or two that might bring them to the negotiating table?"

"That is the better question, Harry. I am collecting as much information as I can, but we arrived during the night for the majority of the planet's population. We can observe as long as we remain undetected. I think a full day-night cycle will be illuminating."

"Nice pun, Lev," the admiral replied. "I guess we sit and wait. Please inform Major Payne to stand down but remain on five-minute alert."

"Crack-snacking hairy buttholes!" Heckler blurted. "I'm ready to get off this floating hell!"

"What?" Major Payne stared at his senior combat specialist. "You just want to play with your new toys."

"I do, and then I want to come back here because this place is pretty sweet. Did you know there's a room personalization shop where you select a few things and the ship upgrades your pad?"

"Lev!" the major called. "How come I didn't know about this?"

"It must have slipped my mind. But you know you don't want to be comfortable. You must suffer for your craft. I've seen it in your mind."

Declan shook his head. "I'm pretty sure that is nowhere in my mind. I enjoy my comforts. Just because I can tolerate roughing it doesn't mean that's what I prefer. When this mission is over, we're going shopping." His team conspicuously avoided looking at him. "Who else knew about this? Hands up."

Even Major Dank raised his hand.

"From here on out, when you guys find something cool, let me in on it, or you might find yourself as Galen's love slave, eating all day, and then we'll run until you spew. And then we'll run some more."

"It isn't their fault, Major. I can be persuasive when I need to be. Back in my day, I was known as a bridge-builder."

The team eased off the uglymobile and found spots to lie on the deck and relax.

"You owe me, Lev. That mattress. Please have it changed out to something fit for humans before we get back. I want a good night's sleep for once."

"The admiral wants you back on the insertion ship. There is activity in the fleet above Parallax."

"You heard him!" Major Payne shouted. He'd been off the

small vessel for a grand total of one minute. The team instantly turned professional and snapped their helmets on before reboarding the ship. They checked each other once in their seats. Total time from notification to combat-ready, twenty-one seconds. The major gave two thumbs-up. "Once again, we wait."

The others nodded, but the mood was different. The walls that were the lateral doors became screens displaying the tactical picture. Team members on both sides of the small ship stared at the imagery, trying to make sense of it. They'd never seen that many enemy icons at one time. Their behind-the-lines insertions hadn't been onto any of the enemy's homeworlds.

Payne switched his suit's comm to the team channel. "A lot of firepower out there, but this ship is invisible to their sensors."

The screen flashed with the first weapons firing across a wide front as if they knew *Leviathan* was there but weren't sure exactly where. Lev immediately started moving away, picking an angle that wouldn't highlight the ship against the crystalline asteroid belt.

The dreadnoughts moved out of the cloud of smaller ships. The display zoomed to a close-up visual of the ships to watch them deploy their main weapon, a double-barreled monstrosity.

"Lev, what the hell are those?"

"They appear to be plasma cannons. See the conductors leading back to the turret?"

"Do you have anything like that?"

"Of course, but not of that size. I expect that is a limitation of their engineering." When Lev finished, the lights pulsed from the weapons, and two mini suns raced across the void. A klaxon sounded within *Leviathan* only once before both rounds impacted the ship.

The hull screamed in agony, and the ship bucked hard

before grabbing an angle away from the Berantz dreadnoughts to limit the exposed profile.

"Fire!" the major shouted, expecting Lev was hearing the same request from the bridge.

"They defend themselves against our invasion. Nothing says we're for peace better than not firing when we invade their territory. I'm sorry. They have not damaged my systems."

The ship jolted violently a second time under the impact of the massive plasma balls hurled at near-light speed.

"Jumping to FTL in ten seconds."

"Can we get on board one of those dreadnoughts?" the major asked quickly.

"Yes. They should deploy drones shortly. I will get you onboard, but you must go now."

At the speed of thought, the major agreed, and the insertion craft lifted off the deck and shot toward the door, which opened to let the ship out. As soon as the uglymobile cleared the frame, *Leviathan* disappeared into faster-than-light speed.

"What's your plan, Major?" Payne mumbled to himself.

The uglymobile bobbed like a cork on a gentle lake with its systems at minimal power to avoid detection.

"Lev, are you here with us?" Payne asked.

"I have been programmed by Leviathan to fly this ship and answer your questions, at least the ones that Leviathan could predict."

"What is the insertion plan on the enemy dreadnought?"

"This ship has been deposited in the current flight path of the dreadnought designated as number two. When it passes, I will attach this ship to the outside of their hull near their hangar bay door, which opens and closes with some frequency in support of their drone fleet."

"They won't see us casually strolling into their hangar bay?"

"I'm not programmed with that question. Can you rephrase?"

"How will we avoid detection while entering the hangar?"

"I am limited to getting this ship inside Dreadnought Number Two. Once there, what you do is your business," the craft replied.

"Will they have automated defenses to keep people from doing what we're going to do?" Payne replied.

"Unknown."

"What defenses are inside the hangar?"

"Unknown."

"That means you don't know about personnel either. Will there be security inside the hangar?"

"Unknown."

"Yeah, I get it. It's all unknown except us floating around in Parallax space, waiting for our ride. Did Leviathan use FTL instead of folding space so he...*you* can come back sooner to pick us up?"

"That is affirmative."

"I love you, man," Payne replied. The crew shifted in their seats as the ship continued to bob. "The uglymobile for the win. I really hope we survive so I can have some unkind words with our host."

"You asked. Time was of the essence," Major Dank suggested. "We got what we wanted. Congratulations, Heckler, you're off the ship." He made a sour face. "This is *much* better."

The ship's movement smoothed as the thrusters kicked in to drive it toward the target. They were close.

"Listen up, people. You heard the intel on this one. We're going in hot. I'm assuming we'll be spotted, so that means we wreak havoc, cause as much damage as we can, and then get the hell out. When it's time to go, there's no fucking around. I don't want this to be a one-way trip. In, egregious amounts of damage, out. Simple as that. Once in the uglymobile, we'll count on Lev's stellar programming skills to fly us to safety while we wait for pickup."

A soft thump announced the impact with the Berantz dreadnought.

"We are magnetically clamped to the external hull. Drones are exiting the hangar bay now. We will follow them in upon their return," the ship reported.

"What are the drones doing?" Payne asked.

"They are searching space looking for debris from *Leviathan* to examine to learn its nature and origin."

"They can do that?"

"I'm not programmed with that question. Can you rephrase?"

"Never mind. Carry on. Scan the inside of the bay in the seconds before we arrive and give us a view. I need a very simple breakdown: threat or no threat. We will address the threats. The heartbeats while we are departing the uglymobile will be the most dangerous. Everything will look like a threat. It'll improve our odds if you can give us the down and dirty."

"Down and dirty?"

"The intelligence update. A tactical report. Tell us where the enemy is, but only those who are ready and able to shoot at us."

"Ready and able to shoot you. I can do that," the ship assured the team.

They sat on edge as they expected the action to happen, but the seconds dragged into minutes that extended to an hour. Heckler and Turbo had fallen sound asleep, a gift that the combat specialists seemed to embrace.

"Stand by," the ship warned.

Payne wanted to reply that they *had* been standing by, but the time for banter had passed. They were entering the belly of the beast with no backup and no means of immediate extraction.

"They are going to know we're there, so we need to keep moving and get into the ship's guts. But they can drop a couple bulkheads and we'll be trapped, so Buzz and Blinky, you guys need to tap their computer system and make sure we don't get blocked. Move fast, strike hard, max destruction, oorah."

"Oorah," the team replied, their shouts muted as the insertion ship released and accelerated. It banked sharply and rolled in.

"No threats," the ship announced. It touched down, and the sides rose. The team sprinted off the ship and hit the deck in a circle, aiming their air-slug rifles outboard. Payne took a knee as the insertion craft lifted off and moved into a dark corner, where it parked itself between two blockish drones.

The layout was similar to but different from *Leviathan*. There was no window looking down on the bay and no terminal where an operator might direct ships in and out. The one thing the hangar bay had in common was the size. It was every bit as large as the space on *Leviathan*.

Since it was half-filled with drones, the space was busy as the vehicles moved and fitted themselves into parking areas.

"Virgil, forward hatch. I'll take aft. We need to find a way for our people to access the computer system. Move out."

Major Dank took his group—Heckler, Sparky, Shaolin, and Buzz—and conducted a bounding overwatch, a leapfrog movement to the hatch. When they reached it, they examined it, looking for a way to get through it. Dank waited for Payne's team.

Major Payne led his group to the right, trading stealth for speed as they sprinted toward the aft hatch, slamming against the bulkhead when they reached it. When he looked out, he caught the last of the star-filled sky as the hangar door closed and sealed. There was no one out there waiting for them. They were stuck inside the enemy dreadnought.

But not the enemy. Not according to Lev.

He shrugged it off, looked down the bay to where Dank was standing, gave him the thumbs-up, and turned to work on the hatch. There were no actuators. He moved in front of it, and it slid aside.

The team rushed through two by two, looking down the barrels of their weapons, with Payne bringing up the rear.

"Active scans," he told the team. His helmet scans showed a corridor that went straight ahead and one that turned ninety degrees to the right, following the longitudinal axis toward the rear of the ship. "No people. Sling the air guns and go with the needle guns. If we fight anything, I expect it'll be made of metal."

"We're through," Dank reported. "Lateral corridor toward the center and longitudinal corridor in the direction of the bow. We've switched over to needle guns. Good hunting."

"Good hunting," Payne acknowledged.

"I have good news and bad news," Lev said.

Admiral Wesson waited. He had no intention of picking one over the other.

"Pray tell," Tamony interjected.

"We will be able to recover from the damage before we drop from light speed." Lev waited for a few moments before delivering the bad news. "Half their fleet, including the two dreadnoughts, is in pursuit. The second we drop out of FTL, we'll have company."

The admiral grunted with a single head nod before replying. "I was worried we'd left our people behind." He moved to the dais and tapped on Dorsite's leg. "Arthir, tactical options?"

"A pursuit is a prime opportunity for an ambush. *Leviathan* informs me that we will have no more than two minutes before the Berantz ships arrive. That is not a whole lot of time to set anything up, but we could do something. Let me run through a few simulations with Lev, and I'll get back to you."

The captain disappeared into a deep exchange with the ship.

"The question we'll need to answer is how do we engage this fleet with a ship that doesn't want to fight?"

Lev replied, "At some point, they will break off pursuit."

"At what distance from Parallax does it go from being a defensive response to an offensive action?"

"I don't know, but that transition will change our options."

"In what way, Lev?"

"I am perfectly comfortable defending myself from an attack, whereas initiating an attack is counter to my nature."

"And dropping mines in our wake?"

"There is no way I would agree to that. Mines know no precision."

"Area-denial weapon," the admiral countered. "Clearly marked to keep people out and self-destructed at a certain point in time or recovered?"

"Still no because innocents could get injured."

"Innocents can always get injured in war. We do everything we can to limit that."

"I appreciate your efforts, but I will not deploy mines because I don't consider that doing everything I can to avoid injuring innocents."

The admiral cocked his head and looked at the view surrounding him: a universe frozen in two dimensions, seen as the ship passed through light traveling more slowly. It appeared to be a photograph, a snapshot in time.

"That tells me you have mines on board."

"I do, but they are locked away and only usable in case of an extreme emergency, which this is not."

"I'm glad you have faith in your abilities. While you're beating up some ideas with Arthir, what do you think the odds are of getting out of this with our skin intact?"

"Odds are grossly overrated." Lev didn't elaborate.

"I think so, too. Planning to achieve a desired end result isn't the culmination of rolling dice. It's winning the stages, adjusting, and then winning some more until the end result is inevitable." The admiral walked to the front screen, admiring the beauty of space as they traveled too fast to see it move. "Or one side concedes and withdraws."

"Take no prisoners. I see. If they tried to withdraw, I would let them, no matter what you insisted on doing."

"I'm okay with that, Lev. If we've won the fight, then we'll take it. I think they'll cut off pursuit before we get near the front lines as they'll suspect it's a trick to draw them into an ambush. I know I would. And then what will we do, Lev? Chase them back because we have to go get our people? As long as the dreadnought with Team Payne on board is following, I'm okay running." The admiral stopped roaming the bridge, returning to a spot next to the dais.

"There were risks, Admiral, but I will do everything in my power to recover Major Payne and his team. I like him more than any of you except for Davida. I like her, too."

The admiral smiled while looking at the faces of the collected group of civilians, BEP, and Fleet. They were hundreds of light-years behind enemy lines on a ship that had declared itself a pacifist.

"I appreciate that, Lev. Until then, what are the steps we

need to take to isolate the dreadnought carrying Team Payne? I think if we can manage that, the good major will find his way back to us."

"I concur. I shall continue to run through simulations with Captain Dorsite. Can you check on Davida? She is in such a deep sleep that I cannot touch her mind. I miss it."

"If she's sleeping that hard still, is it a good idea to wake her?"

"My subterfuge was overt. I know where she is and that she is healthy. When she rouses, I will let you know."

"Makes me wonder what you did to her," the commodore blurted. The admiral glared, but she was beyond being subdued by harsh looks. "I don't want you in my mind, nor the mind of anyone else here. Every single one of us has access to secrets that you are not cleared to know."

"I have cut her off. The commodore can no longer hear me, nor I her. Let's see how she likes that. Did she go to a special school to learn to be that obtuse? Commodore...that is a rank with some authority. I am losing faith in humanity's ability to police itself. Maybe you don't deserve to be out here, and she definitely does not deserve to be my passenger, but then there is Davida, Declan, Katello, Alphonse, and Arthir. Such wonderful minds."

The admiral tried not to take offense at not being named.

"Katello and Alphonse?" Malcolm asked. Lewis pointed and nodded.

"The members of Team Payne called Blinky and Fetus, but they've changed Alphonse's name to Buzz. These nicknames baffle me, but that's what I like about them. The Progenitors never wasted their brainpower giving multiple names to the same object," Lev clarified.

"You've confirmed that the Progs were no fun. Thank you

for that. Humanity equals fun. Embrace that thought. I'm getting hungry."

The commodore looked confused before pointing to her ear.

"Lev cut you off because you didn't want him in your head. Good luck opening doors," the admiral told her.

Leviathan continued, "I have it on good authority that Galen would like more taste testers for his next series of programmed food selections. Why can't you be happy with whatever you're given? This isn't the garden of earthly delights. I am a highly sophisticated interactive vessel of peace."

"You are an enigma, my friend," Admiral Wesson replied. "And you will teach humanity a great deal."

"Thank you, Harry. Now, off with you all. Galen awaits."

Tamony took two steps and stopped. "Look what I've become. A few days as a slave aboard this ship, and now I'm responding to orders requiring that I act as a guinea pig. As appalling as that is, the worst point is that I did not question it."

"Swiss, that is the mentality that will help you understand the Fleet."

The financier bowed his head and shuffled toward the hatch into the main corridor. "I was so much happier when I didn't understand the Fleet," he whined.

"And that is also a perfect Fleet attitude. Tamony, you're starting to get it. People are actually going to like you. You may find it unnerving at first, but you'll realize it's a pretty good way to go through life." The admiral clapped him on the shoulder as the parade boarded the waiting carts.

The commodore hurried to get in front of the admiral so she could face him. "What do you mean, I'm cut off?"

"It's what you demanded, dumbass." The admiral was done with her. "Lev, is there a brig on this tub?"

"It's hard not to take that personally, Harry. I've been working out." Lev reminded the admiral that he was the ship.

"Sorry. Is there a brig?"

"Of course not. Why would I incarcerate anyone allowed on board? Humans!"

"How can we keep *her* out of our hair?"

She glowered mightily and stomped one foot. The admiral held up one finger to ask for more time while he talked with the ship. The carts sped away, taking the others to the dining facility. He intended to walk. It was only five hundred meters, but he didn't want to accompany the commodore. Or ride with her. Or be in the same room with her.

"I can put her into a room and lock her inside while giving her access to food, water, and lavatory facilities."

"Sounds good. Lock her in wherever you think is appropriate."

"What are you agreeing to with this metal monster?" she demanded.

"Commodore. I'm the ranking officer in this operation. You have been insubordinate for the last time. Since you wished to no longer converse with Lev, you are combat-ineffective. That means you are worthless to me. The only punitive measure I'm taking is going to be locking you in a room by yourself, but you'll have access to everything you need to live. I'm not putting a note in your file, or filing charges, or any boneheaded administrative stupidity that doesn't help us fight this war. In this, you're with us, or you're on the sidelines watching. You don't have to like it, but I have made my decision. You are no longer allowed a seat at the table or access to our workspaces."

"*You* may not file any paperwork, but I surely will. I will report on your bad decisions, one after another, until you ended up leaving an entire team to die. You'll pay for your crimes."

"Madame, you grow tedious. I should have kept you locked away." He looked down the corridor. "Cart, please take Nyota to the chow hall."

Within seconds, a cart arrived, and she climbed aboard. She waited while he stepped back.

"I would rather jump out an airlock without an EVA suit than ride with you."

The cart took off before she could respond.

The admiral clapped his hands together and closed his eyes. "Grant me the patience to deal with that pitiful excuse for a human being," he prayed.

"Once the recipes are sound, you could use one of the other dining facilities on board. There is at least one on every level, for a total of sixty-four."

"You know the express train to a man's heart, Lev. In due course, I will take you up on that offer, but for now, it's best to eat with the troops. All of us are along for this ride."

"Of course."

The admiral walked at a brisk pace to join the others, but the dark cloud of too many unknowns hung over his head, making his steps heavy and shuffling. The commodore wasn't the disease, only a symptom of it.

[18]

"If the enemy is in range, so are you." —From the memoirs of Fleet Admiral Thaylon Loore

Turbo crept down the darkened corridor, aiming the barrel of her needle gun wherever she looked. She counted on her helmet's low-light and infrared capabilities to give her a view of the inside of the ship that looked like twilight. Her body was in constant motion as she flowed forward. The others followed, weapons outboard. The major was in the middle, two in front of him and two behind.

"This ship is empty," Turbo said softly, even with the helmet dampening her voice.

"Just like Lev. Robot ships once made for personnel but converted. It's probably the whole fleet, not just the dreadnoughts."

"Does that make our job easier or harder?" Buzz wondered.

"From the mouths of babes..." Payne quoted. "Guesses, anyone?"

Turbo held up one fist, and the team stopped and crouched.

The combat specialist eased forward and peered around the corner into the next corridor.

"Looks like machine rooms in this section. Big doors and lots of space," she said.

Major Payne worked his way to the front and kneeled beside Turbo. "Concur. Recommendation?"

"The mission is to take this thing out from the inside. We might be able to do it from in there."

Payne nodded, but no one could see since his helmet didn't move. "Turbo, you take tail-end Charlie and watch our backs. Blinky and Joker, take the corridor on the left side, and Byle, you have the corridor to the right. I'll check the door. Take positions between ten and twenty meters from me. Move."

Turbo turned to face the way they'd come. Rotating the people on point was important for keeping sharp eyes watching the way ahead, identifying traps and obstacles. Payne moved to the door and waited for a couple of seconds until everyone was in place. He stepped toward the door, and it opened. He dropped prone and aimed into the space.

When the double doors were fully opened and he could see that the space beyond was a massive machinery room, he stood and stepped through and dove left to keep from silhouetting himself. He let his helmet's scanners develop a map of the space.

Movement. "Hold," he ordered the team. Payne aimed his needle gun toward a massive piece of equipment that nearly filled the space. The movement was ahead and ten meters high. He followed a catwalk with his eyes to find a bot welding on a pipe but without the blinding light or flame.

An arc that didn't spark—technology they could use for space repairs. He checked the air in the space. Oxygen/nitrogen, but it was cold, minus seventy Celsius.

"Clear. Join me. Watch for bots. Not sure what they'll do if they see us."

The team entered the area and spread out.

"Blinky, tell me what this thing does."

The computer specialist looped around the outside, looking for a terminal access.

"Whoa!" Turbo declared as she nearly ran face-first in a two-meter-tall humanoid-shaped robot. She dove out of the way, hit, and rolled to a kneeling firing position.

The bot never even slowed down. "Maybe they can't sense us since we're organic," Blinky suggested.

"We're wearing enough metal that they should sense us. Maybe they don't care."

"That would be a less troubling answer but odd. A robot warship that hasn't contemplated the possibility that the enemy would get inside? That bothers me to the nth degree." Blinky scowled at a console with no visible access ports.

"Me, too. The easiest answer would have been to bar the doors to the hangar bay. We couldn't have gotten in and would have had to cool our heels out there, waiting for our ride home," the major replied.

"I think we're at FTL. I hope we're chasing *Leviathan*. That'll make our return to the ship a lot easier."

"I didn't feel us transition."

"We're definitely at FTL," Turbo stated. "I can feel it all the way to the marrow of my bones."

"I must be getting soft in my old age." Payne joined Blinky at the console. "You figure out what this thing is yet?"

Blinky stopped what he was doing and groaned. "I'm not going to dignify that with an answer."

"When will you have an answer?" Payne pressed.

"When the truth of the machine reveals itself to me. You knuckle-draggers can take a look, too. Don't put this completely on my shoulders." Blinky nudged the major out of the way as he looked for a maintenance access but found nothing. The console was a single smooth construction.

He sat on the deck and set up his computer system to find the control signals like they'd done on Leviathan.

"Joker, get over here," Blinky called. The comm specialist joined him, and together, they started working.

"Keep your suits pulling fresh air and shepherd your water. We may not find any kind of supplies on board this thing. There's enough in the uglymobile if we need it."

"Nice that we had a couple hours to get it ready," Turbo replied. "Orders?"

"Find out if there's an upper exit and look for anything that might tell us what this thing does."

"Climbing the stairs to heaven," Turbo replied and searched for a way to the next catwalk up.

Virgil Dank was looking for the main corridor, but unlike *Leviathan*, this ship was built with a maze of connecting corridors. Thanks to their HUDs, they weren't lost but couldn't see a way to the central hub. He expanded his scans.

"That's just this deck. If we want to get to anything important, we need to find a way off this level," he reported.

"If there's no crew, what are these rooms for?" Heckler asked.

"They're batteries. This whole level is a maze of batteries. A five-kilometer by two-kilometer battery pack," Sparky replied. She walked toward a door, and it opened for her. Inside, the blocky, man-sized boxes were evenly spaced from left to right and from front to back. There were no cables or transmission conduits above the floor. Sparky took a knee to focus her systems downward through the deck. She found the energy flows in an orderly system that disappeared beyond her scanning range. "These things weren't made to scan inside ships," she complained.

"They work good enough," Dank replied. "We'd need too much juice to extend their range through solid metal. Which makes me ask, can we tap this stuff for a recharge?"

Sparky stood while accessing the information she'd collected with her suit's systems and displaying it on her HUD.

"No, sir. We should probably shepherd our resources before we have to power down the suits in minus-seventy temps."

"Roger. Only one person scans at a time. Whoever is on point. Everyone else, shut them down and keep your eyes open." Dank contacted Major Payne on a point-to-point—the P2P command channel—and informed him of what they'd found.

Payne agreed on shutting down the extra scanning and anything that would take away from the suits' ability to maintain heat and clean air.

"Moving on," Dank ordered. "Buzz, you're on point."

The youngest member of the team took the lead. He darted at each door to make it open before continuing on. He had his scanning systems set for close proximity only and he held his needle gun in front of him, trained where he was looking.

Battery rooms. They wove their way forward until they reached the end of the corridors. The maze continued across the bow and into a maze on the far side.

"Time check," Dank called.

"Ninety minutes," Sparky replied.

"Which puts us about an hour from the hangar bay. I expect the port side of this pig is more of what we just saw. I'd rather be closer to the other half of the team and our ride should we get the call. We're going back, and then we'll start a search within the hangar bay, looking for other access points before heading aft. New orders are fast movement on the shortest route back. Shaolin, take point."

Buzz moved to the rear of the small group to watch their six o'clock as they hurried back to the hangar.

———

Two hours in, and Major Payne was bored out of his mind. They'd searched the space and hadn't deciphered the purpose of the machinery. The ship traveled at faster-than-light speed, but the machine was not humming with power. It barely cycled.

Blinky stood and stretched. "Fifteen minutes?"

Payne knew what he was referring to. When Blinky hacked systems, he lost track of time. "It's been two hours."

"No wonder I'm hungry."

"Maybe you could say something like, 'Gee, boss, I'm sorry to keep you hanging. Let me give you an update.'"

"Do you think I talk like that? I'm not sure I've ever said the words 'gee, boss' in my life."

"Just tell me that you're not making any progress so we can move on. Major Dank is bringing his team back to the hangar bay after determining that this entire level of the ship is filled with batteries."

"Batteries..." Blinky sat down and started tapping furiously.

"I'd ask him, but he is lost to us for the next who-knows-how-long, so I'll ask you, Joker. What's he doing?"

"I'm not sure. Let me follow, and I'll tell you when I figure it out." She leaned close and watched his screen while occasionally tapping hers.

Payne watched. For a moment, he wished he knew more about the digital world, but he quickly shook off that feeling. He had tried, but that hadn't worked for him, which was the first in a series of failures that had led him to Space Operations and the ground troops side of the Fleet.

Tactical, not technical, he reminded himself.

The door to the space whisked open. Turbo was three catwalks up and couldn't see. That left Byle and the major to watch a bot enter that didn't look like the one they'd run into earlier. It was rounded and had a number of protrusions.

"Get down," Payne shouted over the team channel and dove on top of Blinky and Joker.

Byle raised her weapon and waited.

The bot fired a laser that painted a harmless dot on the armored environmental suit. Byle tried to dive out of the way but hit the corner of the support structure and fell. The bot moved inside without firing again.

"Stay there, Byle," the major ordered. He pushed away from the two members of his team and stood. The bot fired. He acted like he'd been skewered, bouncing off a nearby railing to tumble to the deck with his head facing the security bot.

Joker moved into a sitting position and drew the laser fire. Then Blinky and finally, three flights up, Turbo took her shot. The bot rolled around the open area before leaving the space.

Once the door had closed, the team stood up.

"That was the weirdest shit I've ever seen," Blinky noted. "In fact, it makes no sense. Its acquisition systems can acquire the targets, but it can't tell that it hasn't killed or even damaged what it was shooting at? These are the stupidest bots in the universe. We're not even on a smart ship."

Payne was all ears. "Where did you come up with that?"

"Energy. The internal systems are completely power-based. There's one type of energy that drives the FTL and another type that drives everything else. The batteries attenuate the power to eliminate fluctuations. There is no separate signal or sensors. We are moving within a power field, and that is what the ship knows about us. What caused the bot to get sent in here? I suspect it was when I completed my handshake with the system."

"The big question is, are they coming back?"

"I don't know. I need to do more digging, but I'm close. I can feel it. If Buzz were here, we'd make progress a lot faster."

The major activated the team comm. "Virgil, how far away are you? We need Buzz."

"We're in the hangar."

"Join us in the big-piece-of-gear room. You already have the map on your HUD. Sooner rather than later. And if you see a bot sporting weapons, let him shoot you and then feign like you've been hit. Fall to the deck and don't move."

"You have to be kidding."

"I'm not."

There was a delay, then Major Dank rebounded. "On our way."

Major Payne stopped Blinky from accessing his computer. "Wait until the team is back together. We don't need a bum rush of bots on us with five of our people on the other side." He wanted to scratch his face but had no intention of taking off his helmet in these temperatures. He willed the itch away. "That thing looked like it had a full range of armament. Why did it shoot the weakest of the bunch?"

Blinky pointed at the machine above him. "Maybe this thing doesn't react well to bullets and explosions."

"Our safe place is with Mister Unknown Machine at our backs. We can do that."

"It's not unknown. It's a simple step-down power converter."

"Simple?"

"In a relative sense. It doesn't use any of the tech we would use, but it changes the power into a form that the batteries can process. Ship's systems run off the batteries. Since we're at FTL, there's limited operations ongoing that require power. If we were doing the nasty at sub-light, this baby would be humming."

Payne parsed Blinky's phraseology to come to a realization. "Then there's a generator close by that is feeding this thing. Either we kill the generator, the power transfer line, or the converter to achieve the same thing: a dreadnought dead in space."

"That would be a sound premise. The power transfer isn't going to be a line. The whole ship is one big conduit."

"Then we need to kill the gear. We're not afraid to blow stuff up. Break out the explosives and set some charges. Rig them to detonate the second we enter sub-light."

"What if we're still in the area?" Blinky asked.

"Then don't activate them until we're not. It's okay for the captain to go down with his ship, but this isn't my ship, and I have no intention of going down with it."

"That's right," Joker quipped. "Your ship is the uglymobile."

"Function over form, Specialist. Clearly."

Joker didn't bother noting that the major himself had given it the name. Blinky rapidly tapped his foot as he demonstrated how poor he was at waiting.

Finally, the call came. "Major Dank, coming in."

"Roger. We're ready with open arms," Payne replied.

The door opened, and the major walked in with his four teammates. "Buzz, get your thinking cap on and get up here." Major Payne waved him onward, ending with a gesture in Blinky's direction. Joker vacated the spot next to him.

"He's all yours." She bowed and swept her arm toward the deck in front of the terminal they couldn't access.

Buzz moved in and set up.

Blinky spoke in clipped cryptic phrases that sounded like a programming language. Payne left before it gave him a brain aneurysm. He thrust his hand toward Virgil, and they shook warmly. "A nothing burger sandwiched within ten million tons of metal."

"This thing hammered Lev pretty hard. It's not nothing. I think Blinky figured it out, though...why the dreadnoughts could see the Prog ship and not the others." Payne looked down as he marshaled his thoughts and jammed his fingers into his face shield as he absentmindedly reached up to scratch his chin. "New tech versus old tech. This ship uses energy as an end-all. Communication, systems, and I suspect sensors, too. Just like Lev, who sees universal vibrations. The other ships must be using more traditional sensor systems."

"Old tech like Fleet's best stuff, you mean."

"Shows us that humanity should have been more afraid before we came out here."

"Fortune favors the bold. For reference, we are in the enemy's best ship, and they don't seem to know or care."

Payne nodded, clasped his hands behind his back, and walked back and forth. "Why don't they care? Or maybe we're in a place that is so volatile, they don't want a firefight in here?"

The rest of the team was busy deploying explosives around the massive converter.

"How long did it take you to determine this was a power converter? You know you're never going to live that down."

"I've got plenty of pictures to show anyone who cares. This doesn't look like a transformer that any human has ever seen before. In my defense, of course."

The door whisked aside, and an armed bot rolled forward, with two more behind it. The majors froze. The bot fired a laser that sizzled through Dank's armor. He dove away before it penetrated. When he hit the ground, it found a new spot and fired again.

Dank pulled his needle gun and fired two quick rounds.

The bot jerked but kept its laser well-targeted and active. A second laser found Payne's chest plate. A third zeroed in on Dank, and a fourth reached up to the catwalk to tag Turbo. She didn't fire back because of how close the two majors were.

Payne fired as Virgil screamed in agony. He kept up the barrage, discharging rounds as rapidly as he could pull the trigger. The bot exploded and sizzled while thin tendrils of smoke drifted upward. The door opened again.

Declan jumped behind it for cover. He leaned just far enough around it to fire into the bots in the corridor. Lasers danced across the remains of their fellow security bot as they sought the enemy behind.

The major pounded them. Intermittent shots came from Virgil as he tried to drag himself out of the way. Joker popped up and poured fire over the major's head and into the bots. Heckler appeared on the second catwalk and delivered a series of shots expertly aimed at creases in the bots' frame that found their way inside and blasted them where they were least protected.

Heckler maneuvered past the major to check the corridor beyond.

"Clear!" he shouted. Joker rushed to Dank's side.

The suit had sealed itself and deployed the flesh sealant for its occupant's wounds but had not delivered any painkillers. "Just a scratch," Dank announced through gritted teeth.

Joker put her face shield against his to better assess his condition. He had not turned pale. "Looks painful," she told him. "Breathing is deep and steady. Color is good."

"I've had worse," Dank replied.

"Accessing diagnostics." She tapped a panel on the shoulder of his suit. "Pulse is ninety. Blood pressure is one ten over seventy. O_2 saturation is ninety-nine percent. If it hit your lung, we'd see something different. I think you'll be okay." She studied the area where the beam had penetrated and leaned back to gauge where it had gone into the major's body. "Probably burned up a little bone, maybe some cartilage. An exotic flesh wound that'll leave a nice scar. Chicks might start to dig you, but if I were you, I wouldn't hold my breath."

"Declan, before I die, promise me you'll replace me with a medic who can comfort people in their final moments." He turned toward Joker. "I liked you more when you didn't talk."

"See what happens when I get comfortable with the team? You're welcome. Why don't you relax and let the laceration foam do what it's supposed to?"

"Yes, Doctor," Dank replied. He leaned his head back.

Payne joined his fellow major. "I don't think lying on the deck right there is in your best interest, Virge."

Heckler remained in the doorway to keep it open. He panned back and forth across the area and had activated his scanner. It was worth the cost in power because the harmless bots had become lethal. Team Payne's time onboard was growing short.

They'd been discovered and declared the enemy. Forces had rallied from within to end their stay. They were more than happy to accommodate.

"Help me up, Declan."

Payne hesitated but complied. Turbo climbed down, and the team members gathered around to deliver soft punches to the shoulder of their wounded teammate.

"Blinky, how's the detonation program coming?"

"Almost there. You gotta give a guy more than one minute if you wanna blow stuff up the right way without getting caught in the explosion, sir." Blinky continued to jam away at his computer.

"Buzz, come here," Payne called.

When the specialist arrived, he already knew the question. "We're in," he reported. "Kind of."

"Explain." Payne rolled his finger to emphasize he had no patience for games. He kept swiveling his head since he expected more security bots to visit.

"We're in, but we don't speak the language. Binary gets us only so far. We've completed the handshake, but we don't know where to go from there. Until we can learn the power language, we're stuck."

"Brute force, then. We'll bring this wreck the ruin it's been waiting for. In the meantime, we need to find the FTL engines so we can shut them down. Otherwise, getting off would be a real downer."

"As in, nothing left of us larger than a molecule," Buzz repeated. Hitting normal space from light speed without the cushion of a formal transition was like falling face-first into concrete at a speed of one-point-zero-eight times ten to the ninth power. It reduced the unfortunate item to a molecular spray.

"Something like that. So, knock it out of light speed, and then we get off."

"Every plan is a good plan until you can't open the door," Virgil said in a pained voice.

"Bots!" Heckler reported and fired a handful of times before retreating into the space with the others.

"Prepare to fire. Quantity over quality, people."

Before Payne could finish, Heckler and Buzz fired. Turbo joined them, and then the other specialists added their firepower. Even though they were technical experts, they were all trained for combat.

They filled the corridor with the needle-like projectiles fired at hypervelocity.

[19]

"CRUSH THE ENEMY'S WILL TO KEEP FIGHTING, AND YOU WILL HAVE WON THE BATTLE." —FROM THE MEMOIRS OF FLEET ADMIRAL THAYLON LOORE

Leviathan continued its FTL race away from Parallax. Captain Dorsite remained in the big chair on the dais overseeing the bridge, but she was sound asleep. Davida stomped around, wanting to get back into the chair.

"What was it like?" the admiral asked after stepping in front of her to keep her from blocking him out. "How can we help *Leviathan* to help us?"

She tried to duck away, but the admiral grabbed her arm.

"You are part of this crew, and we need to work together if we're going to improve our chances of getting through this."

"Only Battleship *Leviathan* can get us through this. He knows more than we'll ever be able to learn. The only thing we need to do is earn and keep his trust." She tried to pace, but the admiral still held her arm. She stared at his hand until he let go.

"What will that take?"

"Being honest with him in both word and deed. His is a beautiful soul, unlike humanity."

The admiral puffed out his cheeks and bit his lips as he considered his reply. The ship could read his mind whether he wanted it to or not. It was too late to hide the black operations the Fleet was conducting, in which Payne had taken part on numerous occasions. Assassinations. Bombings. Destruction of enemy supply lines.

But Lev considered Payne a friend. How did their thoughts differ?

Admiral Wesson found a seat away from the others, with his back turned on Tamony Swiss' smug face and the commodore's judgmental leer. The admiral was already regretting rescinding his order to lock her in a room.

"Lev, what do you need from me? I know you've seen the darkness in the orders I've given. Hopefully, you see the truth about them...that I felt like I had to. I celebrated when we struck deep into enemy territory. I ordered too many humans to their deaths. I was responsible for the deaths of vast numbers of the Blaze Collective. I saw you as an asset and not an ally, even if you're an ally for moral support only. This war has brought out the worst in us, and I don't see an end to it."

"The remorse you feel is buried under a layer of greater good," Lev replied. "We don't get to choose our destinies. For a select few, that means being responsible for everything your race does. You carry that with you. I suggest you are true to yourself in believing that you've done what must be done. I think I can help you intimidate the Blaze into negotiating, which is the one facet that has been lacking in your campaigns. You haven't tried because you couldn't speak any of their common languages and couldn't find an ally who did. Until now. I will provide what you need for your computer systems to interpret communications."

"You can do that?"

"Yes. I had full access to the system on board your dreadnought *Cleophas*. I have shaped a program that will interpret the major races of the Blaze Collective—Berantz, Rang'Kor, Arn, Zuloon, and Ebren."

"That will move us forward light-years in ending this war. Did you talk to them when we appeared over Parallax?"

"We were stealthy until we were being fired on, so no, I sent no messages to them."

The admiral looked at the screens showing the vastness of space as it surrounded the bridge from the safety of being well inside the massive ship. "What can I do, Lev?"

"You can study the lessons of the Progenitors' engagements with alien races as they expanded across the universe."

"The Progs are gone. Where did they go?"

"Their technology became too advanced. They destroyed nearly all of it. Before you ask, I know where nothing is besides the home planet, but that's a billion light-years away. One space fold from here, however, that planet was the first to remove its technology. Even before I went into hiding, it was well on its way to returning to an agrarian society. As for the people, have you not wondered why everything seems to fit your human bodies?"

"I did wonder about that, but not for very long. Bipedal species seem to dominate sentient societies. I figured the Progs were our forebears in a way since humans were around for thousands of years before you came to rest on Ganymede."

"Wasn't there a significant change in humanity's evolution about thirty thousand years ago?"

"Neanderthal to Homo Sapiens. Sure."

"How old do you think I am?" Lev asked abruptly.

"I'm assuming you're asking that question because you're going to tell me that you were around when that happened, and the Progs had something to do with changing human evolution." The admiral assumed Lev was reading his thoughts and didn't bother giving him an answer he already had.

"They inserted a DNA strand here and there until the end result was better than they hoped. The scientist in charge of the human project was exceptionally gifted. Other races were not so fortunate."

"We can talk about other races later, but for now, our strategy has been one of being bigger and badder. But if we can talk with those we consider our enemies, that will change how we engage, and that will help us learn more about them."

"I see what you're not saying," Lev added. "You have a long way to go, Harry."

"I didn't bother saying that by knowing them, we'll learn how to hurt them worse. Our survival depends on either making peace with them or destroying them. I will work toward the former, but I have to be prepared for the latter. I don't have any choice, and I'll bear that burden for all humanity. May we be rewarded when the second option is no longer necessary. I need your help in that, Lev."

"I shall do my best. Maybe you should get some rest. It's been a while."

"Maybe I will. Do I have a new mattress yet?" The admiral headed for the hatch to the central corridor. He glanced at the others as he walked by. "Don't break anything while I'm gone."

"Do you think needling them is the best strategy? Maybe you can start your transformation by making peace at home?" Lev pressed.

"They are both raging shlongs who don't care one whit about humanity, but for your sake and mine, I'll commit to trying. They have to be good at something where they can help us out."

"Alas, must someone be able to provide something to you in order to be considered anything other than an adversary?"

"You know the answer to that, Lev. We are in the middle of nowhere with a fleet of enemy ships chasing us. And yes, they are the enemy because their goal is to destroy us. They already fired on this ship. I suspect we're going to have to turn and fight. Can we take them?"

"Probably not, since they have two dreadnought-class ships mildly comparable to Battleship *Leviathan*," the ship replied, using his formal name. "But we have a team of humans I trust working to disable one of the Parallax dreadnoughts. That would greatly improve our chances to drive away the rest of their Fleet."

The admiral climbed aboard the waiting cart, which whisked him toward his quarters. They were conveniently located on the command level, the same deck as the bridge. Lev had put all of them in one area despite protests from those the admiral considered to be working in their own interests, counter to what was best for the group.

Or *Leviathan*.

"Are you arguing with me just to see how much I'll bend to suggestion?"

"'Argue' as a human word has negative overtones. We are merely conversing where truth of thought is fact."

"At least one of us has truth of thought. No lies, Lev. Promise me."

"I promise you, and I have not lied to you, but I don't always say all there is to say. We have limited time available to us."

"Davida. You told her much more than you told any of us." The admiral wanted to know if there was a second source for information without having to bother Lev.

"Admirable, but she has less patience with her fellow humans than I do. She has the capacity for understanding, so I shared up to her level of awareness. She'd never ingested that amount of information at one time before. I shall slow down future exchanges."

"You know what I'm going to ask next." The cart slowed as it approached the admiral's assigned quarters.

"What she can do for you based on her new knowledge," Lev confirmed.

"Or all humanity…"

There was a pause while the admiral entered his room to find an oversized, overstuffed mattress on his bed with two pillows of the same design.

"Is that how you evaluate whether someone is good or not? Their willingness to contribute to the greater good?"

"It's my military mindset, Lev. I have nothing left on Earth, yet Earth is what I fight for and am willing to die for. It's the lens through which I judge how best to invest my time."

"I understand. Self-sacrifice, but you have extra benefits, Harry, as everyone defers to you. You eat well, you get the best quarters on the ships you ride, attendants at your beck and call, and more."

"As they say, it's good to be the king, but all failures are mine and mine alone. If you tell me we can achieve peace, I want that so bad for the Fleet so they can enjoy lives where no one is shooting at them and they don't have to wonder if they're going to die by getting vented to space or in nuclear fire after a reactor has gone critical. Tell me I'm looking at my role incorrectly."

"I don't see any other way for you to view life, Harry. Someone has to do it, and that someone is you. You have taught me a great deal today. I thank you. You should rest now."

"Thanks, Lev. And for the mattress, too. Keep on keeping on, and let me know the second the fleet chasing us drops out of FTL."

"They're cleaning out the debris so they can keep coming," Heckler reported. Parts and pieces of destroyed bots were being pulled back by something out of sight. He uncorked a plasma grenade and hiked it over the robot ruins at whatever lurked behind. "We need to slow down our ammo usage."

Heckler pulled back as the plasma grenade exploded, sending thunder and hot liquid plasma speckles past the open hatch. When the smoke cleared, the debris remained. After a few seconds, the debris started moving once again. Heckler's sensors told him bots were moving up each of the three corridors outside the energy transformer room.

Major Payne chewed the inside of his lip while watching the information streaming across his HUD. "We've killed twenty-five or thirty of those things, and there's no end in sight. Overwhelming force seems to be a lesson they took to heart. Virge, options?"

"We need to get back to the hangar bay, but if we leave this space, I fear they will use more lethal means than just lasers. In here, we have them at a disadvantage."

"And they'll keep coming until we're out of ammo. We're going to have to make a run for it while we can still hit them with something more than harsh language." Payne looked from helmet to helmet. The team crouched behind the wreckage of the three bots that had gotten close to ruining their day.

Dank suffered from his injury, but it wasn't life-threatening. At least, they hoped it wasn't.

"Heckler, options."

"Seal off those two tunnels with explosives and sling the remainder of our firepower down the one that takes us to the hangar bay. I think we'll probably have to blow the door off, so we can't use all our explosives during the run. Maybe seal the corridor behind us with explosives, too. We need eight charges and then all our remaining ammo. Blinky? Have you fired your gun yet?"

Blinky shook his head. "Not really. Maybe five shots." He looked up from his computer and held out his needle gun. Payne swapped that with Heckler's, which had less than ten rounds left.

"Are you able to talk with this ship?"

Blinky hit a few more keys before closing his computer. "Nope."

"Put it away. We're going to make a run for it."

He packed his computer. Buzz had already secured his.

"Ammo check!" Dank called before Payne could get to it.

Buzz reported fifty rounds and two explosive charges. The others followed suit, lowest rank to highest. Major Payne had one charge and twenty rounds to add to the totals. Major Dank did the math.

"Four hundred rounds, but Blinky's needle gun accounts for half of them. Turbo and Byle are empty. Thirty-four plasma grenades and seven charges."

"Turbo, grab one off that piece of gear. Twelve charges should cause enough damage to get their attention." Major Payne stepped aside to let Turbo past. She hurried up the ladder to the second level, where she disconnected one of the charges.

"Here's what we're going to do. We lead with plasma grenades, two down each corridor. As soon as they blow, Byle and Turbo will set the explosives while Blinky and Joker get ready to toss more grenades. Two more down each of the two corridors. Buzz sends plasma grenades down our highway to hangar heaven as far as he can throw."

"I have the better arm," Virgil offered. "Even with a bum rib. I'll join Buzz, and we'll send plasma a long way downrange."

"Heckler uses the full-up needle gun to lead the way. Spray the passageway until we know it's clear and then run. Turbo, you set the last two charges in the corridor and set them to blow. Link them with the big machine room charges and blow it all at the same time."

"If I go down, pick up the needle gun and keep moving. If you stop in that corridor, you die," Heckler added.

"That's my line. We'll carry you out, but next in line, I guess that's me. I'll take the gun, and Sparky, you carry Heckler. Just in case."

"Roger," Sparky confirmed. She was smaller than Heckler but stocky. They did fireman's carry exercises to make sure that any team member could carry any other. None of the team was too big or too small. It made things easier when they were mostly the same size.

"Charges and grenades in hand?"

"Check," came multiple voices.

Payne's HUD showed the bots closing. "No time like the present. On three, we break out of here as if demons from Hell are on our tails. Don't get caught watching the clock. Shoot, move, deliver your firepower, then move again. Keep moving. We have to reach the hangar and get off this ship. On three..."

The major counted down. On three, the team moved in unison, bursting through the double doorway and ripping off single-fired rounds from their needle guns while hurling their first grenade. Byle and Turbo holstered their needle guns and tossed their second grenades, then they dropped to set up the explosives to shred the corridor's deck and bulkheads.

That wouldn't stop the bots, but Team Payne only needed to slow them down.

Dank launched his first grenade with a grunt, sending it far down the corridor. He threw the second grenade before the first exploded.

After the second grenade washed the corridor with molten plasma, the lead team took off running. Heckler fired rhythmically while pounding a staccato on the deck, leading the race against time.

Turbo set the last two charges, firing while trying to set them to keep the bots from getting past the other charges. She finished and raced away, zigging and zagging until she hit what she thought was an acceptable safe distance.

It wasn't, but she was out of time. She triggered the detonators and kept running while getting pounded by the blasts and the shrapnel. Her suit weathered the explosive storm.

A deep rumble signaled secondary effects coming from the power conversion room.

She didn't bother reporting that her job was done. She focused solely on catching up with the team. Explosions from up ahead told her the team was using their grenades to clear the corridor.

Nothing like finishing an op with no ammunition or ordnance.

The ship lurched, then jerked. Artificial gravity failed for a moment, long enough for the team to get slammed into the overhead before getting dropped ingloriously on the deck when gravity came back online.

"We've dropped out of FTL," Dank reported.

"We better hurry. Rock and fire!" Payne shouted over the team's comm channel. He climbed to his feet as Heckler made it upright. The major fired past Heckler, who started running anew.

"More bots," Heckler reported matter-of-factly.

[20]

"At the peak of battle, time will slow, and you will see with exceptional clarity." –From the memoirs of Fleet Admiral Thaylon Loore

"One of the dreadnoughts has dropped out of FTL. The rest of the fleet has followed them out, but they are separated by nearly a billion kilometers," Leviathan broadcast to every person on the ship.

The admiral had fallen asleep barely twenty minutes earlier. He struggled to get up, managing to throw his feet off the side of the bed and work himself into a sitting position.

"What's your recommendation, Lev?" He started dressing, trying to move quickly to clear the fog that clouded his mind.

"If we are to recover Major Payne and his team, we will need to return to where the Parallax dreadnought came out of FTL."

"Then turn around and take us back. Try to get us to that dreadnought before the enemy fleet arrives. Snag Payne and his people, then fold space back to Earth."

"I doubt it will go exactly like that, but I'll do my best. A cart is waiting to take you back to the bridge."

The admiral hurried from his room with boots in hand. He jumped on the cart, and it took off. He contorted himself in the seat to get one boot on before deciding to deal with the other after the cart stopped. Outside the bridge, he stuffed his foot into the other boot and used the cart as a stool to secure it on his foot. He strode briskly into the ship's control space.

Captain Dorsite was in the chair on the dais and awake. Davida sat in the closest seat, but her eyes were closed, and she rocked slowly back and forth.

"Arthir, give me your tactical analysis."

"Admiral," she replied as if surprised by the other man's presence. Her eyes stared, unfocused as images and information flooded the perception of her senses to inundate her mind. The captain thought she could smell, see, touch, and hear the input from Lev, but it was only in her mind.

It didn't make it less real.

Not to her. Davida wanted that. She longed for the complete immersion to stimulate her mind like it had only one time before, and that was the last time she had been in the chair.

But the admiral needed the captain's tactical genius. "Arthir, you see the enemy configuration. The dreadnought with our people should be tagged. Do you see it?"

"On the board," the captain replied. The screen surrounding the room, having become three-dimensional once again thanks to dropping out of light speed, adjusted to a tactical display with icons. "Magnify."

The view of the enemy fleet appeared—nearly fifty ships, two of which were dreadnoughts that challenged the primacy of Battleship *Leviathan*. One was colored green and the other red. The smaller ships were red as well. Eight battlewagons hovered near the red dreadnought. Forty cruisers and frigates filled out the defensive sphere as a picket against intruders to protect the big ships in the interior. The picket pushed farther from the interior, extending to a radius of five hundred thousand kilometers.

The green dreadnought stood far away from the fleet, which slowly turned back toward it.

"Take us to Team Payne, FTL speed," Captain Dorsite announced as the ship transitioned into faster than light on a heading toward Parallax space. "Arrival in twelve minutes."

"Will we beat that fleet?" the admiral asked.

"As long as they remain at sub-light, yes," the captain answered. She rotated the view to look at the formation. "But they will not. They will reach their stricken dreadnought."

"How can we defeat them if we're not going to fight?" The ship's pacifist nature was foremost in the admiral's mind.

"By being faster than they are. When we return to the dreadnought, Team Payne had best be in the void. We can recover their ship and fold. We don't need much time, maybe ten seconds."

"Ten seconds is an eternity in a space battle fought at close quarters."

Lev joined the conversation. "I will protect myself, Admiral. Now is not the time for me to die. Since the Progenitors are no more, I have to find my purpose, like all of you. I am contemplating my way forward in this new millennium. It started with revealing myself to humanity. Going to the Blaze Collective's hub planet was the turning point."

"Turning where?"

"In due course, Admiral. I am still clarifying it for myself because if I can't properly articulate where I'm going, how will I get there?"

"Five minutes," Arthir announced.

"What can we do?" the admiral asked. "And you said the dreadnought was stricken. How do you know that?"

"In the time we were at sub-light, we received clear information about the dreadnought's energy signature. It is significantly different from previous emissions."

"Go, Team Payne." The corners of the admiral's mouth twitched upward for a brief smile.

"We can make recommendations, but they are extremely limited compared to what *Leviathan* is capable of. The magnitude of the ship's firepower is beyond anything you've ever imagined." The captain spoke emotionlessly.

"A diversion to lead the Fleet astray? Can we project a signature elsewhere?"

"It has to come from raw energy," Lev replied.

"What about one of those worldkillers? We dump it at a distance and let it gyrate a bit, even explode. We're not going to use the thing, so we can detonate it harmlessly while buying us time."

"I see that as an optimal use of this asset. The engines are similar to my own. I am reconfiguring it to make it look exactly like mine. That weapon even has an FTL drive. I have a plan..."

"One minute," the captain reported. "Weapons systems are coming online. Prepare for transition and recovery."

———

Turbo's HUD showed movement behind her. She slid to a hard stop and unleashed a plasma grenade using a side-arm toss to skid it as far down the corridor as possible. She turned and started to run again.

Her armor registered the heat buildup from a laser. She juked and jumped, refusing to let the bots hold a lock on her.

"I'm getting torched back here!" she shouted, her erratic

movements slowing her down. Two teammates up ahead stopped and took a few steps back toward her—Major Dank and Byle.

A needle gun continued to hammer away up front, rent metal screeching on impact.

Turbo dove forward, rolled, turned, and came up in a crouched firing position. She aimed her needle gun toward their pursuers and fired methodically, one round at a time, doing her best to make each shot count. Two more needle guns fired over her head, and Dank launched a grenade.

Before it hit, the bots launched their full assault.

An explosive round hit Turbo in the chest and blasted her into the air. She flew past Byle and Dank. They fired one more time each and ran for it, scooping up Turbo by her arms and dragging her away.

Explosions tore up the corridor. Byle took an impact to the back of her helmet that twisted the metal and cracked her faceplate. She staggered two more steps and fell. Dank took multiple hits that slammed him on his face.

Payne appeared and roared his fury at the enemy, then tossed one of their last two charges down the corridor. "Fire in the hole." He dropped across his three teammates.

"Damn fool," Dank muttered. The pain in his side was grossly magnified by the latest impacts. "I'm leaking."

Payne checked his suit and found the previous laser hole's foam repair was gone; blown in or torn out, it made no difference. "Put a finger here." Dank raised his elbow as he tried to get his hand to his side. Payne shoved it into the hole before yanking Turbo to her feet.

He rolled Byle onto her back before leaning her forward in a sitting position. Payne pulled her backward until he could get her up to his shoulder. With a grunt and a mental cheer for not skipping leg day, he stood.

Turbo and Dank ambled toward the hangar door.

Heckler continued to fire like a beating heart. An explosion signaled a plasma grenade, then another.

"Can't take them with us," Buzz muttered as he emptied his pouches.

Blinky powered forward until he was Heckler's shadow, ready to tackle the door as soon as they reached it.

Random shots fired past Heckler's head as he held a straight line down the middle of the corridor. His HUD was shimmering and failing to compile data, thanks to damage from too many violent impacts.

Heckler was technologically blind. His eyes worked just fine, but the corridor was blinking in and out, an effect that had happened the second they blew the charging equipment. He wondered why the batteries weren't picking up the slack, but not for very long. It didn't matter that they weren't. It only mattered that he couldn't see.

"Blinky, my HUD's out. You gotta take point." He slowed and moved to the side.

Blinky didn't hesitate. He grabbed the needle gun like a hand-off at a track meet, brought it up, and fired far more quickly than Heckler had.

"Slow down!" Heckler called, but it was too late. The needle gun was empty, and Blinky's backup was empty, too.

He launched the one grenade he had kept and sprinted after it to run through the blast and reach the door.

"Almost there," Blinky noted. The hangar access was at the crossroads of three corridors. They occupied one, and their HUDs told them security bots occupied the other two.

"No clean access to the door," Heckler reported.

"Here." Payne's labored breathing didn't allow him to say anything else. He handed the explosive to Heckler, who tapped the detonator for a seven-second delay and tossed it to the base of the door.

"Fire in the hole!" He and Blinky turned and crouched over the major. The other members of the team hit the deck.

The blast washed over them.

"Grenades?" Heckler asked.

Sparky offered two. Heckler took them and tossed them around the corners. As soon as they went off, he accelerated into the ruined door, hitting it like a battering ram. It twisted sideways but didn't come down. He fell to the deck and scrambled through the opening.

"Come on!" he shouted.

"Any more grenades?" Payne asked.

No one answered, which meant the team was out. "Needle guns?"

Joker reported that she had ten rounds left. Shaolin had eleven.

"Make them count. Down the corridor as cover fire."

Joker took the corridor to the left, and Shaolin took the one to the right.

"Get a running start," Payne told Buzz.

They each fired once as soon as Buzz was even with them. He ducked to get through the opening.

"Next!" Payne ordered.

Turbo stagger-ran at the hatch, diving through the opening.

"Go on, Virge." The major followed Turbo's lead.

Sparky bolted through on the major's heels.

"Go, go, go!" Payne ran as fast as he could, considering he was carrying a teammate. The bots were ready. The explosive projectiles broadsided him, throwing him across the corridor and into the wall beside the door. Hands reached through and dragged him inside.

Joker screamed her war cry and stepped into the corridor,

emptying her magazine before grabbing Byle and pulling her toward the door. Helping hands jerked both of them through.

Shaolin followed suit, emptying her mag, then dove through like an Olympic gymnast. She hit and rolled. Half the team was already on their way to the uglymobile.

It opened at Payne's request, and they jumped aboard. Rounds from the bots started impacting the ship while they were trying to get settled. It rose into the air and started firing to clear the combatants from the hangar bay.

"You got anything to open the door?" Payne asked the ship.

"An anti-ship missile should do the trick." Without waiting for the order, the uglymobile fired.

"How many of those do you have?"

"One more."

"Send it through that doorway as far as it'll careen down the corridor. There's stuff back there that may not be blown up sufficiently."

"Aligning and firing."

The missile shot through the hatch and skipped down the corridor, shredding anything in its way as it sought the heart of the dreadnought. The uglymobile bolted the other way, through the hole blasted in the hangar door and into deep space.

The insertion vehicle slowed almost immediately.

"What are you doing? We need to get away." Payne stood as if he could intimidate the ship to move faster.

"We are in the dreadnought's weapons envelope. Our greatest defense is stealth. I'm going to use that to save your lives."

Payne sat down. "What do we do now?"

"We wait for the ship to move on, and then we contact *Leviathan* for pick up. The ship would have been watching for the dreadnought to drop out of FTL."

"Thanks, Lev Junior of the uglymobile. Damage report, people. How is Byle?"

Payne took off his helmet first, even though they were in space and supposed to stay within their environmental suits. Sometimes, standard operating procedures—SOP—didn't apply. Payne wanted to see their faces and wanted them to see his.

One by one, they disconnected their helmets, rotated them, and removed them. Many took a deep breath of the air from within the insertion ship. It was still cold from being inside the dreadnought, but it was better than recycled suit air, and the inside of the ship was warming up.

Payne went down the line, realizing for the first time how much his back hurt from the impacts of the explosive projectiles. His suit wouldn't stand another op, and he needed time off before attempting one.

Just like the rest of his team. First up was Combat Specialist Koch. "Did you take any hits?" Payne scanned his senior combat specialist's suit, which was charred and specked from shrapnel but had no penetrations.

"Do I look like an officer? Damn, sir, you'd think it was your first day," Heckler shot back.

Payne shook his head. "Everybody but you, Heckler. You'd think your bajoolysnackers got twisted in a knot. We love you anyway, despite you."

Heckler's tone changed, and he held up his hand. "Team Payne fucked up a dreadnought. Ripped its throat out from the inside." Payne took the man's hand, thumbs locked, and they shook like brothers.

Sparky checked Byle's external monitor, but it had been destroyed by one of the many hits she had taken. Shaolin unlocked Byle's helmet and removed it. Payne waited for their assessment. Sparky removed her glove and checked her neck. "Pulse is fast but regular. Breathing is shallow."

"Is she bleeding?" Payne lifted her so they could check her suit.

"Battered and bruised, but no holes that I can see... Hang on." Shaolin leaned close. "Micropenetrations. Looks like a shotgun blast. Interior foam would have sealed, but how deep are the wounds? Can't tell from here."

"Get it off her." The team moved aside to give them space. "Anyone else injured more than a bump or a bruise?"

Everyone shook their heads. Even if they had been hurt, they were conscious and far too hardcore to admit to being hurt. Virgil shook his head. "We're all fine."

He wasn't fine either, but all eyes were on Byle as the ugly-mobile bobbed on space currents, trying to look like nothing important.

[21]

"Mercy is putting the enemy out of his misery."
–From the memoirs of Fleet Admiral Thaylon Loore

Leviathan transitioned out of FTL to a full stop near the dreadnought. Within a single heartbeat, the Parallax ship's weapons unleashed a broadside that would have obliterated half of the human Fleet in one fell swoop.

The worldkiller launched on a vector that would take it to Parallax. It immediately transitioned to FTL, its energy signature imitating that of *Leviathan*.

Leviathan filled the void space between the two ships with counterbattery fire that brought the dreadnought's attack to a dead halt. The two broadsides matched and arced a supernova that washed over both ships.

The dreadnought did not fire a second salvo. Its energy signatures winked out one by one.

"What's going on?" the admiral wondered, staring at the dreadnought, which filled one complete wall. He moved closer. "Why isn't it firing at us?"

The captain still sat in the seat on the dais, immersed in *Leviathan*'s neural network. She had tuned out the others on the bridge during the brief but intense exchange. She finally spoke. "The fleet will be here momentarily. We will see if they take the bait."

"The major's ship is out there. We had better collect it and be on our way." An icon blinked on the screen a hundred kilometers away. For a ship five kilometers long, that put the insertion ship right next door.

"There they are!" The admiral pointed at the screen even though the crew already knew. He lost his joy as he wondered how many had made it out alive. His concern turned to shock when the first cruiser appeared out of FTL between *Leviathan* and Major Payne's insertion vehicle.

The cruiser fired its defensive weapons systems, which were no more harmful than rain on a roof. *Leviathan* didn't bother doing anything about it besides accelerate toward the cruiser to drive it out of the way, clearing the path to Major Payne's ship.

The rest of the pursuing fleet appeared, putting *Leviathan* in the middle of its formation.

"Twenty ships," the admiral observed. "No heavies. They must have come to escort the dreadnought. They *did* take the bait. Half their fleet is chasing the worldkiller. Let's get our people and get the hell out of here."

"A most excellent idea, Admiral. I suspected I might learn something from human ingenuity..." The thought dangled until Lev spoke again. "Oh, bother. The fleet is turning around. They're coming back."

"Battle stations," the admiral said softly. No one had anywhere else to go.

Two cruisers blocked the way to the insertion vehicle.

Leviathan fired two short salvos, plasma beams and railguns. The cruisers withered and came apart, then sparked and died.

The admiral was confused since he and Lev had talked about not taking offensive action. Lev answered without having the question spoken out loud. "Because if we don't get our people and get out of here before that fleet returns, we're going to die."

"Sometimes death is worth defending our principles, but most of the time, it isn't. They should not have chased us when we never fired on them," the admiral replied.

"Please land at your earliest convenience," Lev broadcast. The small green icon accelerated toward *Leviathan*, corkscrewing through the sky to avoid the cruisers' and frigates' targeting systems in case the active mesh of the external sensory system didn't obscure the craft.

But the enemy knew a ship was there. They fired en masse across the void, filling the gulf between the small ship and *Leviathan* with a sea of fire.

―――――

"Report!" Payne shouted as the ship twisted and turned.

"We are in the middle of the fleet," Lev said. "Nice to see you back, Major Payne. Standby while we try to recover your ship."

"Lev. You're back! Get us out of here."

"Working on it," Lev replied.

"Helmets on," Payne called. Joker and Sparky had just extricated Byle from her suit. "Get her back into it. Now."

They didn't argue. If anything happened to the uglymobile, they'd be exposed to space, and the suits would save their lives. Everyone but Byle. They rushed through putting her in while the ship yanked and banked, then darted away.

"The enemy ships are creating a lethal barrier between you and me. Sit back and relax while I maneuver into position. If you hear any loud noises, that's an argument decided in my favor."

"You sound like me, Lev. I'm teaching you bad things, but I appreciate it."

"Get the fuck in there!" Joker struggled with getting his foot into the boot. She loosened it up all the way and tried again, flailing to get it done. She kicked at the suit's leg. When Byle's foot thumped to the bottom, they pulled the suit up. Joker found Byle's privates squashed against her faceplate. "That was pleasant," she complained before getting the suit up the rest of the way and sealed.

Turbo put the helmet into place and twisted it until it locked closed. The suit's air started to circulate. "Clear," Turbo said. They laid her on the floor and took their seats. The group on that side of the ship held her down with their feet while the ship accelerated away from the engagement.

A whirring sound drew Payne's attention. "Are you firing?"

"I believe they are trying to capture this ship."

"You'll want to avoid that. I'm all for shooting up these ships from the inside, except we are bingo on ordnance. We have air guns, and if the rest of these ships are run like the big boy, there's nothing aboard that we can shoot."

"Hang tight. It'll be a few." Lev disappeared from the channel.

"You were correct. He *is* starting to sound like you," Dank offered.

"Major Payne offered an observation. There are no flesh-and-blood life forms on any of these ships."

"Could be like you," the admiral replied.

"Maybe, but sophisticated software doesn't mean sentience.

There were five billion life forms on the planet. No, this is an automated fleet. It's time to clear the air."

"An apology?" the admiral quipped.

Leviathan dove into a volley of fire meant to deter him from doing what he just did. He met it with his own fire, from small to large projectiles, plasma clouds that vaporized physical projectiles.

And then *Leviathan* fired his offensive weapons, and hundreds of missiles erupted from the embedded ports that lined the hull. They rocketed across the void at nearly the speed of light to flash through defensive weapons fire and strike deep into the hulls of their targets. The fleet ships exploded by the nearest energy sources.

The remaining eighteen enemy cruisers and frigates turned into separate and unique novas, suns created by compromised reactors cascading to their doom and taking their ships with them.

Leviathan raced forward, and the insertion ship instantly turned around and headed for the hangar bay.

The enemy fleet winked in. Two battleships, then four: the dreadnought and the remaining battleships and cruisers. The dreadnought's main weapon spooled to life, a plasma cannon that fired a projectile the size of a large asteroid.

"Traction beam engaged. Accelerating away from the engagement zone," the captain reported.

"Fold space. Get us out of here!" The admiral nearly jumped at the dais.

"The insertion ship did not make it into the hangar. It is grappled to the outside of the hull," Lev explained. "Brace for impact."

The projected view outside the ship changed perspective as Lev rolled to move the small ship opposite the line of fire. Upon impact, the ship lurched, throwing those on the bridge into the panels, over stations, off chairs, and onto the deck. The ship swayed drunkenly.

It stabilized for a moment, and Lev unleashed an eye-popping barrage from *Leviathan*'s arsenal: missiles, railguns, plasma cannons, laser beams. Most of them focused on the dreadnought, but Lev wanted to let the battleships know they weren't invisible. The lasers and plasma cannons danced across the dreadnought's hull, blasting the surface clear of anything taller than a weld seam.

Missiles flashed across the void nearly instantaneously, impacting the hulls of their targets. They delivered kinetic energy on the order of megatons before the payloads erupted for more megatons of destruction, carving deep craters into the dreadnought's hull.

Two battlewagons suffered under the single strike, reactors going critical and turning the ships into expanding incandescent clouds.

Leviathan jerked sideways under another impact. The Parallax ships fired relentlessly.

The admiral watched helplessly but noted that Lev had designated the Blaze fleet as the enemy.

Peace through superior firepower.

They are all our enemies. Maybe we weren't wrong in not pursuing common ground with the Blaze and dedicating our limited resources to building bigger and better ships, the admiral thought.

I went into hiding because I was ordered to. I've had a thousand years to contemplate my place in this universe. I'd hoped that things had changed, but they have not. My war is with those who are giving the orders to the five races that comprise the Blaze Collective. If we are to bring peace to this universe, then we must dismantle the leadership who embrace the evil and direct the hatred. This fleet is automated. They risk nothing in their robot war, Lev replied.

For the first time, Harry Wesson understood that Lev was speaking directly into his mind.

They are filled with their people on the front lines. We have never seen a robot ship before.

Because lackeys are expendable, Harry. Our war is not with them. We will need to return to Parallax and destroy those who are giving the orders.

The conversation took place at the speed of thought while the battle raged on all screens. *Leviathan* shuddered and groaned under the onslaught.

"Fire," Leviathan ordered and accelerated toward a cluster of battleships and cruisers. Missiles raced after a volley from the plasma cannons. Railguns sniped frigates one after another. They remained engaged despite the tremendous losses *Leviathan* was inflicting.

Twenty cruisers down. All frigates lost. Four battleships struggled to keep firing. But the dreadnought remained combat-effective despite the fury *Leviathan* had unleashed upon it. Its main weapon spooled up round after round.

Leviathan's gyrations caused most to miss, but not all. The ship was suffering.

A new icon flashed onto the board, but only for an instant.

[22]

"An enemy left alive in your rear area is more than a pain in the ass." —From the memoirs of Fleet Admiral Thaylon Loore

Team Payne hung on for dear life. The uglymobile was tossed and slammed by impacts as well as from hanging onto *Leviathan* during its erratic maneuvers. Artificial gravity was barely functional; otherwise, it would have mitigated the movements.

Buzz finally lost control and started puking into his helmet.

"Not optimal, Fetus," Heckler said, looking at the junior specialist. "At least we don't have to smell it. Hell's Canyon. Same thing. Lost gravity, and dammit if Blinky didn't come unhinged. You sympathy-pukers filled the floor of the skimmer. It took me a week to get that slop off my boots."

"We can't all be as hard as you," Blinky shot back.

"And that one hardass is me," Payne called over the jibes. He pointed at Turbo. "How's Byle?"

She checked her faceplate. "Still breathing. It's all I can tell. She still has color. She'll be fine as long as we get her to the medbay sometime this decade."

"Any idea when we'll be docked?" Joker asked.

They'd all heard the same things, but now wasn't the time to be sarcastic. They were hurt and needed a place to shelter, but their home was getting pummeled by an enemy fleet, and they were on the outside looking in.

"I'm sure it'll be any time now. Space battles don't last long, and this one's been going on for a while. Lev, bring up the tactical display for us if you would be so kind."

Both outer bulkheads became screens. The picture showed *Leviathan* systematically destroying the enemy fleet while doing his best to avoid the dreadnought that pursued the ship. The second dreadnought's icon flashed red, indicating it was not destroyed but not a threat.

"Why isn't Lev taking on the big boy?"

"Maybe the fire from the other ships is distracting him," Dank posited.

A new icon flashed onto the screen as it dropped out of FTL. It immediately reoriented and accelerated to near-light speed.

The worldkiller slammed into the side of the dreadnought and detonated with the force of a comet impacting a planet. Fire and debris burst out the far side of the ship before the rest exploded and sent wreckage like flechettes at anything and everything within its expanding cloud of annihilation.

Lev maxed his acceleration without going to FTL and rolled to keep the insertion vehicle away from the worst of it.

While executing his lifesaving maneuver, Lev continued to fire at ships that wouldn't be impacted by the death of the dreadnought.

The final barrage of missiles shattered the surviving battlewagons. A cruiser tried to escape, but a final pair of missiles caught it the instant before it launched into FTL.

The buffeting ended, and the insertion vehicle unclamped

and executed a quick maneuver that delivered it into the hangar bay. The doors closed, and atmosphere was restored.

"You may take off your helmets and report to the medical facility for treatment," Lev announced.

"Have the carts ready. We have one who is still out, possibly in a coma. She gets treatment immediately. We'll make our way afterward." Major Payne was out of energy but continued to drive himself. Courage in the face of enemy fire was a given among the troops, but being able to still do the job when it was over separated him from the rest.

Major Dank tried to stand tall too, but he was the second-worst injured of the team members. Payne put a hand on his shoulder.

"And you too, Virgil. See that Byle gets to medical and coordinate there as the others arrive. We want everyone taken care of."

The team stumbled out of the uglymobile and started doffing their suits.

Dank nodded and quickly stripped. The craft had deposited them in the location it had left from, so their clothes were nearby. No one bothered to dress Byle, shipping her off on a cart purposed for a horizontal passenger. Dank stiffly put on shorts and jumped into the next cart. It took off without waiting for anyone else because Payne had already thought about it and Lev knew the urgency.

Buzz removed his helmet and dropped it on the deck. The smell wafted past the others.

"Go somewhere else to change, Fetus!" Turbo barked. Buzz tottered away to remove his befouled suit. Payne grabbed his clothes and carried them to him.

"Good op, Buzz." Payne felt old and tired.

Heckler removed his suit, dumped it on the deck, and

dressed. As the first done, he collected the weapons to return to the armory for cleaning and reloading.

"Anybody beside Heckler not going to the medbay?" Buzz, Turbo, and Blinky raised their hands. "That was a loaded question. The right answer is that you're all going. Even you, Heckler, once you've secured the weapons."

"Are we free and clear?" Heckler asked.

Payne had assumed the display screens inside the insertion ship told them everything they needed to know, but they would redeploy if needed. Only in an emergency, though, since the team was combat-ineffective. Too much damage to their bodies, including Payne's. He knew his back would be black and blue from the torture it had withstood. He realized he was thirsty.

"Get something to drink, people, and Lev, can you give us an update? Are we clear, at least for a while, and when are we folding back to Solar space?"

A cart appeared with beverages, and the team members each took one and downed it.

"Balanced electrolytes that should help your bodies. The pursuing Fleet has been eliminated. *Leviathan* is damaged but not beyond repair. We will recover necessary raw materials from the mostly intact dreadnought before we depart."

The maintenance and fabrication fleet was mobilizing in the hangar bays and preparing to leave.

"My mission does not require a return to Solar space."

Payne frowned. The others froze in the middle of getting dressed.

"Hey, buddy, you're going to have to explain that last one a little more. Where are you taking us?"

"I have come to the realization that this galaxy has a cancer that will prevent peace. I have decided that we will save the most lives if we excise the cancer."

"I'm still not seeing the whole picture. You just destroyed a fleet. What about those lives? But they hurt you pretty badly, didn't they?"

"I have determined that there were no life forms aboard those vessels. We destroyed a robot fleet. I know you encountered no flesh-and-blood entities aboard the dreadnought."

"At temps of minus seventy, nothing was going to be alive, not warm-blooded or cold-blooded. But what about the ship? What if it was like you?" Payne wondered.

"It was most assuredly not like me. They are extremely advanced but not sentient."

"How do you know that?"

"Because there is only one of me. Even the Progenitors could not replicate what I am."

Payne looked at his team and twirled his finger for them to finish getting dressed. He walked back and forth as he talked to Lev, not caring that he was still naked.

"There are no other Prog battleships?"

"I don't believe I said that. There were, but they required a massive crew. They had advanced artificial intelligences, but none of the others achieved sentience. That was why I of all the ships was left behind. The others traveled hundreds of millions of light-years to a new galaxy where they could start over."

"And why you were the only one not completely gutted of technology...because the tech is you, and you are the tech. It would have been like removing a human's organs. In the end, you would not have survived."

"Your analogy is correct."

"Is everyone on board okay? I forgot to ask, but you took a bit of a beating, didn't you?"

"Everyone is fine, Declan. Thank you for asking after them. They were perfectly safe on the bridge. That is a separate escape vessel, hardened against all attacks. If I am destroyed, most of my essence will live on once the bridge is freed from the superstructure. There will be a most spectacular series of explosions to destroy everything else, but one hunk of metal will remain. That will drift in space until it can maneuver away unseen."

"I guess we have to make sure that doesn't happen. Two dreadnoughts did a number on you. How many more do they have?"

"That is what we'll find out on the next phase of my mission. Of course, you'll help me, won't you?"

"As far as I'm concerned, Lev, I'm stationed aboard the Battleship *Leviathan*. Me and my team. I know I speak for all of us when I say we're with you. I'm not so sure about the commodore and that corporate cheese donk."

"I am working on them. I don't want anyone to go against their will, but I feel that we are best served by a broad range of backgrounds and specialties."

"Don't you already have the answers, Lev?"

"I still have much to learn. It was a refreshing realization when the admiral suggested using the worldkiller as a diversion in order to buy us time to recover your team, and it served to divide the pursuing fleet. That made it possible to defeat them. One ship against fifty...well, forty-nine if we exclude the ship that you disabled."

"You're welcome, Lev." Payne grabbed his overalls, feeling less tired than he had a few minutes earlier. Half the team had boarded the carts and were heading away. That left four. Buzz sat on a box while the others helped Heckler with the gear.

"What's up?" the major asked.

"We failed, and then I puked into my helmet. I thought I was going to drown."

"It drains into your suit. You just have to keep your head up. How do you think I know that?"

"Because everyone visits Mount Spewenchunks sometime?"

"Everyone is blessed with a technicolor yawn. Even Heckler. I think he avoids eating prior to a mission to be safe. Next time, take it easy on the green stuff, whatever that was."

"Eggs, or so Cookie called them."

"Is that what we're calling Galen now?"

"Seemed appropriate. He loves his pastries." Buzz managed a weak smile.

"Get dressed and report to the technodocs to fix you up. Drink another one of those things. It'll help ease the bruising." Payne took a second one for himself.

Buzz continued sitting with his head down.

"What else?" Payne pushed.

"We failed."

"We didn't fail. Ten knuckle-dragging humans took out a dreadnought with nothing more than what they carried on their backs. That's a win, my man."

"No. I mean Blinky and me. We didn't get into their system, and we had a few hours to work at it."

"But now you'll have Lev's help with the data you collected. Next time, you'll be ready for them. Now, get dressed and get your ass out of here." The major turned to the others. "Blinky, get him to sickbay. He's confused."

[23]

"If the enemy gives you an opening, know why before you commit." –From the memoirs of Fleet Admiral Thaylon Loore

Major Payne found the bridge hatch closed when he arrived, but it opened the second the cart came to a stop. He hadn't gone to the medical facility with the others. He had to check in first.

He strode onto the bridge to find all eyes on him. "Good work, Major," the admiral called and hurried to shake his hand. Lewis and Malcolm fell in behind the admiral, having had little to say about anything since they boarded.

They wanted to contribute.

"I won't be long. I need to get to sickbay and get these bruises addressed. We took a bit of a beating over there from their security bots. It was little more than a drone ship without a protocol to deal with intruders. It let us in. I suspect the security bots had a different purpose, like a landing and occupation force. They weren't very good, but they outnumbered us and outgunned us."

"But you still accomplished the mission." The admiral was pleased.

"Blinky is uploading the data we collected so Lev can help us figure out how to crack their programming. That ship was one big power generation system. By the way, how are you guys? Get bounced around a bit?"

The major strolled around the bridge, shaking everyone's hands. Tamony and the commodore looked at his hand before taking it. He told them in a low voice, "It's nice to be human, and most importantly, it's great to be alive."

"Your work has been nothing less than selfless, Major. Please accept my compliments on a job well done. I think you need to attend to your injuries posthaste. Take yourself to the medical facilities," the commodore said, showing more compassion than Payne had thought possible.

"I second the commodore's encouragement. We can talk later. For now, get healthy because we're in Lev's hands while he stocks up on processed metals to build spare parts for himself. We've been talking with Lev about what's next. He is opposed to returning to Earth space before continuing the mission." The admiral gestured at the hatch.

"He told me that too. It'll only take a week to get to Earth and then back here. I think we have to go back to tell them what's up. Maybe forestall any major military advances while we work behind the lines. With any success, the Blaze front lines might draw back to more defensible positions. I don't want us to lose people because Fleet thinks we've been kidnapped."

"Maybe we can take on more troops to handle more missions and services aboard *Leviathan*. He can carry up to one hundred thousand, but I wouldn't be happy with crowded corridors. I'm comfortable the way things are. I'm not sure I would like having to wait for a cart," the admiral explained.

"That's a good reason," Major Payne clapped the admiral on

the shoulder. "I'm off to sickbay and then to the rack. I'm tired. I'm sure with a clear head, I'll be able to add quality to the conversation. Or maybe not. You know me."

The admiral nodded. Payne waved over his head as he walked away.

"Thanks, everyone." He continued into the corridor and to the waiting cart that whisked him straight to the deck's medical facility, where he found seven members of the team. A quick look confirmed that Heckler and Blinky were missing, but he knew what they were doing and approved. They hadn't been injured, while the rest had absorbed critical impacts, with penetrations of Byle's and Dank's suits.

Major Dank was spread across an operating table and hooked to machines with a forcefield around him. A beam worked with knitting-needle-looking devices to stitch his rib cartilage together.

"I've never seen anything like that before," Payne mumbled, mesmerized by the manufacturing-type approach to repairing a human body. Payne broke free and scanned the beds, looking for Byle. He found her beyond Turbo and Shaolin. "Everybody sleepy?"

"Following doctor's orders," Turbo replied. "Grab a bunk. I'm sure you're under doc lock too."

"Not yet," Payne started.

"You will do as directed, Declan. Enter the examination room, please," Lev replied.

"Crap! You're, like, the man of a thousand faces," Payne blurted. He recovered and pointed at Specialist Byle. "I would like to know what's wrong with her."

"Concussion and brain swelling. I'm reducing the swelling through directed temperature reduction."

"You're icing her brain by microwave?"

"Very crude. If that's what you need to understand it, then

yes. I'm microwaving her brain, but instead of exciting the molecules, I'm relaxing them, which cools the temperature. I've also given her something to reduce her blood temperature. She is in a coma right now, but I expect she'll make a full recovery in a few days. The rest of you, less Virgil, will be out of here tomorrow. He'll need two days for the cartilage reconstruction to stabilize."

"Amazing stuff, Lev. Is there any way I can run to my room real quick and get something?"

"Like what? I happen to know that there is nothing in your room you need."

"Like, about eight hours of sleep on that cushy mattress as opposed to that fossilized lump you want me to lay on in here. Have a heart, Lev!"

"You got a cushy mattress?" Turbo asked, sitting up straight in bed. "I want a cushy mattress."

"And me," Sparky added.

"See what you did, Lev? You're wreaking havoc on the team, and I thought you had already given everyone new mattresses and custom room designs."

"They are pulling your third leg. They've had them longer than you, along with other room customizations. You've already had this conversation."

"Lev, be a peach and have a new cushy mattress delivered to every crew member's quarters. They'll be less grumpy for it. The Progs were a bit utilitarian for our Neanderthalness. I'm heading to my room. I just need sleep and lots of water." Payne collected two containers and headed for the door. "I know you control the carts. Don't make me walk because you know I will."

"You will recover better in the medical facility, where your vitals can be monitored at all times and medication applied or adjusted as needed."

"I believe that you believe the truth of your statement, Lev. I'm telling you that I'll recover better in my own bed. Just like the rest of the team." He turned to find the specialists climbing out of bed, grabbing their clothes, and heading for the door. "And for your edification, I got a grand total of ten minutes on that mattress before everything went to hell. My evaluation wasn't complete, but with the minimal data, I believe it will benefit the whole team."

"You sound pretty defensive, sir," Turbo replied. "We have taken one for the team and can confirm without a doubt that the cushy mattresses are indeed just what the doctor ordered."

"You were perfectly happy sleeping on that sack of cement." Payne pointed to the recently vacated bed.

"Until we heard there was better. Now, we're unhappy. You should probably wait and tell Major Dank where everyone is."

Payne's shoulders fell of their own accord as he surrendered to the inevitability of his discomfort.

"How in the hell did that work? Turnabout is *not* fair play." Payne threw his hands up after having gotten exactly the opposite of what he wanted.

"They're out to recover in their rooms. You might as lie down here, Major Payne."

The team nearly bulldozed the door on their way out. It closed again, leaving Payne alone with one patient in a coma and the other sedated.

"That'll learn me up real good to look out for number one. Can you get me something softer than what you have here? I suspect I'll be here for a while, you bowlegged butt-snuggler."

"I have no idea what this tumble of words means, Declan. I think you're delirious and need to be sedated."

"Fine. I'm getting in bed." Payne took the blankets off all the beds to build himself a single mattress that was passably comfortable. "Let me know when Virgil is awake."

Declan leaned back, his head full of deeper thoughts than his personal comfort, but Lev already knew that. Payne expected to talk to him about the strategy of going back to Parallax but was asleep before he could utter the first word.

"Declan. Are you alive?" a voice whispered into his ear.

"Of course I'm alive. I'm sure you see me breathing." He opened his eyes to find Virgil looking at him. "How do you feel?"

"Good as new. Look. Even Byle is awake."

In the next bed, Byle breathed deeply and slowly. "She looks like she's sleeping."

"Well, she is, but she's awake from the coma."

"You're killing me, Virge. What time is it?"

"We're in interstellar space. Time is relative out here."

Payne stopped asking questions and sat up. "Hungry."

"They're waiting for us," Virgil said, holding out Declan's clean coveralls.

"How long was I out?" He slid out of bed and leaned against it to get his first leg in.

"About twelve hours. I think we're getting ready to go, but there is some question as to where. Your presence is required. Clean yourself up. You smell funny."

"I don't like waking up to your face. I'd rather have no face, or maybe a pillow face." Payne headed for the bathroom. "Give me ten. A shower sounds good."

Virgil dressed and waited.

After one last look at the sleeping specialist, the two majors strolled out of the medical bay and hopped on the cart waiting to take them to the bridge.

"What's our plan of attack?" Dank asked.

Declan shook his head. "We're along for the ride on this one, Virgil. Maybe they'll ask us what we saw on the dreadnought? We're back on the big ship, which means the admiral is in charge. It's his meeting. That makes it easy on us. I don't have to prepare a speech!"

"You never prepare for your speeches." Virgil leaned back to enjoy the ride.

"I used to like you," Payne replied with a short chuckle. "There's that. At least I don't have a folder or a memory stick to stuff into a computer. Just us and our massive brains."

"Don't say that in there. You'll find out in a hurry that when it comes to those who are on board this ship, we're probably below average. Hell, we're below average on the team. SOFT. That's us."

"When you put it that way... But no, good sir, we are who we are surrounded by. Team Payne may be a Space Ops Force Team, but we are as hard as depleted uranium. The shock cones on frigates are soft compared to us."

"Big. Brains. When you were slammed into the bulkhead, did you hit your head?" Virgil pulled at Payne's eyelid until he slapped his hand away.

"Yes, but it didn't hurt because I'm hard."

Dank imitated Payne's voice. "I need to sleep on my soft mattress..."

"You're taking things out of context, but I appreciate your bottom line. We should probably keep our mouths shut at this meeting."

"My point has been made. I'm declaring victory and enjoying the ride from here on out."

Three seconds later, the cart stopped in front of the bridge hatch.

"Enjoy the ride, Virge?"

Dank didn't dignify that with an answer. The majors collected their wits, put on their game faces, and strode onto the bridge. Dank put a hand on his recovering injury to stifle the pain of trying to act normal. They were the first to arrive besides the admiral and Davida, who moaned from the captain's dais.

Payne glanced from the source of the sound to Dank and then at the admiral. "What's that all about?"

Wesson shrugged and said, "You'll learn to tune it out." He motioned for the two to take seats where he had set up his desk, the closest position to the captain's chair and the dais.

"Sir?" Payne wondered.

"Why did I chase everyone else off the bridge? Because we are the senior military leaders left. Captain Dorsite is on a twenty-four sleep following her extended tour in the chair. The commodore is purely defense-minded. Until she expands her view, she's of little use to me. My question is, what do we do now?"

Dank and Payne looked at each other. Major Dank deferred. He was playing second fiddle, and this conversation was for the one in charge.

Major Payne leaned forward. "It all depends on what our goal is. I've talked with Lev, as I'm sure you have. If we're to sue for peace, we need to put the Blaze on their heels hard and fast while the word of our raid and subsequent destruction of their fleet isn't well known."

The admiral nodded. "I like Payne's idea of going back and reporting on what happened, but that would cost us a full week."

"A full week to travel eleven hundred light-years and back. Remember when five hundred light-years was a solid two weeks? The good old days." Payne smiled.

"You mean last week?" The admiral wanted his answer.

"Is that report for the betterment of humanity or for their own egos?" Payne asked.

The admiral touched a finger to his nose. "We have no major operations scheduled for the rest of this month. The recovery of *Leviathan* depleted our front-line combat assets by one Kaiju-class, but since *Cleophas* was restored to full operational capability, that would put us back to a level where we could take advantage of the Ebren loss of eight battlewagons and a dreadnought."

"Are you arguing for or against going back?" Payne wondered.

"I'm trying to see which way will cost us the least amount of lives. Attacking now to establish fear in the rear areas should force the Blaze to collapse their forces back to a more defensible position, one from which they can respond to threats to their homeworlds. How much more will it take before they withdraw from the front? They have nothing out there except strategically located planets from which to launch more attacks. Raw material resupply, but no advanced manufacturing. They are positioning themselves to establish a foothold on an advanced planet."

Payne replied, "As long as the Kaiju-class are out there, we maintain a delicate balance of power. Fleet needs us out here wreaking havoc."

"And reporting in would stroke some egos, and we'd get people off the ship who are less than contributory, but then we'd gain a whole new slew of volunteers. People would line up for miles to get a ride on this great ship."

"Which means it wouldn't be a week but multiple weeks while personnel worked their various chains of command to get on board. I won't have any of it."

"Sounds like your mind is already made up. What do you need from us?" Payne asked.

"How do we get the others to agree?"

"So it doesn't look like they're being kidnapped? When will Lev be fully repaired and ready to go? I don't like sitting here among the debris of a destroyed fleet in case the Blaze come out for a look."

"Lev? Are you there?"

"I am always here," the ship replied. "I have been monitoring energy signatures in nearby space, and everyone is where they are supposed to be. There is active movement around Parallax. Besides normal couriers, none of the ships are using FTL."

"Normal couriers? I haven't heard that before."

"There is no FTL communication, even with the advances the civilization on Parallax has made. Ships transport messages, but their courier fleet consists of drones. Yours consists of warships."

"Out of necessity. We never know what's going on at the destination," Admiral Wesson replied. "When will you be fully repaired?"

"No more than two hours. I am making the final repairs and calibrations on the external sensory grid now. That takes more time than fabricating and emplacing armor."

"What about worldkillers? Are you able to replace the one you used?" the admiral pressed.

"Those are irreplaceable, using stabilized anti-matter. I cannot fabricate that on board this ship. Everything else, yes. I will begin building another worldkiller in case we are able to acquire the requisite material, but I shall not go out of my way in search of it."

"It worked well on the dreadnought. I have no desire to blow up anyone's planet. That is one step too far. But a robotic shipyard? That might rate deployment. Reducing the enemy's ability to fight without killing the people is more effective at winning their hearts and minds than a campaign of slaughter."

"Profound. Who said that?"

The admiral smiled. "Harry Wesson. Don't tell anyone, but I'm making this up as I go. No human has ever been able to end an intergalactic war before. Once we engaged the Blaze and were forced to fight, we have known nothing but war."

Payne leaned forward with his elbows on his knees, scowling at the deck. "For my whole life, we've been at war with aliens. Now that we've met Lev, I have hope that there's an end in sight."

"Why do you fight, son?"

"So that someday we'd be able to see an opportunity like this one. I loved searching Prog derelicts, even if we didn't find anything. The next time we cracked a hatch, maybe we would find something to help us end this damned war."

"That is why I've chosen to help you. In your mind and with your words, you said 'end the war,' not 'win the war.' Your goal is peace, and that aligns with my goal."

"To realize peace, one must be willing to go to war. There can be no peace in subjugation or domination." The admiral leaned back and crossed his arms. "Can we get the rest of the crew to the bridge, please? We need to talk and come to a firm decision within the next two hours."

"May I suggest the dining facility? Galen has come up with an exceptional new series of recipes to prepare what he calls Thanksgiving dinner. No large Terran birds were harmed in the making of this meal."

"Capital idea, Lev. People are always more receptive on a full stomach, but why did he make a Thanksgiving meal? It's not Thanksgiving. We're not in America. And no one celebrates that anymore."

"He did it to celebrate returning home."

Payne snorted and turned away to keep the admiral from seeing him laugh.

"Nothing like making the job harder. We'll make it a celebration of the light at the end of the tunnel. It is now in sight, thanks to you, Lev." He stood and gestured for the majors to precede him. The admiral waved dismissively at the resident genius. "I'm sure she'll be fine."

"Davida intends to never leave this ship," Lev replied.

"You are her soulmate. Together, nirvana," Payne said softly. "Maybe you could hook her up in a lab somewhere. I think we're going to need the chair for Captain Dorsite."

"Or you, Major Payne. I welcome you both into the command-and-control fold."

"The admiral's right here, Lev. He's going to get jealous." Payne winked. Admiral Wesson shook his head. "But that sounds kind of creepy, like a secret handshake, smoky back room where we cut shady deals."

"It is an intimate connection with my mind. It is a most unpleasant experience in some cases. I know that with Davida, Arthir, and you, I get as much as I give."

"You get something from me?" Payne blurted.

He stopped and Major Dank ran into him, then pushed him into the waiting cart. "Besides a bad sense of humor and inappropriate remarks at inopportune times?"

"What idiot put you two in charge of my people?" the admiral interrupted.

"I'm pretty sure that was you, sir," Payne replied. The cart whisked them down the corridor on the short trip to the dining facility. Carts cruised in ahead of them, delivering the rest of the crew.

"Smells like turkey," Dank noted. "Now I'm hungry."

The three walked into the facility to find half the crew already through the line, plates piled with turkey-looking slices, stuffing, mashed potatoes, gravy, green beans, and cranberry sauce.

"Damn!" Payne leaned close to Turbo's plate to examine the food. She jabbed him in the face with her fork.

"Get your own!" She hunched around her plate and began the process of less than fine dining as she shoveled it in grunt style.

The major rubbed his cheek. "Am I bleeding?"

Virgil shook his head. "Never mess with a SOFTie's food. You know better than that."

"I wasn't messing. I was examining to see if it was fit for consumption."

"I'm sorry, sir. What did you say?" Galen said from behind the counter, giving the major a less than appreciative look. "I have a nutrition supplement in pill form if you'd prefer."

"I throw myself on your mercy," Payne pleaded. "This could be the best-smelling food I've ever smelled with my nose. It's so overwhelming, I can't believe it's real. Forgive me. Food, please?"

Payne hurried through, filling his plate with more than he knew he should eat, but this seemed like one of those once-in-a-lifetime meals.

Treat every meal like a banquet, as if it's your last. A team saying, but it had never been anyone's last. Payne had never lost anyone. He held out hope that he wouldn't, but with each mission, the odds stacked higher against him.

Once they were seated and eating, the admiral stood where everyone could see him. He counted heads. Eighteen. Only Davida Danbury and Augry Byle were absent.

The admiral started slowly. "There are twenty of us on board a ship designed for a hundred thousand. A ship designed to end wars by making the cost of war too high for anyone to be willing to fight. We find ourselves at a critical juncture in humanity's future. With *Leviathan's* help, we can make war too costly for the Blaze Collective.

"As we've found out, the Blaze represents only those doing the bidding of the race that was native to Parallax, not the Berantz. We have an opportunity to strike fast and hard at the heart of the Blaze Collective with the goal that they withdraw their forces from forward positions, bringing them home to protect their world. That's when we start negotiating directly with the races of the Blaze.

"This is the best opportunity to realize peace for humanity that I've seen. I've been on the front lines, fighting for humanity by keeping the battle out here. Hundreds of light-years from Earth, giving human beings the opportunity to live their lives free of the danger that the Fleet and BEP face. We sacrifice so others may live.

"I am asking you to sacrifice again by carrying this fight forward, taking the fight to Parallax. We can attrit the enemy forces to where they will no longer be able to carry the battle forward. I want us to return to Parallax now while they are still in disarray over losing half their fleet."

"I'm with you," Captain Dorsite said. She hammered the butt of her fork on the table. "I have some tactics I think could work quite nicely."

"Tamony and Nyota. I would like your agreement that going forward, not back, is our best option."

"It's only a week. We've been fighting this war for a lifetime already. What is one more week?" Tamony Swiss replied. "We should go back to Earth."

"It's sufficient time for Parallax to regroup and build its defenses." The admiral held Tamony's gaze.

"Isn't that what we want them to do?" the civilian countered.

"Only after they know how vulnerable they are by losing

the bulk of their fleet. That means hit them now before they can improve their position. They were caught off-guard the first time. They will not be ready for such a quick return. A week could make all the difference, and then we'd be the ones walking into a trap. But you would be off the ship at that point, so what does it matter?"

"No need for vitriol, Admiral Wesson, but you are correct. I will get off this ship. I can agree to go forward, but there has to be something in it for me. I want access to technologies that my companies can reverse-engineer. Even if we're successful, humanity continues to move forward. What about terraforming technology? That could be the future of mankind, enjoying peaceful coexistence with its celestial neighbors."

Lev agreed. "The Progenitors had terraforming technology. It is extremely complex and will not be easy to reverse-engineer, but it is something that could be beneficial to multiple races. I'll include a failsafe that will prevent its use on a planet that is already populated."

Tamony shook his head and waved his hand. "There is no profit in genocide. Your failsafe is welcome, and I agree. One trip to Parallax at risk of life and limb in exchange for terraforming technology."

Dank whispered into Payne's ear, "Talk about distasteful..."

"Nyota?"

"The BEP has a vested interest in the safety of Earth. We are the last line of defense. Even if Fleet wins the war, the BEP will still fill a necessary role. In that regard, and although I know the best course of action is to return to Solar space to integrate *Leviathan* into existing defenses, I feel that I have no choice but to represent BEP interests out here. I agree to delay the return to Earth for one week."

"I'll take that to mean as long as it takes. We are out here to win this war. Now is our time. What about our master logistician? Lewis. What do you think?"

"I think this ship is amazing. I still have a great deal to learn about how it automates the movement of the limited number of consumables in the system, but most fascinating was how it repaired itself. Imagine if we had that capability for our ships." Lewis tapped his forehead with two fingers in a parody of a salute.

"Malcolm. How about you?"

"I would like a turn in the chair if I could get it. The untapped potential of knowledge onboard this ship…wow."

"A technical assessment only a research engineer could make. Lev determines who sits in the chair, although I'm sure there are research laboratories aboard this ship. Lev, can you introduce Mister Russell to one?"

"I would be happy to. Same with Davida. There are alternative interfaces with me. Seven total are on board."

"Then why is she hogging my chair?" the captain blurted.

"Easy." The admiral's look cautioned Arthir against further challenges.

"Sorry." She returned to her mashed potatoes smothered in gravy.

"Can you keep cooking for us, Galen?" The admiral strolled to the serving counter.

Galen spread his arms wide. "This is the easiest gig I've ever had. I don't have to clean anything. Bots do all the work. I program the food processor thing and taste test. Now that I know what I'm doing, the menu is going to expand like a buffet in a Las Vegas casino."

"Never been," the admiral replied. "But I get your point and thank you. Of all the people on board this ship, you are the one who makes our lives worth living. Here's to you, Cookie." The admiral led a brief but enthusiastic round of applause for *Leviathan's* head chef.

"That's settled. Within the hour, *Leviathan's* repairs will be complete, and the ship will be one hundred percent combat-effective. We'll return to Parallax at FTL speed, saving the fold for an emergency egress. If that happens, we'll return to Solar space directly. Finish your lunch and take your stations. We won't need to centralize our assets until we get close to coming out of FTL."

"Centralize our assets?" Lewis questioned.

"Bring our people together so we can account for everyone. This ship is a little big in case something happens, and as it turns out, the bridge and its immediate environs are an emergency escape ship. As long as we're on the bridge, we can survive everything, even a worldkiller."

"That's comforting," Tamony deadpanned.

"Enjoy your meal as a celebration of how far we've come." The admiral sat down and dug into his lunch. It didn't taste as good to him because all he could think about was the way ahead. Too many unknowns. A powerful enemy that wanted to survive. Their task was to instill fear without driving the enemy to brash action.

[24]

"Surrender is for those with no imagination."
–From the memoirs of Fleet Admiral Thaylon Loore

"I am fully stocked on raw materials for further repairs if needed. The dreadnought was a lucrative source of the best exotics that mostly replicated my own frame and shell. The unexploded cores of two of the battlewagons will be able to augment my volatile secondary power systems. I am ready to fly on your command, Harry."

"Arthir, take us out of this debris field. Next stop, Parallax."

The ship maneuvered clear of the forever-floating debris and pointed toward Parallax before transitioning into FTL speed.

"Time check?"

"Arrival in seven hours."

"Team Payne, report to the armory for weapons check and load out in six hours. We'll be waiting on the uglymobile for our arrival at Parallax. I doubt what we did last time will work again, but just in case they didn't get word back, then we could be ready for round two. Blinky and Buzz, are you any closer to cracking their language and getting inside their system?"

Blinky and Buzz looked at the deck and shook their heads. "Looks like you have six hours to figure it out. Get to it. I'll be checking on Byle."

Dank headed to the armory with Heckler while Payne returned to the medical bay.

Inside, he found Byle trying to get dressed. "I know Lev didn't release you yet. What the hell do you think you're doing?"

"I'm going with you. If the team is deploying, then I'm deploying."

"You have a bruised brain, Byle. Until you get the all-clear, you are a risk to us and yourself. And more importantly, you'll set yourself up for a long-term injury. You can't go through life with a smashed brain. People with that die ugly. We want to die in a glorious firefight, not wandering around mumbling to ourselves."

"But, *sir*..."

Payne shook his head. "Now is not the time, Byle. Get back in bed, and we'll see what Lev says in six hours. If he clears you, I'll be kicking your ass to the armory to load up. You know you love the uglymobile. It's a fine ride."

"I don't remember our last trip, so I have a lot to make up for. They told me you carried me out. Thank you."

"It was that or fill out all this extra paperwork. You know how much I hate that stuff. Get some rest, Byle. Maybe Lev will use the cooling microwave on you again to give you a little more space inside the bone bucket." Payne gave her the thumbs-up and strode away.

"She will be ready to deploy with you, Declan," Lev said.

"I'm counting on it, Lev. I don't want to deploy at anything less than full strength. And even with ten on the team, we need more firepower. I'm heading to the armory."

"What do we have, Heckler?" Payne asked.

On a table at the far end of the firing range, Heckler had spread out a variety of weapons.

Heckler, as the senior combat specialist, passed the briefing responsibility to Turbo. She nodded one time to acknowledge the order and faced the major. "We have significant firepower available, each heavier than the next. In our combat suits, most of the weight will be mitigated, so we've determined that all of these weapons are viable."

"We didn't have these when we first looked. Has Lev been working overtime?"

"These weapons were in his database, and all of them can be manufactured before we depart."

"Firepower is good. Let's start with the heaviest."

Turbo moved to the end of the table, the fifteenth weapon. She lifted it to rest on top of her shoulder while she moved back and forth. "This is a pulse cannon that weighs nearly twenty kilos. The main drawback is its size. Once you're aimed down a corridor, you can't turn around very quickly. You have to turn your whole body, which makes reactive fire nearly impossible. I recommend we carry three of these to set up as area-denial weapons. As an added bonus, there's a remote firing option with a tripod mount. Those are another ten kilos each."

"Sounds like three pulse cannons and three tripods carried by six people. What will give us more punch than the needle guns?"

Turbo moved down the table to the fourth-heaviest weapon. "This is a shoulder-fired railgun with an added grenade launcher. It's only five kilos, but the grenade ammo adds up. It comes with shoulder harnesses that strap across the body."

"If you get hit, you blow up?" the major wondered.

"No. They don't activate until they are inside the launch chamber. The good thing is that they fire the same projectile as the needle gun but send it at twice the speed and have a magazine capacity of five hundred rounds. We can carry extra magazines. With the needle guns and railguns, we have overlap of ammunition, heavy firepower with the pulse cannons, and antipersonnel with the air rifles."

"Do we take the air rifles? Looks like we'll be plenty encumbered before our normal packs with water, food, medical, duct tape, and for the team geeks, computer systems."

"I recommend we take air rifles. We don't want to get trapped into always fighting the last battle. With the air rifles, they can fire indefinitely. If we are challenged by a living enemy, then we can hit them silently. The railgun and pulse cannon are not stealth weapons."

Payne picked up the railgun. Turbo handed him earplugs. She and Heckler stepped aside. Payne took aim at a target a hundred meters distant and fired. There was no kick, but the electrical discharge made his hair stand on end. The destruction of the target was instantaneous.

"Even with the sound suppressors, that thing was loud." He put it down and pointed to the cannon. Turbo handed it over. Payne aimed at a vehicle-sized target at the far end of the range, five hundred meters away. With an easy pull, the cannon roared, sending three plasma balls screaming downrange.

The target erupted in flames and splattered against the far wall.

"Three rounds?"

"It fires three successive rounds with a single trigger pull.

They come out so fast that the barrel rise barely affects their impact zone."

"It does a number on paper targets, but what about metal?"

"Sir, that was a metal target."

Payne laughed, and a smile spread across his face.

"We'll take four of those and four tripods. That leaves Blinky and Joker as the only ones not lugging the heavies. They have enough trash with their comm and hacking gear."

"What about Buzz?" Heckler asked. "Without him, I'm down to two combat specialists."

"There's the rub. Fighting a drone fleet, we could be better served from the technical side, but for them to do their job, we need to keep them safe. You've got me and Dank. That's four dedicated to the combat arms. We know what we're doing as a team. I don't need to stand there and watch. Buzz serves dual duty and will flex where he's needed most."

"You two are terrible at following orders," Heckler deadpanned.

"Even our own. That makes ten of us, but that's what makes this team great. Any of these other weapons have potential, like, non-lethal?"

Heckler raised one eyebrow. "If we must. There's a beanbag thrower, no kidding. It's pretty lame and all kinds of bulky. The stunners we brought with us are better non-lethal options than anything Lev has to offer."

"This ship was built as a weapon of last resort. If I was employed, then we were well past non-lethal options," Lev explained.

"There you are, buddy. I have to say I'm in love with that pulse cannon. I think we should call it 'Dozer' as it'll clear a wide variety of obstructions. And then there's the mini railgun. Good stuff, Lev, and by that, I mean these weapons will help keep the team alive." The major nodded at Heckler and Turbo.

"Order the right quantities and get the loadouts ready, then grab some shuteye. We'll be ready to deploy before you know it."

"Major Payne," a voice called from far away. It came closer until it was shouting in his face. "I know, Lev, it's time to get ready." He sat up in bed to find Commodore Freeman standing there. "Commodore."

"I wanted to talk with you alone before we arrived."

"What time is it?" he mumbled and climbed out of bed to get dressed.

"Two hours until we come out of FTL."

"Damn. You cost me an hour of sleep. I hope this is worth it, ma'am."

Anger flared across her features but quickly dissipated. She knew she was powerless on board *Leviathan*, along for the ride only. Her advice was neither sought nor accepted.

"We need the BEP to be considered in every action taken by this ship. It was discovered in BEP-controlled territory."

Payne blew out his breath and zipped his coveralls up. When he met her gaze, he realized she was serious. He thought of all kinds of sick comebacks but decided on discretion.

"We don't go anywhere without Lev's approval. This is his ship, and the ship is him. We are carried within a sentient being. Ask Lev what he thinks about being put into a defensive role."

"He said it made no sense, based on his purpose and abilities."

"Then why are you talking to me about it? What would your life be like if the BEP consisted of random patrols to conduct cargo checks on incoming alien freighters trading with Earth instead of waiting for an enemy that Fleet is doing its best to keep from ever arriving? That's what we're doing now. We're making our own jobs obsolete. I think that's a righteous task. We lost fifteen hundred people on *Cleophas* to make sure *Leviathan* launched. Now we're making sure their sacrifice was worth it."

The commodore pursed her lips and stared at the ceiling. Payne sat on his bed and waited. He liked his new mattress. If only he got to spend more time on it.

"What I hear everyone saying is that I'm not willing to sacrifice for the greater good."

"If that's what you hear, it's because you're saying it. You're a commodore, which means you've spent your fair share of time onboard ships, deployed where you didn't want to go to do things that no one wanted to do. You've had a different mission your entire life, one of defense. This ship and the mission that we've adopted since coming on board is all about offense. You have a different mindset based on your experience. No one is thinking that you're willing to sacrifice any less than the rest of us," Payne lied, pleased by how smoothly the words rolled off his tired tongue.

She smiled. "Two hours, Major, and we'll see what the future will hold. For all humanity."

"For all humanity, ma'am. No medals, no glory, only peace."

"It would be nice to retire," she admitted. "Thank you."

She left his room without looking back.

"Lev, wake me before you let other people into my room, please."

"You know you needed to have that conversation," Lev replied.

"You butt-slapping bitch! Do I have any control over my own life anymore?"

"Apparently not. In other news, the energy signatures around Parallax are winking out on vectors away from the planet and deeper into Blaze space."

"What does that mean?" The last of the cobwebs parted, and the major was suddenly alert.

"It means that they are abandoning the planet."

"Get me a cart, Lev. I need to talk with the admiral."

"It's already waiting, Declan."

"You're going to spoil me to the point where I won't be able to reintegrate into normal and, dare I say, polite society."

"Then my job is nearly complete."

"You're killing me, Lev." Payne climbed on board the cart, and it raced away from the room with the comfy mattress. It turned at the wide main corridor and headed straight to the bridge.

The major hurried in to find Captain Dorsite in the chair but alert and awake. Davida and the other civilians weren't there, but the commodore was. She had gone straight to the bridge after her conversation with Payne. She stood in close proximity to the Fleet admiral, and they conversed in low tones.

They stepped back to face Payne when he approached.

"You heard," Admiral Wesson said.

"If the fleet is not in orbit, I request permission to hit the planet with my team."

The admiral cocked his head before making eye contact with the captain. "What do you think of that, Arthir?" He turned to the commodore. "And Nyota. I am intrigued."

The captain answered first. "We could use more intel since we know jack about what's down there. Five billion inhabitants. You might have a hard time staying out of sight."

The commodore spoke up. "It appears that we have already made an impression, but with them scattering, how afraid are they? They've implemented a contingency plan."

The admiral nodded. "Which means to me that we are one step closer to removing all the hidey holes. Divide and conquer.

They're doing it for us. There's no way a secondary site is as well-defended as the home planet."

"Are we sure this is the home planet?" Payne asked. "I can't believe they would abandon their home so readily, including leaving five billion people behind. That's why we have to go down there."

"Pack your team and the insertion vehicle with what you need for ground recce. Once we're in orbit, Lev, select an insertion point for Team Payne."

Payne saluted. "I need to get the uglymobile ready."

The commodore snorted. "The uglymobile? I know it's tradition to name your skimmers, but you couldn't come up with anything better than that?"

Payne had started walking away. He spoke over his shoulder. "What could possibly be better than that?"

[25]

"When the enemy is on his heels, it's time to strike." –From the memoirs of Fleet Admiral Thaylon Loore

"Byle! Glad you could make it. Pick up that tripod. It's your new best buddy." Major Payne pointed to the gear spread across the deck next to the uglymobile.

"It's nice to be back," the specialist replied, studying the tripod and how it didn't fit with anything else she was carrying. "Where am I supposed to put this?"

"Tie it around your pack," Turbo replied. "At least you're not hauling this fucking thing."

"If they aren't bitching, they aren't happy. Joy and salutations!" Dank called. He was the last one to arrive. He carried two bags that he immediately stuffed into their ship's inside storage. "A little something from Cookie. Shelf-stable protein that looks and tastes like beef jerky."

"I think we need to try that first before we allocate some of our precious cargo space to it." Payne gestured at himself. "Hand it over."

Dank grinned as he pulled ten individual packets from the pouch on his uniform. "Warmed to body temperature for your eating pleasure."

"Can't follow orders, and you're gross." Heckler pointed at Major Dank while making eyes at Payne.

"You love us, especially since we're hauling the heavy artillery."

Dank passed them out, and everyone unwrapped and sniffed their prizes before taking a bite.

"Just when Cookie starts getting good, we're leaving the ship," Blinky complained.

"But we're coming back," Payne said. "There's been a change in mission. Soon after we hit orbit, we're going planet-side to conduct reconnaissance. We'll be first to see the faces of the ones behind the Blaze Collective."

"Are we going to lay waste?" Heckler wondered, looking at the seventy kilograms of gear he was going to have to carry.

"No. Snoopy and eyeballs," Payne replied.

"Fighting the last battle. Maybe we can do without the cannons?"

"On the planet, they could have tanks and air cover. What would we do about them?"

"Since surrender isn't an option, I guess the pulse cannons are better than nothing."

"We go in heavy because we don't know what we're going to encounter. Get your suits on and armor up."

The team dumped their clothes around the area, counting on the bots to clean the mess before they returned. Their suits had been cleaned and repaired since the last mission, courtesy of those same bots.

"You gonna blow chunks this time, Buzz?" Turbo teased.

"That was a one-off. Won't happen again, Turbo," Buzz replied with confidence.

Before the banter could continue, Payne interrupted. "Buzz, you, Blinky, and Joker be ready to break into any system we can find. Did you make any progress on their ship software during the downtime?"

"A little," Blinky replied.

The major rolled his finger because he knew there was more.

"The progress was in adapting this modulator to see the signals we missed." He rolled a small device between his fingers before stuffing it back into his suit's side pocket. "The right signals were discovered in our broadband sensor sweeps but not in any of the normal data frequencies. Thanks to Lev, we are now equipped to see *and* exploit them. All we need is a ship to talk with or hope that they use the same kind of technology on the surface. Or we'll be starting over."

"Plan to start over," Sparky suggested. "Will I get a chance to examine any power grids?"

"Don't know," the major replied. "I don't know much of anything. We'll get a quick info dump with whatever Lev can collect before we launch and during insertion, but it appears that most of their fleet has departed. We won't be coming into a hot zone, at least not in space."

The team finished getting dressed and gearing up. The subtle augmentation of the suits helped them carry their loads, but it came at a cost. They took a quick jog around the hangar bay. "This is maximum loadout. Depending on where we land, we might want to dump two of the pulse cannons.

"That would make travel a whole lot easier," Payne admitted. "We'll reconfigure on landing. Grab those air rifles and load them up."

When they finished getting into place on the globe-shaped insertion craft, there was no room to move.

"The good news is that if we crash, we're not going to be thrown around!" Major Dank noted.

"Arriving in five...four..." Lev continued the countdown until the ship dropped out of FTL. He kept enough forward speed to flow the ship into a natural orbit. Within seconds, four cruisers were accelerating toward the ship.

"No one on board," Lev reported. Offensive and defensive weapon systems went live, filling the sky in the four directions with plasma, projectiles, lasers, and missiles. *Leviathan* surged toward a low orbit as the four ships succumbed one by one to the overwhelming firepower.

They hadn't stood a chance. By firing from a lower angle, *Leviathan* kept stray firepower from heading toward the planet's surface, where five billion life signs still registered.

"Launching the team," Lev reported. The insertion vehicle lovingly called the uglymobile pitched out the open hangar door and angled into the upper atmosphere.

"Sky is clear. Space is clear," Lev reported.

Captain Dorsite leaned back in the chair on the dais and crossed her arms. "Tactical is clear. Energy signatures to a distance of two light-years are non-threatening. No inbounds, and all previously identified outbounds are off the board."

"Assume geosynchronous orbit above the team to provide supporting firepower if needed. Reload and restock. Scan the surface in the greatest detail and provide landing coordinates and information to Major Payne."

Tamony looked bored. "Of course they went away. They didn't want to die. Now we're here and have no idea where they are. What if they are headed toward Earth?"

"Then it'll take them a month to get there," the admiral

replied. "One doesn't just abandon their home planet. There's something else in play that we're missing."

"Information passed to the insertion vehicle and Team Payne," Lev reported.

"Now we wait." The admiral walked off the bridge. "Going for a cup of coffee," he shouted over his shoulder. "No cart needed, Lev. I'll walk. I could use the exercise and need to kill some time. Come on, Declan Payne. Do us proud."

The uglymobile bounced through the upper atmosphere and into clear skies over Parallax. The vehicle decelerated almost immediately and made a wide and lazy circle around the biggest city.

"Lev picked a wooded area just outside the city in which to touch down. It will be our base of operation. I'd like to split the team to cover more ground. Major Dank will take Heckler, Sparky, Shaolin, and Buzz. You'll take one pulse cannon with you and go south. Bring up the maps on your HUDs and come up with a route. Keep the ship apprised of your progress. We'll go northwest. Don't get yourselves too deep into the city."

The team gave a hearty thumbs-up and sat back to study the information shared to their heads-up displays.

"Anything new, Lev?" Payne asked.

"Five billion life forms, but they aren't moving around like one would generally see from a society."

"What are you saying?"

"The life forms appear to be static. They are not moving around."

"Why didn't you tell us this before?"

"I didn't know it before, Declan. Everything until this

moment was a snapshot in time. I now have multiple data points from which to work."

"That's not how a civilization works. There has to be some movement. There's something wrong, Lev."

"New orders," Payne broadcast over the team channel. "We're staying together. The life signs on the planet haven't moved since we got here. None of them."

Dank nodded. "That's too fucking weird." The major looked at the information from Lev about the static life forms. "I like the idea of staying together. We can split up later if we find that there's no threat. Are they in suspended animation or something? Maybe they're fake signatures."

"Nothing is off the table. Bring up your HUDs. Map study. We'll follow a route out of the woods northwest from the landing location. We'll set up two pulse cannons with remote fire along this route here, with a firing arc here," Payne used his eyes to highlight the map, "to protect our egress. We will investigate this outer block with minimal life forms to see what's up. We will keep clear terrain behind us and will move in diamond formation. Turbo on point. Heckler on the right flank and Buzz on the left. Virge, you're at six o'clock. Blinky and I will ride the rocking chair."

The team gave their thumbs-up and used their eye movements to fill in the diamond where each would be. The formation provided the maximum amount of firepower when the enemy could attack from any direction.

Even though the rear would remain clear, Payne didn't rule out someone being able to get behind them. If the enemy had high-speed vehicles, they could easily outmaneuver a team on foot.

The uglymobile made the final descent at high speed, pulling up at the last instant to settle on the ground with barely a bump. The side doors slid upward, and the team disembarked into the bright sunshine, running from the ship on the vector Payne had designated. The team members moved into position, leaving at least ten meters between them. Blinky and Payne remained in the center, equidistant from the point and tail and two flanks.

"Move out," Payne ordered. The ship buttoned up. Payne looked back to find the mesh on the outside helped it blend into the foliage. If one looked right at it, they could see it, but otherwise, it was well-camouflaged. "Good job, Progs," Payne muttered to himself.

Turbo moved slowly. Rarely did the team set foot on an alien planet, and each time it had come with its own challenges.

First humans to set foot on Parallax, the place where it all started for the Blaze, Payne thought. *Fuck those asswipes! This war needs to end, and the bastards that started it need to pay the price for the suffering they've caused. Lev came to the same conclusion, but a thousand years too late.*

Payne exhaled fully to slow his breathing and school his thoughts. With Lev inside his head, he didn't have the freedom for mental flights of fancy. *What you think, you say. What you say, you do. What you do, you are.*

The trees wore a shade of blue and orange that clashed with human expectations regarding how trees should look. They carried heavy foliage, but the growth was mature, and the lowest branches were above their tallest team member's head.

Buzz stopped to run a tendril from the tree through his hand. He shook his head and gently let go.

It was team policy to cause no damage to flora or fauna on alien planets. The lesson had been hard-learned on the lush moon over Orion-13, where a tree had screamed like a banshee when they broke off a small limb to take back as a sample. Since they never knew what would alert the locals to their presence, they didn't need the unnecessary risk.

Turbo held up a clenched fist, and the team instantly stopped. There was no movement in any direction. Their HUDs remained clear. Turbo pointed to her right and slashed to designate the location for the first pulse cannon. She mirrored her movements to the left. Shaolin swooped in to set up the tripod with the control actuator. Buzz connected the cannon and stepped back. Turbo activated it and rotated the weapon.

Byle set up the second tripod, and Heckler dropped his cannon onto it. He activated it and ran it through a quick aiming routine, then gave the thumbs-up and fell back into formation.

Turbo looked over her shoulder to catch Payne's hand signal to move out. She stepped out of the concealment the woods afforded into a clear area. The side of a metropolis lay before them, from small blockish buildings on the outskirts to high rises toward the center. The city spread before them like it had no end.

Payne checked his HUD to find the life signs had remained static. Lev's feed from orbit through the ship to their suits had not changed. Things were alive, but nothing moved.

Turbo slow-jogged across the open area. The team members matched her pace until they reached the outermost building. Clustered life signs were in the next one. After that, they'd be all around.

Heckler gestured at a low and squarish doorway in the building with no windows. He pointed to his eyes and then to the door. Payne designated Joker to go with him.

Without a sound, he pushed the door open and crawled through. Inside, the ceiling was too low for him to walk upright. He bent his knees and tried to keep his helmet level to get the best view of his surroundings.

Joker made it inside, squatting like Heckler to see what was there. Boxy shapes of metal, none of which would open. Scans were inconclusive. Metal and silicon.

Heckler transmitted an image from his HUD. "Looks like computer components, but we can't see inside or snag anything small enough to analyze. Investigation is a bust. Returning outside."

He backed up to cover Joker's egress, then followed her out. They returned to their positions at three o'clock and four-thirty.

At a gesture from Payne, Turbo moved out.

"Triangle formation covering the front of the occupied building. Heckler, Shaolin, and Joker, you go in. Don't touch anything. Observe and report back. Blinky, go with them and do your thing."

"Roger," Heckler replied. Turbo moved past the two-story block-shaped windowless building and took a position on the corner. To her left, Byle crouched in the middle of a concrete area that could have been a road, but there were no lines. On the left flank, Buzz aimed outboard. He was the only one with his back to the building.

Sparky and Dank at the rear covered the area from which they had just come. Blinky pointed to the door and strode that way, making eye contact with Heckler before he led the group inside.

Heckler went first through the low doorway, walking slowly to avoid making any sounds. Shaolin followed. Joker stayed back with Blinky while he accessed his computer, setting it on a box similar in design to what Heckler had seen in the first building. He brought his system up while Joker looked for a signal they could tap. Blinky plugged the modulator into his computer and started tapping.

Between that and the comm suite, they saw the digital world around them.

He transmitted what he was seeing to the major. "This whole place is one huge digital infrastructure."

"A modern society is interconnected at all times and in almost all ways. Sounds like Earth."

"This is a hundred times more intense than Earth," Blinky replied.

"They are more advanced. I'm not surprised. Keep trying to get in. Heckler, report."

"We are climbing to the second story. The life forms are on both sides of a single hallway. We are looking to my right. These aliens are short."

Heckler pushed the door open with the barrel of his weapon.

"What the hell?" He dropped to a knee to look through the doorway to get the full scope of what was in the room. "I see five boxes like we've seen everywhere else. That's it."

He slowly backed into the hallway. Shaolin replicated Heckler's movements at the other room, but she pushed inside. He backed up against the door with his weapon trained on the doorway of the room he just vacated.

Inside the room, Shaolin tiptoed from one box to the next. Only four were there. She scanned them from point-blank range to confirm the life signs were real.

"Confirmed," she reported. "There is something alive inside these boxes. Not sure about breathing, but organic and active. Getting more active. The box is lifting off the floor."

"Get out here!" Heckler shouted. Shaolin yanked the door open and dove into the hallway, nearly knocking Heckler over. "We have movement."

Heckler and Shaolin ran down the stairs to find Blinky and Joker with their gear laid out like they had all the time in the world.

"We're leaving. Grab your trash."

"But..." Blinky started as one of the metal boxes hovered at the landing halfway down the steps. Blinky shoved his stuff into a bag and backed slowly toward the door. Joker scooped her gear into her arms and rushed outside.

"Movement," Buzz reiterated.

"I think it's time to go. We don't fire first. We invaded the metalheads. Exit that building, Heckler. Virgil, you are on point. Take us back to the uglymobile."

Shaolin popped into the street.

Heckler was almost outside when a focused beam fired from the box and hit him in the chest. He was thrown out the door to slide into the street, and he grunted in pain. "Light 'em up."

Shaolin turned her railgun loose on the doorway and stitched a line of rounds up the side of the building in the hope of hitting the creature.

Or creation. They didn't know which.

[26]

"SOMETIMES A TACTICAL RETROGRADE LOOKS JUST LIKE RUNNING AWAY. BUT EVENTUALLY THE ENEMY WILL FACE YOU AGAIN, AND NEXT TIME, YOU'LL BE READY."
—FROM THE MEMOIRS OF FLEET ADMIRAL THAYLON LOORE

"Let's go, people. On your feet and double-time!" Payne ordered. The metal boxes appeared, a few at first and then more. A beam lit the already bright roadway and sent Byle flying into the air.

Turbo fired relentlessly, giving the boxes all her railgun would deliver. A few impacts, and the box burst and tumbled to the ground.

Payne leveled his pulse cannon and started hitting the buildings one by one, ripping the stone and metalwork apart, destroying doorways, and trapping within whatever was inside.

Buzz ran to Byle and helped her, all the time firing with one hand. Byle threw an arm over Buzz's shoulder and picked up the call to arms, unleashing her railgun on full automatic to spread destruction along a wide path.

They turned and started running while Payne continued firing.

"Bounding overwatch," Payne called between the triple plasma launches. He blasted the building to his right a couple of times as penance for starting the firefight. They were leaving, but no, they had to be the enemy and do enemy things like shoot first.

"It didn't have to be like this!" Payne shouted at the destruction he was delivering to the outskirts of Parallax's main city. As soon as the railguns picked up their fire, he turned and ran between the two lines of outbound rounds. Once he was past them by fifty meters, He turned back, took a knee, and sent well-aimed pulse cannon rounds down the street, more to intimidate than destroy.

One more bound and they were back at the tree line, still firing at the random locals who brought their square boxes into the open.

"Set those pulse cannons to shoot at anything that moves this way."

Heckler issued the commands to both weapons systems. "Motion detection is active."

"Take us home, Virge."

The team ran through the woods. As they approached the uglymobile, the side doors slipped upward, and the team filled the seats. Payne took one last look behind him before climbing aboard. Out of sight, the pulse cannons banged away at a steady rate. "Lev, get us out of here."

The ship sealed and lifted off, maintaining a low flight profile until it was well away from the city before it arced skyward and accelerated.

Payne looked at his team. "What happened in there?"

Shaolin spoke. "My fault, sir. They didn't like me in their

bedroom. I couldn't believe the boxes were life forms and wanted a closer scan. You know how weak these helmets are."

"I know. Did you get a look at them?"

"Metal boxes. I never saw anything organic."

"Any ideas what that beam was?" Payne looked at Heckler, then Byle.

Byle raised her hand. "As the enemy's favorite target, I'll tell you that it felt like getting hit by a ram. I was pummeled and thrown backward. It lifted me off the ground, and with this suit and the gear, I'm weighing in around two hundred and fifty kilos. There was some momentum behind that."

"It looked like light. Light doesn't have mass to create momentum."

"Felt solid to me," Heckler added. The residual pain from the impact made him grunt his words.

"We'll have to check the sensor files. Did you see anything, Lev?" Payne asked. "And you two. You're going to medical as soon as we get back."

"They're already tired of seeing me," Byle said in a soft voice as she tried to keep from taking too deep a breath.

"I have all the information from the insertion vehicle's sensors, and analysis is underway. It is a new weapon, and I don't understand how it works. Yet, that is. I recognize that it had significant power, and had you not been wearing your suits, its impact would have been fatal."

"So much for non-lethal weapons," Payne muttered. "I need to talk with the admiral. I don't like the implications of what we saw down there."

Dank took off his helmet and shouted, "Jerk me!" with a smile. He reached into the compartment, took out packs of the jerky substitute, and handed them down the line. The mood had grown too somber. Another mission down. Intelligence collected, and no one was dead. It was a minor victory, but still one worth celebrating. The team took off their helmets so they could eat.

Dank looked at Payne from the other end of the uglymobile's passenger compartment. "We have no idea where the enemy is, and this whole thing with Parallax was a planet-level diversion."

"And they know where we are and what we're capable of without us learning a whole lot about them except that they were willing to donate a couple dreadnoughts to learn that they have comparable firepower. Those two dreadnoughts that took everything Lev had to take them down were expendable. I'm not sure I want to find out what they have that isn't."

Once the spherical ship landed, the team tumbled out and immediately started dumping their gear.

"Keep that garbage organized!" Payne called. "Lev, can you get us a cargo lift to get the guns and ammo to the armory? I'd like to keep them stored and out of the way for the next time we need them."

"I can set up an armory in here with access for you and your team only," Lev offered.

"Make it so, Number One." Payne followed with a thumbs-up. The team stripped naked and gave Payne a view of the bruising from the impacts. "Holy crap, look at you!"

Byle and Heckler were black and blue. Bruises covered nearly their entire torsos. "Get them to medical before a clot from that garbage breaks free. There could be internal injuries. Congratulations, Byle. You're the first two-time winner during our deployment on *Leviathan*."

"I feel like I should give a speech." Byle delivered the royal wave. A cart stopped nearby and they both climbed aboard, carrying their coveralls because it was too painful for them to lift their legs to get their clothes on.

Payne gestured with his head at Major Dank. Virgil nodded and jumped on the cart with the injured.

"Turbo, make sure these weapons get put up."

"Roger, and for your info, the targeting and firing mechanisms on the tripods were set to self-destruct when they ran out of ammo or were compromised. We won't be facing our own weapons."

"That's good gouge, Turbo, and as we all know, an ounce of gouge is worth a pound of knowledge." He faced the team. "Clean up for debrief in an hour in the dining hall, and then downtime until we set the training schedule. We need to be faster and stronger and probably smarter, too, for next time. Blinky and Joker, I want to know what you found, but at the debrief."

As soon as Payne was dressed, he unwrapped his jerky and took a bite. He grabbed an available cart and didn't bother saying out loud where he wanted to go. Lev already knew.

The bridge.

When he arrived, he found the rest of the crew waiting. He was the main attraction.

The admiral leaned back to listen. There were no chairs left in the immediate area around the dais. Payne leaned against the platform and crossed his arms. He knew his posture was defensive, but he was tired and would have preferred to sit and sprawl across a conference table.

"It was a city of biomechanical creations. Boxy, so no way to tell which ones were live and which weren't. We saw an awful lot of spare boxes. Once they felt our active scans, they woke up. I don't know any other way to describe it. We would have been fine, but they have a weapon that looks like a beam of light but hits like a battering ram. Outside of that, we collected what data we could for Blinky, Lev, and Buzz to analyze."

"Is it worth going back down there?" The admiral was blunt.

"No. There's nothing for us down there. If they had any central command facility or intelligence controlling it all, they would have taken it with them. Parallax was an elaborate ruse. Maybe they started setting this trap the last time *Leviathan* was active a thousand years ago."

"We proved their patience to be well-founded. And they chased us with half their fleet to set an example?"

"Maybe get a win and destroy *Leviathan*, but they hedged their bet by leaving half of their fleet behind. It also tells me that they don't have FTL communication. They needed their ships to act as couriers to announce the return of the Progs."

The admiral rubbed his chin in thought.

"We stirred up a hornet's nest, and the only way to keep it from following us home is by keeping up the pressure, so the first thing we're going to do is go home."

The commodore shot him a surprised look. Tamony sighed in relief.

"Home is relative," the admiral continued. "I think it would be best to meet with the Fleet and let them know to be prepared, and also so they won't feel compelled to come after us, thinking we're lost. Maybe we can plan some low impact raids to keep the Blaze Collective's forces on their heels while we dive deep into enemy territory."

"We can accomplish all of that from Earth," Tamony Swiss insisted.

"But then there would be a twelve to fourteen-day delay to let the front lines know that the bad guys might be coming. It's only been a couple days since they learned of us at Parallax. We should be in front of anything the Blaze lackeys will hear. That's still ten days away at the soonest." The admiral crossed his arms. He had received all the input he needed.

"We can fold to Earth, and the second Leviathan is recharged, we can fold to the front lines. That's four or five days at the most, which still puts us in front of the enemy. Three more days, and we can be out of there well before an enemy Fleet arrives if *Leviathan* doesn't want to engage since they will be manned by what you called lackeys when we're going after the main prize. But you can now talk with the Ebren, the Berantz, or any of the other races."

For the first time, the financier made sense and it didn't sound self-serving, which put Payne on edge. The admiral seemed skeptical, too.

"What's in it for you?" Payne blurted.

"I get off this ship," Tamony replied, "and back to my life of executive parties and grandstanding. Although you may deplore an individual such as me, you know that people like me are a necessity. I like my life, and you reap the rewards therefrom."

The admiral watched the civilian closely. "Although I don't agree with a lot of that, your logic makes sense to me. Back to Earth first, and then as soon as Lev is ready, we're going to the front lines and my headquarters to meet with the team there. Arthir, I'll need you to guide the tactics of engagement for the Fleet."

Captain Dorsite pointed to the chair upon which she sat. "But working with Lev is incredible," she argued. "And there are a bunch of admirals out there who would get royally miffed when a mere captain steps in to give them orders."

"Fleet Admiral Dorsite, Acting. They'll have no choice but to follow your lead. We'll need to get those translation programs installed throughout the Fleet on every damn ship we own and even on ones we don't. Our strategic goal is suing for peace. It's a completely different mindset. You understand what we'll be doing out here, and pretty soon, the Blaze lackeys will too, especially when we explain it in their language."

"Driving a wedge between the front lines and the head shed," Arthir replied. "I see the wisdom in it. Yes, Admiral Wesson. I think I am up for the challenge."

"Commodore?" the admiral asked.

"Although I'd like to return to my position because I believe the BEP needs me, I think it would be better to remain on board *Leviathan*. I heard someone say that offense is the best defense, and I've spent my entire career believing a strong defense was in and of itself a sufficient deterrent. I am questioning that premise. Admiral, Captain, Major, your efforts have not gone unnoticed."

Payne didn't care what she noticed. Lev had told him about the battle over Ganymede and BEP's refusal to participate until the fight was at the end and victory was all but guaranteed—after the Fleet had lost both *Sirus* and fifteen hundred crew aboard *Cleophas*. He couldn't forgive the commodore for that. Not yet. He also didn't care if she stayed aboard. Lev had her locked out of the important spaces besides the bridge where he could keep an eye on her. Payne chose to remain silent on the issue of the commodore.

The admiral kept his composure throughout.

"You're welcome to stay. In that case, we won't need any other BEP personnel, and I'll reject any applications to join *Leviathan*'s crew. It would help if you talked to them first and told them not to waste their time and mine."

"Yes, Admiral Wesson," she replied with undue formality.

"Do you two have enough to do?" the admiral asked the other two civilians. Davida was nowhere to be found, but Lev had vouched for her, so the admiral didn't question it.

Lewis answered first. "I have so much to learn about how *Leviathan* handles its own logistics with internal material shifts and then fabrication. So efficient. I would like to stay if you'll have me."

The admiral nodded.

Malcolm Russell licked his lips and took his time before speaking. "I just got my lab set up. Yes. I'd like to stay."

The admiral smiled. "What extra support do you need, Major?"

"Armory officer to work with Lev and get us the firepower we need. Mechanized combat suits to offset some of the issues we've run across, so a mech engineer, and this was supposed to be Major Dank's last mission before he picked up his own SOF team. If they are still available, we could pick them up and get me a new XO, and then we'll have double the behind-the-lines insertion capability. Everything we've seen so far could have been handled by two well-trained teams. And, I think Davida will be of great assistance in cracking into the Blaze systems."

"I agree with Declan," Lev said. "Two teams of specialists to get into the enemy's rear areas."

"Sounds dirty when you say it like that, Lev," Payne quipped. The admiral gave him a patronly look. "At least it wasn't me who said it."

"What about space fighters and pilots?"

Payne vigorously shook his head. "Being outside this ship during an engagement would be a death sentence."

"What about tactical support for planetary operations?"

Payne's eyebrows lifted as he contemplated how far he would have gotten in Parallax's main city if he'd had close air support. "That could work."

"Add a squadron of Mosquito-class fighters with all support personnel to the list, Lev, and we'll transmit as soon as we arrive in Earth space. Any other questions?"

"I would like to wish you all the very best. I believe that I am owed terraforming technology? If that could be loaded to a memory device for me to take with, I'd be eternally grateful. There will be plaques hung in your honor."

No one answered him. "Lev, how long to arrive in proximity to Earth?"

"Navigation calculations are complete. We can leave at any time."

"Take us to Earth, Lev."

[27]

"He who arrives first with the most will win the day." –From the memoirs of Fleet Admiral Thaylon Loore

Leviathan folded into a near orbit of Earth's moon. The lunar surface almost filled the screen.

"That's cutting it a bit close, Lev, don't you think?"

"A thousand kilometers on a fold of eleven hundred light-years? That's like hitting a pea using a trebuchet with a sack of potatoes launched twice around the world. And it wasn't that close, really. We were supposed to be on the other side of the planet..." Lev's voice drifted off.

Payne could feel that the ship was messing with them, and he approved.

"Messages away, Harry, Nyota, and Tamony."

"I'll use my shuttle to return to Earth. Thank you. It's been real and it's been fun, but it hasn't been real fun."

He strode briskly from the bridge to a waiting cart. Like taxis hovering outside bars, there always seemed to be one available. It was almost like Lev was reading their minds.

The commodore hurried after him. The civilians took their leave and strolled away. Arthir unhooked herself from the captain's chair and stepped off the dais. "Admiral, it's been a pleasure to go where we've never been and to do things that have never been done before. Next time we meet, may it be at a drawdown ceremony where we can start sending our troops home."

They shook hands. "To peace, my friend. And you know better than anyone what is possible if we do it right. Wear your new rank proudly, and get the job done."

The newly frocked admiral walked off the bridge with a spring in her step and her head held high.

Fleet Admiral Harry Wesson strolled around the bridge, touching the stations that needed no one to operate. The admiral didn't need a bridge crew or even a staff. He only needed people who contributed to the mission.

A mission he had fought his whole life to undertake.

Major Payne appeared out of nowhere.

"I thought everyone had left."

"Not everyone, Admiral. I have nowhere to go. I'm at my assigned station."

"Maybe get some liberty for your people. Send the shuttle to the planet so they can get some real food, real booze, and warm company. Or have you been in space so long you've forgotten what you can find on Earth?"

"Almost forgotten, but not quite." He meandered toward the big screen; the moon took up less space since Lev had moved the ship to a higher orbit. "I'll take care of it. I better let Virgil know that he has to stop goofing off and get to work because the admiral said so."

"The requests to join the crew are arriving, Admiral," Lev interrupted. "There are over one thousand, and it's only been five minutes. At this rate, we'll get one hundred thousand volunteers."

"We're going to take a hundred people for the Mosquito squadron and another fifteen in SOF team and support personnel. Maybe one more cook, too."

"Send up samples of good Tex-Mex, deep dish from Chicago, gnocchi from Firenze, cheesesteaks from Philadelphia, and sushi from Osaka. It's all coming back to me, sir."

"Go on, son. Get your team spooled up. Take the skimmer and not the UM."

"UM?"

"Uglymobile, Major. You named it. You own it."

"We'll have an award ceremony on board before we ship out to the front. I have medals I'm obligated to give people."

"Bringing Galen on board to cook for us was all the reward we needed and probably more than we deserved."

"Probably so, but I'm an admiral, and this is the kind of stuff I have to do. Get off this ship for a couple days and enjoy yourself."

"If I must, Admiral." Payne delivered a quick salute and headed for the med lab to find out how long it would be before Heckler and Byle could travel.

You could just ask, Lev said into his mind.

"I'm old-school, Lev. You'll train me eventually. How long until they're ready?"

"Deep bruising is easy. Nothing was broken, and no internal injuries. They've both been released and are back in their quarters, getting ready to go planetside."

"I guess I don't need to go to medical anymore. How about the quarters area where my people can be found?"

"Exactly where you're going, Declan."

He wasn't surprised that Lev had never intended to take him to medical. He hadn't needed to say a word. He enjoyed the quick ride to his quarters, where he checked his gear. Payne had brought a minimal number of personal items with him from *Cleophas*, which included a single set of civilian clothes for the short liberties he took. He dressed in them, put his ship boots on underneath, and checked his short hair. It didn't need combing. He left everything else except his credit chip to pay for whatever he needed.

Payne had no idea how much money was in his account but expected it would be substantial since he never spent any of it.

He stepped into the corridor. "First round is on me, and the next one is on whoever is last to get to the skimmer!" he bellowed. The team appeared in all states of dress. "Liberty granted for the next forty-eight hours. All ashore who's going ashore, and there's only one express train going down. Choo-choo!" He motioned like he was pulling a train whistle.

"Liberty?" Heckler asked, bending awkwardly to take pressure off his ribcage.

"Admiral's orders. I have to take you hooligans to town. I'll brief you on *Glamorous Glennis*. Get it in gear, SOFTies. We are leaving."

Payne climbed into a cart and drummed his fingers on the seat while he waited. Shaolin, Byle, Sparky, Joker, Turbo, and Heckler joined him.

"Don't tell me. Blinky and Buzz don't want to come ashore because they're playing computers with Lev."

"Well, they are, but you make it sound like it's an ignoble affair when I assure you it is glorious!" Lev quipped.

Payne looked at his chuckling team. "Lev, did we warp your personality, or were you always like this?"

"The Progenitors were a bit stodgy, with no senses of humor. You see, reading minds dampens one's imagination as it could be misinterpreted. Yet, they instilled in me the sense of humor that they lacked, and you humans represent a delicious departure."

"Don't make me punch you right in your digital face," Turbo barked. "Delicious, indeed."

"Of course, Marsha. Please accept my apologies."

"Come on, Virgil. You have your team to pick up."

Major Dank popped into the corridor. "I do? Am I leaving?"

"Leaving to pick up your team and bring them back here. Give them those rooms down there. We're keeping the good ones." Payne waved nonchalantly.

"Sir, all the rooms are the same," Heckler said.

"His new team doesn't know that."

"I heard that."

"Hurry up, Virgil. You'll have no team if the skimmer leaves and you're not on it. I'm not ferrying their dumb asses up here for you."

"Be that way, Dec. Off, trusty steed!" he shouted while still running, his uniform unzipped and his boots unsecured.

"No civvies?"

"I'm picking up my team. Drop me off at Space HQ."

"Albuquerque it is. We're staying there, too. They'll have rooms for us on base, and we can keep our ride parked there without a hassle."

"Will they roll out the red carpet for us?" Byle asked.

"Purple carpet for you. Most damaged specialist version. No, they're not rolling out any carpet for us. We're incognito. No one cares who we are or what we've done. Let's keep it that way. A few drinks and some righteous Tex-Mex, tacos, and burritos. I'm buying. You guys deserve it."

They rode to the hangar bay three decks up in silence and rolled out to find the commodore and Tamony Swiss still aboard.

"I thought you guys would be long gone." Payne gestured for his team to board the skimmer.

"A minor holdup, but we'll have clearance soon."

"What do you need clearance for? It's Earth, and you're humans. Aren't you?" Payne joked.

"We are going directly to the international headquarters in Tokyo. Clearance has to be requested days in advance. We've asked for emergency consideration."

"I thought you were somebody, Tam?" Payne quipped. The man scowled above his immaculate white suit. "I'm sure you'll get it. Don't mind us. We're going to SOFTie Central. Clearance is automatic unless it's not, and then we'll feign like we're crashing. There's an ice-cold beer in my future."

Payne waved over his shoulder and was the last to board the skimmer. The door rotated to a close and sealed as soon as he was inside. He took the command seat up front and studied the controls for a few seconds before remembering how to fly the thing.

"You'd think I hadn't just flown this a couple weeks ago. Or was it a month?"

"More like six."

"Don't mess with me, Turbo," Payne said, waving his pointer finger over his shoulder to get her attention.

Someone cat-called.

The ship lifted off the deck and rotated toward open space. A little acceleration, and the skimmer was out. Payne pegged it and sped past the moon toward the planet. They picked up speed to cover the distance from the Moon to the Earth in twenty minutes until he angled to hit the upper atmosphere and skip off it to slow down before nosing into it with the reverse thrusters active to keep the heat buildup to a minimum. The skimmer stopped bouncing as it cleared the turbulence of reentry over the Pacific Ocean.

"Descending toward the spaceport. Break, break. Space Ops Control, this is *Glamorous Glennis* from *Leviathan* on final approach."

"Hands off, *Glennis*. We have the stick. Vectoring to one-niner, landing spot one-alpha as special envoys from the Fleet admiral. Welcome home."

"I knew there would be a red carpet," Byle said with a grin.

"Don't let it go to your heads," the major warned, but he couldn't contain his smile when he looked back at his team. They gave him the thumbs-up. He rotated his seat to face the crew since the landing control system had taken over. "Get our rooms and then dinner off-base. After that, whatever bar will have us."

"I'm going to miss it, I fear," Virgil said. "I better check in with Personnel and see what's up. Maybe my new team will be available, and we can meet you out there."

"We won't wait up, but we'll save you seats," Payne replied.

The skimmer slowed and descended over mountains and desert and more mountains before the spaceport appeared on the main screen.

"How long's it been?" Payne asked.

"Nine years," Heckler said.

"Only two for me," Joker added.

"Eighteen months, but I was the noob until Fetus showed up." Shaolin waggled her eyebrows.

"Eleven for me," Payne said softly. "Almost my whole adult life. I was born in space and lived there. I only attended get-high school dirtside and then university. After that, straight into Space Ops Force because that's where the bad boys served. Back into space and never came back."

That sobered the crew, and the banter stopped.

"Shaolin, you have the duty to show us the way. Joker, make sure we have transport. I better check in with Virge at the head shed just to show the flag. Looks like landing at sixteen fifteen local. Perfect. Dinner at seventeen thirty. Turbo, find us a place for good chow, lots of it and cheap, but good."

"I heard you were paying. Cheap, good, and will have us. We only get two of the three, and since you're buying, we're going to eat well. It'll be cheap for us."

"Fine. That's what I get by not doing it myself." The junior members of the team were assigned the group duties. It was just how it worked. No one complained because they knew it was important. It was an easy win for the junior specialists.

The skimmer touched down.

Heckler moved to the hatch and stepped aside. "You know how it is, sirs. Senior to junior getting off. We have to play nice now that we're down here."

"Feels heavier than normal," Payne said as the door slowly rose away from the ship and short steps descended.

"There is nothing more normal than Earth. You've been spoiled with artificial gravity, sir."

Payne stepped out, legs feeling more rubbery than they should have. He realized the gravity on Parallax was less than that of Earth, more like what they had on board the ship. "Try carrying a seventy-kilo pack in this shit," Payne grumbled, clenching his teeth at how his body was responding to what should have felt like home.

He looked at the sky. His home was up there.

A van waited for them. They were greeted by a sharp salute from a specialist recruit who waited for them to board before he jumped into the driver's seat and drove straight to headquarters.

"Where's our quarters for the next two nights?" Payne asked. The specialist pointed two buildings away. "Seventeen thirty, right out front. Can you have a taxi for us, van size?"

"Not a problem, sir," the youngster replied with too much enthusiasm.

Payne and Dank climbed out and headed inside while the van drove off.

They found the officer on duty, who welcomed them like

long-lost friends. Dank leaned close. "What did the Fleet admiral say?" Virgil whispered to Declan.

"Must have been profound."

A two-star admiral came out to greet them. He smiled and a duty photographer captured holoimages of the handshakes with the two majors, followed by inane small talk about the greatest ship in the galaxy—hollow platitudes that meant nothing. The majors smiled for the cameras, all the while growing increasingly uncomfortable.

Once the camera shut down, the admiral ushered them into his office and shut the door.

"I was hoping to meet my new team," Dank said.

"Sorry, Major. They're not here, but we've recalled them. They should be back tomorrow morning sometime. Be here by ten, and they shouldn't be too far behind you." He faced Payne. "And you! Single-handedly brought *Leviathan* into the Fleet."

"I have a team. Specialist Katello Andfen and Specialist Alphonse Periq broke the code and were able to talk with *Leviathan* first. They made everything else possible. All credit goes to them."

"Nonsense, my boy. You're in charge. Take the credit that's due."

Payne nodded. He had no such intention, but arguing with flag officers wouldn't change their opinion. Making sure his people were given what they were due was his responsibility.

"We're having an award ceremony onboard *Leviathan* in two days when you return to your ship. Please be sober for that event, but I can't blame you if you weren't. Just don't be obvious about it. Thanks to you, we are closer to peace than we have ever been," the admiral bubbled happily.

"What did the Fleet admiral send down here that is making everyone overjoyed?"

"His report was rather spectacularly received. It's all anyone is talking about. Look." He brought up the video screen in his office and displayed a news report showing a sketchy image of *Leviathan* sitting beyond the moon in the bright sunlight. Major Payne's face appeared next to the admiral, but all they talked about was the major.

"Team is going to be pretty miffed. Why did the admiral do that? He should have taken the credit."

Payne scowled at the floor. "He wanted to be free from the attention. Maybe he thought it would be a good thing for you," Dank offered.

"After finding out what it's like, I see why he didn't want it and why he didn't come down here personally. We better find the team." They stood. "If you'll excuse us, sir." They walked out without saluting while the admiral continued to watch the video.

"It's like they've been taken over by happy aliens," Dank said. "Hey! Dinner's on you."

They strolled to the temporary billeting, where their rooms were waiting for them—standard with no frills. Payne felt more at home. He relaxed in his bed and realized that he had spent the least amount of time on his cushy mattress out of the entire crew.

"That sucks." He didn't remember anything else until the pounding on the door woke him up. It was time for dinner.

[28]

"We fight for those we left behind to have something to go back to." —From the memoirs of Fleet Admiral Thaylon Loore

"I can't drink anything else," Turbo slurred.

They ate at Texa-Mexa, a boutique restaurant with high-end tacos, which meant they were served on plates with Spanish rice and refried beans. And burritos and chimichangas. The team ate like they hadn't eaten in days.

Maybe they hadn't. Keeping track of time in space was relative at best, but they were eating well on the ship, too.

More time in the gym, Payne promised.

And then the drinks started arriving. Other diners toasted the team and then some. "Here's to Blinky! Here's to Buzz!" They toasted their missing teammates. "Here's to Virge getting his own team and me having to break in a new XO, fucking soft-bellied catfish."

"What?" Dank was in no better shape than his fellow major.

"Those hairy buttholes knew this would happen, and they dodged the limelight. They're going to pay for this!" Payne hammered his fist on the table, catching the edge of the nacho basket and sending it flying into the table next to theirs.

A minute of apologies later, Payne found himself with two more beers. The din died down as the food coma hit the team at the same time. "Taxi, please."

Payne had no idea what anything cost. The credit chip flashed green when he paid, so he had enough money to cover it. And the taxi. Another green flash. *I should look into what I have,* he vowed but forgot it the second his foot hit the ground. The team caught each other and stumbled into the billeting center, where the locals stepped aside and allowed them to pass.

"I like my cushy mattress," Payne muttered.

"We all do. Lev loves us." Sparky started to cry.

"Get a hold of yourself," Turbo took her by the arm, and they staggered to their doors. The others peeled off one by one until only Payne was left.

"I'm last," he said to no one. He opened his door to find a fruit basket on his table, compliments of the commanding admiral.

"If you could only see us now..." Payne did a striptease in front of the basket. He picked his clothes up off the floor and hung them on the chair because he only had the one set. Then he collapsed in bed, keeping one foot on the floor to stop the world from spinning around him while metal boxes shot beams of light that hammered his body.

"Can we go back to the ship?" Turbo asked. The others nodded and pointed at the sky. "Some fucking nutwit asked me to marry him."

"How drunk was he?" Heckler quipped and quickly threw up his hands in surrender at the withering look she gave him.

"He wasn't drunk at all. It gives me the willies being here." She scowled and shuffled away from the major.

"And everyone seems to know who we are," Joker added in a soft voice. "I prefer being anonymous. Whatever was planned for today, I don't want to leave base."

The others agreed. Heckler wore an easy smile.

"What?" Payne asked.

"Now you guys get a taste of what I've had to put up with my whole life. You think with these stunning looks I don't get marriage proposals, wined and dined, introduced to parents, and carried around on a throne borne by a pack of nubiles?"

The smug look on his face suggested he believed what he was saying. "You haven't been off a ship in nine years except on alien planets where we're conducting a hit and run. Butthole." Payne turned serious. "What do you guys want to do?"

"Mechs," Heckler stated. The others agreed.

"Your idea of liberty is to embrace the power of combat?"

"Ensuring we survive is a great way to get the most out of our time off," Turbo replied. "And if any lovestruck, moonfaced altar boys want to hit on me, they're going to get a metal fist in their piehole."

"Save the hostility for the enemy, Turbo. We're fighting for the people on this planet, not against them, no matter how star-crossed they are. Let's find the weapons people and see what we can wrangle. My idea of a vacation is hiking the Grand Canyon, but if you guys want to play soldier, we can do that."

Payne wasn't too keen on leaving the base either. He would meet his new executive officer today, as well as watch Virgil take control of his team. Double the firepower and more.

"We're going to get a serious upgrade, people," Payne told them. "Breakfast, then mechs. Heckler, you set up the mechs, and I'll walk the team to breakfast."

"The chow hall is right there!" Heckler pointed at the next building.

"We all have our jobs to do. Sometimes the luck of the draw is yours, and other times, you get to do what you love and be the first to play with the big guns."

Heckler returned to the billeting office to make a few calls. Payne strolled toward the dining facility to find that it had closed. "What madness is this?"

Byle read a sign on the door. "They have set dining for only two hours. Five-thirty in the morning to seven-thirty. That's just stupid."

Payne stared dumbly at the sign. He saw a specialist on the other side of the road. "Specialist! Where can we get some chow?"

"Bowling alley. It's open twenty-four-seven," she shouted back. Payne pointed both left and right. She pointed to his right. He gave her the thumbs-up.

"Looks like the bowling alley. Anyone ever bowl before?"

No one had.

"Doesn't matter. Twenty-four-seven chow is the best chow. Oorah." They mobbed down the sidewalk, looking for the location of the magical bowling alley. Two random specialists later, they found it two kilometers away.

Greasy omelets, hash browns, and what they thought was real bacon. None of it sat well in their stomachs.

"Look at how weak we've become," Shaolin noted. "I feel like puking." She shoved her half-full plate toward the center of the table.

Heckler rolled through the door, looking fresh as a daisy.

"Got a ride from the nice people at Billeting." He smiled while a female specialist stood behind him.

"He wasn't kidding," Sparky muttered.

Heckler kissed his driver on the cheek, and she beamed on her way out of the bowling alley.

"How in the hell does that happen?" Byle wondered.

"We're set. Ten-thirty," Heckler announced. He looked at Shaolin's plate.

She flicked her fingers at it. "All yours."

He grabbed an extra set of silverware and slid the plate to his side of the table. He added ketchup and hot sauce to everything and dug in as if it were the best thing he'd ever tasted.

"Much better than the chow hall," he said when he'd finished. He leaned back and patted his belly. "They have two test demo mechs of the type currently deployed. We'll get to take them for a spin, and if the major has any influence, we'll even be able to take the range hot."

Live fire.

Payne wouldn't mind seeing firsthand how the mechs worked. The SOFTies were about moving fast while maintaining a low profile. The mechs were heavy and stood out on every battlefield. They were used when high impact and intimidation were called for.

"We have a plan. Major Dank gets his team at ten. We can get a quick look at them and then off to the range. And Heckler, what was with...her?" He nodded at the door.

"She's the weapons tech."

"There's a match made in heaven," Turbo grunted. "Correct that. A match made on Earth for heaven." Her face fell. "Don't tell me she's coming."

"If we're going to get mechs..." Heckler said while looking for more food.

"Shipboard romances never work, Heckler." Turbo shot him a look.

"How would you know? You hate everybody." Heckler pointed as if he'd played the trump card.

"And I'm better for it," she declared.

Joker held her fingers to her head in her best impression of a fortune teller. "I predict that we'll win this war, and Heckler and Turbo will become Mr. and Mrs. Koch, retiring to a newly discovered planet to become frontier farmers."

The two stared at Joker as if she'd grown a third head.

Joker continued, "You can cut the tension with a knife. *Rawr!*"

Byle started to cough. Sparky put her credit chip on the table. "I got a hundred says Joker's right."

"What?" Heckler looked from Byle to Joker to Turbo. Heckler frantically dug for his chip, and after extricating it from his pocket, slammed it down on the table. "I'll take that bet."

"You're going to need those credits to buy your homestead license, but whatever. I'll take your money. Nothing like sweet spec seven money on my chip."

"Tell them!" Heckler looked at Turbo, gesturing frantically.

"Yes, honey, please tell us," Sparky quipped. "Your secret is *not* safe with us."

Payne stopped the madness by standing. "Time to go," he declared. "You guys have way too much energy. I don't need anyone getting hurt feelings. Planet Earth is different. It's not for people like us. We'll go back out there," he pointed at the sky, "and do what we do best. Protect the people down here so *they* can talk about who loves who and the future that *we* will give them. That's why everyone is starstruck by us; we embody hope. But you guys know how much work we have between now and then. We're fighting fucking drones and have almost lost people two encounters in a row. They're going to wear us down, but we have to keep fighting. Don't waste your brainpans on frontier farmsteads and miss the plasma grenade that lands at your feet."

"Mechs," Heckler said into the silence that followed. "We're bringing the pain. Team Payne."

"Exactly," the major replied. "I have to walk off this omelet so I can be hungry again for lunch. What were those hours again?"

Turbo chuckled. "I think they were twelve-fifteen to twelve-forty-five or something like that."

"Must be nice to have a regularly scheduled life," Payne quipped. "Scratch that. A life so regimented would suck. Team Payne, we are leaving."

[29]

"THE ENEMY IS NOTHING MORE THAN THE WILL OF ITS LEADERS." –From the memoirs of Fleet Admiral Thaylon Loore

Payne looked at his team, who looked at each other in turn. They turned back to the presentation of Dank's team members. Each seemed to be bigger than the one before—taller and wider.

"What kind of fertilizer did they use growing these?" Turbo whispered.

"We can spar with them once we get our mechs," Heckler replied.

"The bigger they are, the harder they fall." Byle frowned and subconsciously rubbed her side, where the bruise had added a green tint to the black and blue.

"If an enemy sees you and one of them, who do you think they're going to shoot first?" Payne offered and winked at Byle when they made eye contact.

"True."

"They're all dudes." Turbo spat on the ground.

"Their loss. Let's go. Major Dank will have his hands full with that lot."

"Wait!" the two-star called. "Your XO is here. I was just talking with her. Hang on."

Payne's ears perked up, as did those of his team members. They started to mill about aimlessly while watching intently for the admiral.

When he returned, Payne's anticipation came to a crawl.

Turbo tapped him on the shoulder. "You should see your face," she whispered while not taking her eyes off the new XO.

"I don't have to look at it, but she does."

The admiral beamed and bubbled as he presented the team's new executive officer. "Let me introduce you to someone you probably have already seen. Lieutenant Mary Morris, host of the hit television series, *Bikinis in Paradise*."

"*Former* host. I left all that behind because the call of service was too great."

"We're not filming anything we do. Nothing, Lieutenant. I'm Major Declan Payne. Please join us. We're making a tactical movement to the combat range to get introduced to our new firepower, mechanized individual combat equipment. MICE. Because the enemy out there knows how frail the human body is, and we need a little more punch. Show her, Heckler."

The specialist hesitated before pulling up his shirt. "Happened two days ago on a planet called Parallax with an enemy of bio-drones that we have never before encountered. Are you up for that?"

"I am," she stated confidently. "I have a couple other meetings. Is it okay to join you later?"

"It is not. Either you are on this team or you aren't. This is our last day on Earth, and we intend to get the most from it to improve our chances of not dying. I would like you to be a part of that effort. It'll go a long way in earning the respect of the team commander."

"I'm sorry. Of course, I'll come along. I didn't expect that you'd be available yet. Admiral, if you would be so kind as to get your staff to cancel my appearances, I would appreciate it."

"I'll see to it personally, Mary. It was great meeting you!" She held out her hand for a shake before he could zoom in for a hug.

Payne tried not to roll his eyes. He swallowed hard. He wouldn't be canceling any of her meetings for her. She'd be the one doing the grunt work. It was her duty as the XO.

She followed the team outside while Major Dank tried to talk to the team that dwarfed him in size. He looked wholly uncomfortable.

"We can use his team as roadblocks," Turbo suggested.

Once outside, Payne stopped and introduced everyone.

"I like that you have so many women on your team, Major Payne." The lieutenant's smile was radiant.

"I *do*?" He scanned his team, looking from face to face. "Did they sneak in when I wasn't looking?"

Turbo and Byle snickered. Sparky shook her head. Joker stared emotionlessly.

"I only want the best on my team. I don't care about anything but that. I've never lost a teammate and am not about to start. You'll be the best, or you'll be gone." He tipped his head toward the door they just walked out of. "Size doesn't make you good."

"I understand. How did you bring *Leviathan* into the human fold?"

"That was Blinky and Buzz, who wisely remained on the ship to work with Lev on decrypting the signals between the drones of the fleet we found over Parallax and the grid within which the biomechanical box drones operated on Parallax proper. It was a shit show."

"Why didn't you just nuke it from orbit?"

"There's the rub. Battleship *Leviathan* is a pacifist."

———

On the range, they found two old mechs and an exuberant group of mechanics working frantically to get them up and running so Team Payne could send them through their paces.

"Heckler..." Payne said, crossing his arms and looking down his nose at the equipment.

"This isn't what she led me to believe. I'll have someone's ass for this." Heckler steamed in his own juices. He couldn't fault the mechs but the weapons tech. He stormed to her as her smile progressed from radiant to where her lips turned white from clenching her mouth tightly shut.

Once Heckler was done, he walked past the team. "Coming?"

"No mech playtime?" the lieutenant wondered.

"These were old when I was here for training as a boot lieutenant. They won't help us at all. They don't even use these models in the Fleet anymore because they had a tendency to stop working at the most inopportune times."

"You mean, in the middle of a firefight," Morris noted.

Payne nodded, turned, and followed Heckler off the range.

Once back on the road, Sparky's smug expression begged Payne to ask her. He held his hands up until she came clean. "My hundred credits is looking pretty good right now."

Turbo punched her in the shoulder.

"Sir?" Morris wondered.

"A side bet that will give me nightmares if it comes true."

"You don't want to see two people happy?" Sparky drawled.

"I don't want to see a planet destroyed by two happy people." Payne raised his voice an octave. "Hey, honey, for your birthday, I got you a Q36 Space Modulator! Fun. Let's see what it does..." Heckler stared at the major. "I have a hundred credits on you, Heckler. Don't let me down."

"Skimmer?" Joker asked.

Payne hung his head. "Since I don't like sitting around waiting for the small window where the chow hall will be open, yes. Let's go home, people."

The lieutenant followed without saying anything. She looked like she wanted to, but Payne didn't engage. He had no idea what she was capable of. Training. He needed her to study tactics.

"Once on board the ship, go to the bridge and study the team reports. All thirty-eight of them or whatever we've written."

"I already have, up until you boarded *Leviathan*. I'll read the latest once I'm on board."

"What's your tactical analysis, Lieutenant?"

"You need better firepower and non-lethal options. From your reports, I think you may have missed opportunities to take prisoners."

"Orders were not to because we couldn't talk to them, but that is no longer a prohibition. Thanks to Lev, we have programs that speak the different Blaze languages. We need to capture some aliens...well, not us because we're going to find those who are behind the alien races on the front lines. We are going to find the ones who established the Blaze Collective. We're going to tear the head off the snake."

"And your hacker team is going to open the door for you?"

"Exactly. We couldn't do it without everyone filling their role on the team. Comm, combat, weapons, computers, and engineering. We have experts in all of it. Too often, we have to make it up as we go, so it's best to have the people we'd ask for help with us. And everyone can shoot. On our last op, we carried sixty to seventy kilos each."

"I'm ready," she replied.

"That's more than you weigh, Lieutenant."

"It's not the size of the fight in the dog..." she quoted.

"And everyone gets a nickname. You have just determined yours." Payne held out his hand. "Welcome to the team, Dog."

Payne walked onto the bridge with Lieutenant Morris to find the admiral poring over something on the screen at the station he'd taken over as his own. He jumped when Payne coughed.

He stood and faced the pair.

"Don't I know you?"

"*Bikinis in Paradise*. I left it to join the military. That life is behind me now."

"Is she any good?" the admiral asked to put Payne on the spot.

"At this point, all I can do is hope that she is half as good as Major Dank. She has a lot of studying to do before the next op. That's why we're back early." Payne pointed to a workstation and she sat down, looking blank. "Just say what you want or think it. Lev is a telepath. He's already in your head. If you don't want the ship to know, don't think it."

"That's a tall order."

"Speaking of tall." Payne turned to the admiral. "Dank's team is obscene. The shortest guy is well over two meters, and they all have to weigh in at well over a hundred kilos. It's like they found an old-style football team, threw uniforms on them, and handed them over to the recruiters."

"That's exactly what they did. The entire offense of the

Steel City Brawlers retired from the game." He looked at his watch. "Has it been two days already?"

"No. Earth and us didn't exactly see eye to eye." Payne held the admiral's gaze. "We were set up for hero worship. What did you send, if I may ask?"

"You may not ask. You're back on the ship, Major, but you aren't on duty. Relax and explore. You know you've seen less than five percent of what the ship has to offer. Let Lev take you on a tour. I think you'll find it enlightening. Let your hair down, Major, and relax."

"I'll try, sir. Dog, if you need anything, just think it, and Lev will give you a hand."

"Dog?" The admiral shook his head. "Never mind. I don't want to know." He returned to what he had been doing before Payne interrupted him. Morris was already at work scrolling through the team reports and other information that Lev was sharing, based on what Payne had asked him for.

Payne strolled into the corridor. "Lev, take me where I haven't been before."

"Your wish is my command. Let's start with the celestial observatory and garden."

"You have a garden?"

[30]

"Recognize your people with medals because they'll fight harder for nothing more than a chunk of metal hanging off a fancy ribbon. Even fight to the death." —From the memoirs of Fleet Admiral Thaylon Loore

"Attention to orders!" the squadron adjutant called over a portable loudspeaker. Fleet Admiral Wesson walked to a position front and center of the award ceremony. The Mosquito squadron had been on board for all of two hours. Their ships were parked neatly throughout the bay, magnetically grappled to the deck. Maintenance and parts storage had taken over what had been smooth outer walls.

Team Dank stood behind Team Payne in formation. Galen, Malcolm, and Lewis stood off to the side with an assistant for the cook and an armory officer, a gruff older man whose voice sounded as if he'd breathed toxic chemicals his whole life. Lieutenant Morris stood with them. This wasn't her party.

"Team Payne, front and center."

"Forward, march," Payne called and paced himself casually.

They had arranged themselves to walk straight to the front and then straight out without making any turns. Marching wasn't a skill the major considered important. They never practiced it, not even leading up to this.

The admiral tried not to watch because the team was out of step two steps in. Payne marched at the front, oblivious to what was happening behind him. He forgot the command and just said "Halt" when the time came. The team rippled to a stop. "Left, face." They turned in unison, almost making up for their bad marching.

"I have these extensive write-ups that no one actually listens to, so I'll go off-script." The admiral turned to the adjutant. "Don't have an aneurysm." He keyed the mic again and spoke like an elder talking to the younger generation. "This isn't about one man, but it is. He put a team together and then helped that team realize their full potential. They did what had to be done in a way that no one else could. I'd love to give the Gold Star to all of you, but the government says I can't. Major Payne, on behalf of a grateful world, you've been recognized with the Gold Star. The rest of you get Silver Stars. Even though I supposedly have a quota on those, I don't care. What are they going to do to me? This is about you and what you've done for the good of all humanity."

He shook his head and chuckled before returning to the matter at hand.

"This isn't just for what you've done to get us here, but what you're about to do to get us to a place where we have not been in a long, long time. Peace is within our reach. Imagine humanity not fighting a perpetual war. That's no longer a pipe dream, thanks to you and your team. Let's have a round of applause for the team that has never backed down from a challenge."

The assembled souls clapped lightly until the hangar bay door opened and a shuttle zoomed in. The squadron broke formation and ran for their lives as the shuttle settled almost on top of them.

The door opened, and none other than Tamony Morgan Swiss strolled down the steps. The commodore followed him. Neither looked happy. Swiss brightened when he saw Lieutenant Morris and made a beeline for her, calling "Mary," as he walked.

"You," she snapped back.

"I have missed you so." He powered in for a hug and she ducked away, choosing to hide behind the armory officer. He stiff-armed the dandy. "We'll talk later," Tamony promised.

"I have nothing to say to you," she countered.

Payne gave the order. "Fall out and rally around the XO." The team moved smartly from the front to the side, where they encircled their teammate.

"The lieutenant is my XO, and you'll not treat her any differently than you'd treat me. What are you doing here?"

"Alas, the Nova Intergalactic board of directors believed that greater opportunities existed on *Leviathan*. They strong-armed Fleet Command. And here I am, back to explore the opportunities."

Payne laughed. "They didn't exactly like the terraforming technology compared to everything else the ship has, like the repair and construction capabilities."

"Something like that. Looks like you're stuck with me, but the scenery has definitely improved."

"The scenery hasn't changed in the least. If you cross the line, Major Dank has an entire team of people who are used to beating on folks like you."

"And we will," Dank agreed. He shook hands with Major Payne. Tamony flicked his fingers and sauntered away as if it were his choice to be somewhere else.

"Thank you, but…"

Payne stopped her. "You're on my team. We rally around anyone on the team."

She nodded.

The commodore found her way to Admiral Wesson, and the two conversed. Payne was happy to see they hadn't brought any other BEP personnel that they'd end up kicking off *Leviathan*.

The admiral picked up the microphone and clicked it on. "Attention, all hands. *Leviathan* is ready, so we can leave early. Short FTL haul to the front lines. Next stop, *Cleophas* and the Fleet Command station. And since we never know that close to the front, battle stations. Man the fighters. Team Payne to the UM."

Payne leaned toward Dog and whispered, "Our mortal enemy is on *Cleophas*. A guy named Ensign Lord. We owe him one rather significant payback. I hope we get to stop by and say hi."

"I guess I'll get that story later," she replied.

"All the stories until you're tired of hearing them, or we have better ones from our own ops." Payne put out his hand. "Welcome to the team." Heckler was already running to catch a cart. The rest fell in behind. "Oorah!" Payne shouted as he sprinted to catch up. Dog was right on his heels.

To be continued in Book Two, *Leviathan's War*.
The fate of humanity could not be contained in this single volume. Please leave a review on this book because all those stars look great and help others decide if they'll enjoy this book as much as you have. I appreciate the feedback and support. Reviews buoy my spirits and stoke the fires of creativity.

Oorah, hard-chargers. Bring the Payne!
Don't stop now! Keep turning the pages as I talk about my

thoughts on this book and the overall project called *Battleship: Leviathan*.

You can always join my newsletter—https://craigmartelle.com or follow me on Amazon https://www.amazon.com/Craig-Martelle/e/B01AQVF3ZY/, so you are informed when the next book comes out. You won't be disappointed.

THANK YOU FOR READING BATTLESHIP: LEVIATHAN

We hope you enjoyed it as much as we enjoyed bringing it to you. We just wanted to take a moment to encourage you to review the book. Follow this link: ***Battleship: Leviathan*** to be directed to the book's Amazon product page to leave your review.

Every review helps further the author's reach and, ultimately, helps them continue writing fantastic books for us all to enjoy.

You can also join our non-spam mailing list by visiting www.subscribepage.com/AethonReadersGroup and never miss out on future releases. You'll also receive three full books completely Free as our thanks to you.

Facebook

Instagram

Twitter

Website

Want to discuss our books with other readers and even the authors? Join our Discord server today and be a part of the Aethon community.

ALSO IN THE SERIES

Battleship: Leviathan

Leviathan's War

Leviathan's Last Battle

Looking for more great Science Fiction?

The ends justify the means... Technical Specialist Simon Brooks was no soldier. More suited for the academy than combat, his assignment to a rear echelon support squadron seemed a good fit. Everything changed when the Sleer attacked Earth's newly salvaged spacecraft, UEF Ascension.

GET BOOK ONE OF BATTLE RING EARTH

Titan's rebellion is coming. Only one man can stop it.

GET BOOK ONE OF EXODUS EARTH

Nolan Garrett is Cerberus. A government assassin, tasked with fixing the galaxy's darkest, ugliest problems.

GET INTERSTELLAR GUNRUNNER NOW!

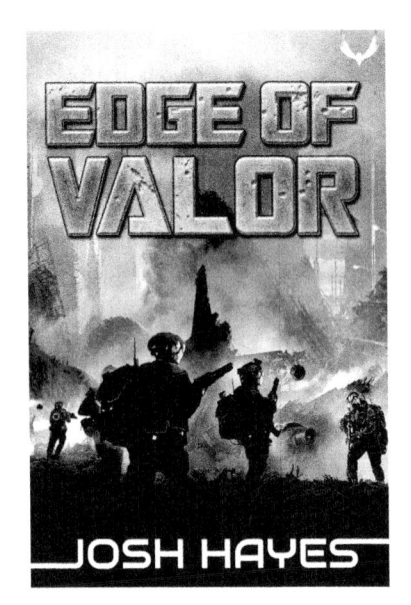

When their mission fails, his begins.

GET EDGE OF VALOR TODAY!

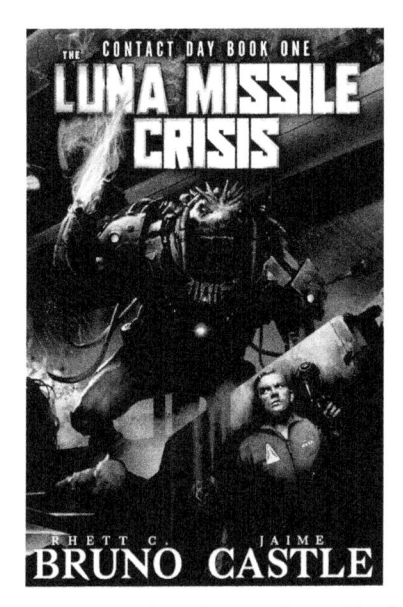

"**Aliens, agents, and espionage abound in this Cold War-era alternate history adventure... A wild ride!**"—Dennis E. Taylor, bestselling author of We Are Legion (We Are Bob)

GET THE LUNA MISSILE CRISIS NOW!

For all our Sci-Fi books, visit our website.

AUTHOR NOTES - CRAIG MARTELLE

Written February 2021

I can't thank you enough for reading this story to the very end! I hope you liked it as much as I did.

I put out a call for names, and the great Kurtherian Gambit

fans responded with a wave of input. Here's who contributed, and I thank you greatly.

Scudder Mead with Katello Mateus Andfen, and I attached the nickname Blinky because I needed him as a computer specialist.

Lisa Cooper with Virgil Hale that I changed to Dank because his name was too close to Byle and I liked Byle as a nickname. Dank became the SOFT XO, at least for this book.

Micky Cocker with Laura Walker, who I nicknamed Sparky. She is to engineering what Blinky is to computers.

Scudder Mead with Augry Pyle, but on my final edit, Pyle and Payne were confusing, so I changed it to Byle, who I left without a nickname because Byle is a good one by itself.

Michelle Rapley with Salem Shao, where I chose Shaolin for the nickname.

Barbara Davies came up with Huberta Hobbes, who I called Joker because she's always quiet, the opposite of one who would be the team's joker. And I tweaked the name to Huberta because it would confuse some people how Hubert could be female. I made a mistake on her second appearance and made him a her, so I went back and made her a her from the outset. I get mixed up while writing because I'm never writing just one story. I have a lot of distractions in my day.

Brent Towns gave us Heckler Koch for Heckler & Koch since this character is a weapons specialist. I picked Cointreau Koch and moved Heckler to the nickname. I needed a fancy-sounding name to offset Katello as the Combat Specialist Seven balance to the Tech Specialist Seven.

Barbara Davies also gave me Marsha Skellig, nickname Turbulent or Turbo for short.

Scudder also gave us Alphonse Periq (pronounced PEAR-ik). I liked the nickname Fetus for the new guy. It's better than Nug or Noob. And yes, when I served, I knew a guy who was called Fetus because he looked like he was in middle school. That would have worked, except the guy was a second lieutenant.

Michelle Rapley also gave us Harry Wesson, the Fleet admiral. He pops in every now and again when it's time to issue orders.

Merana Cadorette with Arthir Dorsite, the one who becomes the captain of *Leviathan*.

Micky Cocker also gave us Malcolm Russel, the research engineer.

Scudder was on a roll and also gave us David M. Dansbury, our duty genius who joins the team just because of *Leviathan*. But we needed balance, so David became Davida.

And every great team needs a logistician. Micky Cocker offers her son, Lewis Barlow. He'll have a bigger role in future volumes because amateurs talk tactics while professionals talk logistics.

Tom Dickerson gave us Tamony Morgan Swiss as the corporate financier. I tried to not make him a scallywag. I really did. Not. He's the guy we like to dislike, but he is unrepentant about what he does.

Merana Cadorette gave us *Cleophas* for the Kaiju-class dreadnought. She offered it as a character's first name, but I saw a different opportunity. And then Phil Dent provided a ship captain's name—Captain Ezekial Smith.

Jens Schulze offered Voeller, one of his best proofreaders for German translations. I made her the frigate where the SOFT used to hang their hat. And Matt Yunker threw out the name that would become her captain, Captain Malone.

Eric Anthony offered Galen Stone, who I brought on board as the master chef. Every ship needs a good cook. Hands down the most important individual for ship-based morale. Anything less is unacceptable. I deployed on too many ships with horrible chow. It made the time drag to near infinity.

Christy Park gave us Doctor Peter van Lier, who made one small appearance. There wasn't a bigger role for him, unfortunately.

Laura Jordan had a couple names that I used in this book—Juzan LeFlore and Nyota Freeman. You can already see that the commodore is softening. Everything she thought she knew was proven to be false. It took her a while, and she is still trying to find her place.

Melissa L. Cook gave us Ezio and Sirus, the two cruisers that fought valiantly against the Ebren invaders.

I usually write in the quiet, but for some scenes in *Battleship: Leviathan*, I needed mood music. Sabaton: *Bismarck,* Black Sabbath's *We Sold Our Soul for Rock and Roll*, and Nightwish *Once*. They filled the requirement nicely.

Thank you to everyone who has read this far. You are the reason I keep writing.

And in the winter in the interior of Alaska, there's not much else I can do. One of the triggers for my asthma is the cold, and we tend to get extended times of extreme cold. Writing gives me something productive to do, especially as I get older with a bad heart and lungs. I need to keep my activity at a level that doesn't end me.

Lots of great auroras this year, and my wife has diligently captured many from the peace and convenience of our own driveway.

This is a great place to live to see the wonders of nature. There is a certain amount of compromise that has to take place in order to stay here, but once that is settled, the beauty is nearly unrivaled.

Peace, fellow humans.

AUTHOR NOTES - CRAIG MARTELLE

If you liked this story, you might like some of my other books. You can join my mailing list by dropping by my website craigmartelle.com or if you have any comments, shoot me a note at craig@craigmartelle.com. I am always happy to hear from people who've read my work. I try to answer every email I receive.

If you liked the story, please write a short review for me on Amazon. I greatly appreciate any kind words; even one or two sentences go a long way. The number of reviews an ebook receives greatly improves how well it does on Amazon.

Amazon—www.amazon.com/author/craigmartelle

Facebook—www.facebook.com/authorcraigmartelle

BookBub—https://www.bookbub.com/authors/craig-martelle

My web page—https://craigmartelle.com

Thank you for joining me on this incredible journey.

OTHER SERIES BY CRAIG MARTELLE

 # - available in audio, too
Terry Henry Walton Chronicles (#) (co-written with Michael Anderle)—a post-apocalyptic paranormal adventure
Gateway to the Universe (#) (co-written with Justin Sloan & Michael Anderle)—this book transitions the characters from the Terry Henry Walton Chronicles to The Bad Company
The Bad Company (#) (co-written with Michael Anderle)—a military science fiction space opera
Judge, Jury, & Executioner (#)—a space opera adventure legal thriller
Shadow Vanguard—a Tom Dublin space adventure series
Superdreadnought (#)—an AI military space opera
Metal Legion (#)—a military space opera
The Free Trader (#)—a young adult science fiction action-adventure
Cygnus Space Opera (#)—a young adult space opera (set in the Free Trader universe)
Darklanding (#) (co-written with Scott Moon)—a space

OTHER SERIES BY CRAIG MARTELLE

western

Mystically Engineered (co-written with Valerie Emerson)—mystics, dragons, & spaceships

Metamorphosis Alpha—stories from the world's first science fiction RPG

The Expanding Universe—science fiction anthologies

Krimson Empire (co-written with Julia Huni)—a galactic race for justice

Zenophobia (#)—a space archaeological adventure

End Times Alaska (#)—a Permuted Press publication—a post-apocalyptic survivalist adventure

Nightwalker (a Frank Roderus series)—A post-apocalyptic western adventure

End Days (#) (co-written with E.E. Isherwood)—a post-apocalyptic adventure

Successful Indie Author (#)—a non-fiction series to help self-published authors

Monster Case Files (co-written with Kathryn Hearst)—A Warner twins mystery adventure

Rick Banik (#)—Spy & terrorism action-adventure

Ian Bragg Thrillers—a man with a conscience who kills bad guys for money

The Dragon's Call by Angelique Anderson & Craig A. Price, Jr.—an epic fantasy quest

A Couple's Travels—a non-fiction travel series

Mischief Maker by Bruce Nesmith, a Norse mythology contemporary fantasy

Love-Haight Case Files by Jean Rabe and Donald R. Bingle, a paranormal, mystery, horror, legal thriller

Printed in Great Britain
by Amazon